Praise for *When You Give a Duke a Diamond*

"Galen creates a lighthearted yet poignant, humorous yet touching love story—with original characters who delight and enough sizzle to add heat to a delicious read."

—*RT Book Reviews*, 4½ stars

"Tinged with danger and darkness, Galen's sexy and dramatic story has depth."

—*Publishers Weekly*

"A thrilling ride, filled with mystery, intrigue, and romance. Shana Galen kicks off her new Fallen Ladies series with an explosion that leaves this reader breathless with anticipation."

—*Fresh Fiction*

"I loved this gem of a story!... Fraught with intrigue and mystery."

—*Night Owl Reviews*, 5 stars

"Absolutely delicious... a witty, suspense-filled historical romance that you will not want to put down until you reach the very satisfying conclusion."

—*Romance Junkies*

"Shana Galen has done it again. She's made me pull an all-nighter with this book. Fast-paced action, smoldering attraction, sexy love scenes."

—*Romancing Rakes for the Love of Romance*

Also by Shana Galen

The Making of a Duchess

The Making of a Gentleman

Lord and Lady Spy

The Rogue Pirate's Bride

When You Give a Duke a Diamond

IF YOU GIVE A RAKE A RUBY

SHANA GALEN

sourcebooks
casablanca

Published by Sourcebooks Casablanca, an imprint of Sourcebooks, Inc.
P.O. Box 4410, Naperville, Illinois 60567-4410
(630) 961-3900
Fax: (630) 961-2168
www.sourcebooks.com

Printed and bound in Canada.
WC 10 9 8 7 6 5 4 3 2 1

For my readers. I have the best readers in the world. Thank you, thank you, thank you.

...and so our flaxen-haired Duchess of Dalliance exits the scene with her Dangerous Duke and becomes a duchess in truth. We suppose this is the last mention of her we will make in this lowly column as we are concerned with the doings of the demimonde, not the haute ton.

Now to the question on everyone's lips: who will snare the next gentleman of the ton? Perhaps one of the two remaining diamonds will set the parson's mousetrap for an earl or even a marquess. The ladies of Society flirt and simper with newfound desperation, fearing their ranks will be further sullied.

And fear they should. Lately, one cannot but note the ravishing Marchioness of Mystery has been courted by none other than the Duke of E—, Lord K—, and even H.R.H. Could the gypsy queen be our next English queen?

Not if the Princess of W— has anything to say about it!

But who is this dark-eyed, enigmatic beauty? From whence does she hail? One dear source insists she is the daughter of a fallen maharaja. Oh, fair Fallon, we beg one paltry clue. We shall feast on the rumor crumbs from your table for weeks.

Diamonds are the hardest natural substances on earth.

One

"LORD KWIRLEY," FALLON SAID WITH A POINTED LOOK at the bracket clock on the brass–inlaid drawing-room table. "The hour grows late, and I would like to go to bed."

Kwirley smiled suggestively, and Fallon's upper lip itched to curl in disgust. But she controlled the impulse, as she had been taught, and imagined Lady Sinclair nodding in approval.

"Why, Marchioness, that was my thought exactly." He rose and held out his hand, seemingly unfazed by Fallon's icy stare. Kwirley was not a small man. He was tall, well-built, and handsome in the most conventional way. Fallon could understand why the *ton* insisted on pairing the two of them. Kwirley with his dark hair, dark eyes, and tanned skin complemented her own dark features perfectly. His height was better suited to Juliette, who was tall and willowy. Fallon was petite, which was Lady Sinclair's polite way of saying she was short. Fallon did not mind her diminutive size. It meant others often underestimated her, and that usually worked to her advantage. Not tonight.

"Why don't you show me to your boudoir, *Fallon*?"

Fallon raised a brow. "You overstep yourself, my lord. I have not given you leave to use my Christian name. Nor have I expressed any interest in taking you to my bed."

"You're a courtesan," Kwirley said, his eyes narrowing in annoyance, "you're paid to take men to your bed."

Fallon was still sitting, Kwirley still standing, and her neck was beginning to ache from looking up at him. What a boorish lout—or, as her bastard of a father would have said, *what a bloody clodpole*. How dare Kwirley stand when she, a lady, was seated?

Simple, she supposed. He did not consider her a lady.

Very well, then. She rose. "My lord, you are exceedingly arrogant."

He laughed, which was not unexpected but certainly not the response she'd hoped for. He was going to make this difficult. She rolled her shoulders. Perhaps *difficult* was not such a bad thing. She needed to keep in good form.

"And you are exceedingly coy," Kwirley said, stepping closer. "I had not expected as much. In fact, I have been led to believe you are quite the tigress in bed. *Roar*." He lifted his hands to make claws.

"Unfortunately, my lord, you will never know. Shall I ring for my butler to show you out or can you find the way yourself?"

Kwirley lowered his hands. "I don't think you understand, Fallon."

"I've told you not to address me as such, my lord."

"I am the most sought-after man in London. I am doing you a favor by becoming your lover."

"Really? The only woman I know seeking your favor is your wife. And, if I'm not mistaken, she is quite heavy with your child at present. Do you not think you should be home with Lady Kwirley?"

He took a step toward her. "My wife is my business."

"Then I suggest you attend to your business, my lord. Good night."

She turned and strolled toward the drawing room doors. She knew she would not reach them unmolested. She also knew she could ring for Titus.

But that would be too easy.

Kwirley was slower than she'd anticipated, and she had almost gained the towering mahogany doors before he caught her elbow and spun her around. "Not so fast—" he began.

Fallon kicked him in the belly, sending him sprawling backward. He knocked over a pedestal holding a jeweled lamp, and she had a moment's worry because it was one of her favorites. But a quick glance reassured her the lamp was not broken.

The glance also revealed Kwirley was getting up. *Blockhead.* "Go home, my lord. I don't want to hurt you."

"Really?" He wiped his hands on his breeches. "Because I would like to hurt you. I don't know who you think you are, but you're going to pay for—"

She sidestepped him, spun, and booted him in his lower back. The blow set him off-balance, and she had a moment to grab a book and hurl it at him. Her aim was perfect, and the book's spine hit him in the center of the forehead. "Ow, you little bitch!" He charged her, and Fallon shook her head. He wasn't even thinking, simply acting blindly. She easily sidestepped him again, and he rammed into a settee, knocking it over. While he struggled to rise, Fallon dug her heel into the back of his neck and pressed him down.

"Had enough?" she asked. "Or would you prefer to go another round?" Because she was tired and wanted to go to bed, she ground her heel into his neck.

"Enough," he mumbled.

"Good." Without lifting her heel, she reached for a little silver bell and rang it. The sound tinkled softly in the room, and the drawing room doors opened immediately to reveal Titus.

Titus was close to seven feet tall and easily twenty-five stone. He had a thick head of bright red hair, shocking blue eyes, and a mouth full of crooked teeth. His hands were as big as puppies and his legs tree trunks. He did not walk so much as lumber, and Kwirley began protesting the moment Titus entered the room.

"There's been some sort of mistake. I didn't intend any disrespect."

Fallon sighed. "Titus, I might have known you would be standing right outside."

The giant shrugged, his shoulders small mountains. "I like to make sure there's no trouble, my lady."

Fallon had told him a hundred times she was no lady, but he insisted on referring to her as such anyway. Who was she to protest? It wasn't as though anyone else was clamoring to call her a lady.

She pressed her foot into Kwirley's neck for good measure then lifted it and stepped away. "Would you be so kind as to show Lord Kwirley out?"

"I'll show 'im out," Titus said. "But I won't be kind about it."

Kwirley gave her a panicked look, and Fallon was sorely tempted to shrug helplessly. But at the last moment, she took pity on the man. "Titus, be nice. Don't throw Lord Kwirley farther than the lamppost."

She strode out of the drawing room, listening to Kwirley sputter and then plead for mercy. Titus was a gentle giant to anyone he loved. He was an ogre to anyone who but looked askance at someone he loved. But she couldn't feel too sorry for Kwirley. Her father—she hoped he burned in hell—always said when you started feeling sorry for those who want to take advantage of you, then you've gone soft and deserve what you get.

Of course, he hadn't said it quite that politely.

She lifted her skirts and climbed the stairs, nodded to Mary, one of the chamber maids, and blew out a long sigh. She was exhausted.

The past few days had been grueling. She'd been to one social event after another—balls, routs, masquerades, soirées, musicales. At this point, if she never saw another ballroom, theater, or pleasure garden, she would not mourn the loss. Normally she enjoyed the whirl of the Season, but without Juliette, everything seemed different.

Juliette, Lily, and Fallon were no longer The Three Diamonds. Now it was only Lily and Fallon, and they both missed Juliette terribly.

And, if Fallon was honest, she envied Juliette. Who wouldn't envy a woman married to a wealthy duke who obviously adored her? Fallon had never really believed in love. Her father hadn't loved her mother. He'd used her charms to run scams or make ends meet. And her mother hadn't loved her father. She'd been a dim woman who needed a man to tell her what to do.

Fallon hadn't loved either of her parents. She thought she'd fallen in love once, but the experience had taught her she'd been right all long.

There was no such thing as love.

Except… when she looked at Juliette and her Dangerous Duke, Fallon wondered.

She strode down the corridor toward her boudoir. Her booted feet made shushing sounds on the thick rug, and even though she was now quite used to living surrounded by opulence, she paused a moment to savor the plush rug, the paintings on the walls, the expensive upholstery on the Sheraton chair she'd just passed, and the fine silk of her gown.

She had no illusions as to how fortunate she was. Unlike the daughters of duchesses and earls Fallon often glimpsed at the theater or a ball, she had not grown up in such privileged circumstances. She had been lucky to have something to eat and shoes on her feet.

She did not take any of this for granted. It could all be taken away from her with the snap of a finger if anyone ever found out who she really was. There was a reason the Prince Regent had dubbed her the Marchioness of Mystery. No one—save Lady Sinclair, Juliette, and Lily—knew the truth about her. The *ton* was greatly diverted by conjecturing as to her true identity.

Some said she was the daughter of a maharaja. Little did they know, Fallon had been obliged to ask Lady

Sinclair for the definition of *maharaja*. Other rumors hinted she was a gypsy queen or a princess from a secret kingdom. Fallon wished there was a tiny kernel of truth in but one of the rumors. Anything was better than the reality.

She opened the door of her boudoir and stepped inside. Strange. Usually Anne had the fire roaring and several candles lit. But the room was dark and cold. Fallon shivered, crossed to her bed, and pulled the cord to summon her lady's maid. She reached out and felt the edge of her bed—the soft silk of her counterpane felt light and inviting as a cloud. Fallon rolled her neck, then sank down onto her bed.

"Ouch!"

She bolted upright and stifled a scream. There was a man in her bed.

An uninvited man.

Two

WARRICK FITZHUGH DID NOT RELISH AN AUDIENCE with the Queen. He did not know how it was he'd become her personal lackey, and he didn't give a bloody farthing. All he knew was the woman was mad. Daft as a resident of Bedlam, if he was any judge. And people claimed the King was mad. Well, those people hadn't met the Queen.

He sat in his club and rubbed his temples. Warrick had no problem taking orders. He'd been taking them from the Secretary of the Foreign Office for years, but now the Queen's cousin had been killed, and she wanted to give orders too.

It wasn't as though Warrick wasn't already investigating the death of his fellow Diamond in the Rough. He'd been turning every stone he could find for weeks now. He might be retired from the Foreign Office, but he wasn't going to leave his friend's murder unavenged. Warrick supposed that spending the rest of his days acting the profligate his father always assumed him to be would have to wait.

And so Fitzhugh sat at White's and waited for

Pelham to meet him for their appointment. He resisted checking his pocket watch and instead surveyed the club. It was filled with the usual stoop-shouldered, gray-haired men with gnarled fingers turning crisply ironed pages of the *Times*. Earlier Warrick had noted his father, the Earl of Winthorpe, seated in his usual chair near a painting of Charles II and his various dogs. Warrick glanced over again and met his father's gaze.

Warrick lifted his glass and saluted. His father gave him a stony look and lifted his paper again.

Warrick drank from his glass—since it was raised anyway—and wondered if his father was going to blame him for the rest of his life. It wasn't as though Warrick hadn't tried to stop Edward.

They'd all tried to stop Edward from joining the military.

Impatient now, Warrick pulled out his pocket watch. Pelham was never late, but he was also a newly married man. He had been less than enthusiastic about leaving his bride to meet Warrick. But Warrick had insisted, most persuasively.

And he could be very persuasive when necessary…as evidenced by the sight of Pelham striding into the dining room. His clothing was perfectly in order, his blue eyes clear and hard, his mouth set in a firm slash. But something was different about the man. Warrick narrowed his eyes. Pelham's hair, perhaps? It appeared a bit…tousled.

He rose when his friend spotted him and didn't hide his grin.

"What are you looking so cheerful about?" the duke asked, taking a seat without being invited.

"Do I look cheerful?" Warrick sat, signaling to the

waiter to bring the port he had already requested. It was a vintage Warrick knew Pelham liked. "Have you done something different?"

Pelham glanced at him sharply and shifted. Oh, now Warrick was going to enjoy this. Making Pelham uncomfortable was one of the few joys he had in life. "Your coat cut differently?" He pretended to study Pelham's conservative coat. "Your cravat tied in a new sort of knot?" He reached out and touched the perfectly tied neck cloth—perfectly tied in the same fashion Pelham had always worn it. "No, that isn't it."

"Stubble it, Fitzhugh. There's nothing different."

"Oh, I think there is." He looked pointedly at Pelham's hair and could all but see the duke leaning back in his chair, away from Warrick's scrutiny. "It's your hair. Why, Pelham. It's positively *fashionable*."

"My hair is exactly the same. Now why the devil did you call me here?"

"I don't believe so."

The waiter set the port in front of Pelham and Fitzhugh waved the man away.

"It looks a bit tousled. That's how the dandies are wearing it these days."

Pelham slapped the table with his palm. "I'm no bloody dandy. Stop looking at my hair."

"Can I assume this is the new Duchess of Pelham's doing?" Fitzhugh asked with a satisfied smile.

"I don't wish to discuss my hair. If that's the only topic you want to converse about—" He stood, and Warrick yanked him back down.

"What the devil are you about?" Pelham adjusted his sleeve. "Have you gone quite mad?"

"No. I have a serious matter to discuss with you."

Pelham narrowed his eyes. "It had better not be the state of my cravat."

"No. I fear we must suspend our fashion discussions for the moment. I need to ask you about one of your wife's friends, one of The Three Diamonds."

Pelham drank his previously untouched port, swallowed, then said, "Why?"

"I'm not at liberty to discuss that. I can say it's a matter of state."

"I thought you'd retired from the Foreign Office."

"On occasion I am still called upon to exercise my skills."

"I see."

"What do you know about the Marchioness of Mystery? She calls herself Fallon, I believe."

Pelham shrugged. "Not much. She's not as friendly as Lily."

"She's secretive," Warrick remarked.

Pelham sipped his port. "I don't know that I'd say that, but I don't believe all that rot about her being foreign royalty or a gypsy queen."

"No, that's rubbish," Warrick murmured.

"How do you know? I don't think Juliette even knows where Fallon came from. And what does a courtesan have to do with a matter of state?"

"I'd love to discuss that with you, old chap…"

"But you can't. Well I will tell you this. I don't know who you're looking for, but if it's a spy or a traitor, looking at Fallon is looking in the wrong direction."

Warrick leaned forward. "Go on."

"She's fiercely loyal—to her friends and to the

Countess of Sinclair. The last time I saw her, she told Juliette she was relieved this business with Lucifer was over and done. She said he was…" Pelham rubbed his fingers together, obviously searching his memory for the exact words. Warrick appreciated his friend's effort to be precise, but then again, he expected nothing less from the orderly Duke of Pelham. "Ah! She said Lucifer was a thorn in the side of the city and had been for years. Struck me as rather patriotic."

A tingle ran up Warrick's spine all the way to the base of his skull and then down his arms. So this Fallon knew of Lucifer. That was interesting because the very existence of the man was not common knowledge among anyone who did not frequent London's gambling hells. And those were certainly not the usual haunts of glittering courtesans like The Three Diamonds.

Pelham didn't know it, but by trying to defend his wife's friend, he'd just confirmed everything Warrick had learned, thereby dooming her.

"I had better be going," Pelham said, rising. "We are leaving early in the morning. I told Juliette I'd take her to Bath."

"One more thing." Warrick rose. "Has the duchess, your wife, ever called Fallon by any other name? Besides the Marchioness of Mystery?"

"Not in my hearing. Do you want me to ask Juliette if Fallon has another name?"

"No. Don't say anything. In fact, I'd prefer if you kept the topic of this meeting to yourself."

"Of course. Good luck with your search, Fitzhugh."

"Thank you. Godspeed." Warrick watched Pelham stroll out of his club. The man was obviously in a hurry to return to his bride. And why shouldn't he be? He was married to one of the most beautiful and notorious women in London. Someone—Warrick suspected the girls themselves—had put it about that the Prince Regent gave them their sobriquets. Juliette had been the Duchess of Dalliance before becoming a legitimate duchess and Pelham's wife. Lily was the Countess of Charm, and Fallon, the one he sought, was the Marchioness of Mystery. Warrick thought the marchioness might not be such a mystery after all.

Warrick gave his father a salute, which the earl ignored, and strolled out of his club.

◦⟡◦

Two days later, Warrick had been to more social events than he normally attended in a year. Fallon appeared to have boundless energy. She and her counterpart, the Countess of Charm, went everywhere and knew everyone. He did not know when they slept because they danced until after four in the morning and then began making calls or receiving callers at ten.

What Warrick did know was that, for a courtesan, Fallon was remarkably difficult to corner. He had tried, quite unsuccessfully, on several occasions to get her alone. It had proved impossible. And so tonight he had been left with no other recourse but to adjourn to the one place he knew he could have a private conversation—her boudoir.

Warrick had been impressed with her staff, in particular her giant butler. The man had almost caught Warrick as he wound his way through Fallon's town house and up to her private chambers. Once in her chambers, he'd had to deal with Fallon's lady's maid. He'd bound her and stashed her comfortably in Fallon's rather large dressing room, and then he'd returned to wait.

And wait.

He didn't know at what point he'd decided to lie down on the bed. He'd only known he was weary and wanted to close his eyes for a few moments. He didn't expect to sleep. He rarely slept. But he'd been startled from a light doze when something—rather, someone—sat on him. He realized immediately what had happened. She had not seen him in the dark room. To her credit, when she jumped up, she did not scream. He heard the hasty intake of breath, but she seemed able to control the impulse to utter a bloodcurdling screech.

"It's about time you came to bed," Warrick said. It was too dark to see his pocket watch, but he gauged the time close to five in the morning. "I've been waiting for hours."

"Oh, how rude of me," she said, her voice quite low and husky in the shadowed room. He could hear her fumbling about and realized she probably sought her tinderbox. "To keep an uninvited man waiting."

A moment later a spunk blazed to life, and she lit one of the lamps beside the bed. Upon seeing him, her brow creased. He was obviously not who she expected. And she was not what he expected. He'd seen her more times than he could count, but he'd rarely been this close to her, and when he had, he'd not been looking at her but planning how to best monopolize her attention. Now she was an arm's length away and, for once, not surrounded by an army of admirers.

Warrick realized she was impossibly beautiful.

But of course she was beautiful. He'd known that. Everyone knew that. She had lustrous chocolate-brown hair and dark brown eyes. Her skin was the color of burnished gold, and her body far more voluptuous than was the current style. But what man ever favored a Greek statue? A man wanted soft flesh and warm curves when he sank into a woman.

And Warrick didn't know why the hell he was thinking of soft flesh at the moment. He was supposed to be working. But he hadn't anticipated the distraction of her mouth. It was wide and red and far too tempting. And then there was the tilt of her eyes—rather exotic the way they turned up at the corners. No wonder people tossed about rumors she was a gypsy queen. Warrick's gaze wandered downward, and he had to take a fortifying breath. It was one thing to glimpse her body across a crowded ballroom. It was quite another to feel the heat from her, to see the rise and fall of the rounded flesh revealed by her neckline, to smell the scent—jasmine or some exotic flower—she wore, and to know if he buried his face in her hair that sweet scent would surround him.

"Get the hell out of my bed," she said in a velvet voice that only made him desire her more.

Warrick didn't even sit. "I have a few questions for you."

"Get out, or I'll call my butler and have you thrown out."

"I don't think so." He put his hands behind his head and leaned back on her prodigious pile of pillows. They were satin and velvet, arrayed in every jewel tone he could imagine. The mountain was quite comfortable except for the occasional beaded pillow whose ornamentation dug into one's skin.

"Oh, really? I've already thrown one man out tonight. I can do so again." She started for the door with a fast, purposeful stride he had not seen before, but before she could reach for the handle, he spoke.

"I would not do that, *Margaret*. Or should I call you Maggie?"

☙

Fallon stilled, not trusting her ears. Her hands had begun to shake, and she clenched them to still their trembling. Slowly, she turned. "I believe I see your mistake now, sir. You have me confused with someone else."

"No, I don't." His hands remained linked arrogantly behind his head as if he had not a care in the world. Fallon felt like pulling all the pillows out from under him so he would knock his skull on the headboard. Then she'd hold those pillows over his face until she smothered him.

Bloody man!

"Mr. Fitzhugh—is that your name?"

"It is, but you may call me Warrick. I think it only fair since I intend to call you by your given name—*Maggie*."

"I'm afraid you are mistaken, Mr. Fitzhugh. My name is Fallon—not that I've given you leave to use it. And I really am going to have to insist you leave now."

"Insist all you want, but I'm not leaving until I get what I came for."

Fallon's blood chilled in her veins. All men were the same. They wanted one thing and would apparently go to any length to take it. She did not know how this man had discovered her real name. And she didn't know what else he knew about her, but she did know if he thought he was going to outwit her, he had a lot to learn.

She had been outwitting arrogant men since the age of five.

She put a hand on her hip. "And I suppose if I do not give you what you want then you will reveal my secret."

"It's called blackmail, and yes, that is generally how it works. Now that we both know the rules…"

"Oh, I make the rules, Mr. Fitzhugh." She sidled closer to the bed. "After all, we are in my bedchamber."

"I…" He trailed off when she dropped her shawl on the floor beside the bed and, lifting her skirts, crawled onto her satin coverlet.

"What are you doing?" he asked.

"Courtesan rule number one," she whispered, crawling toward him. "Don't talk."

His arms dropped from behind his head and he sat forward, looking rather alarmed. Oh, this was going to be easier than she'd anticipated. She had thought to arouse him and then, when he was sufficiently distracted, knock him over the head and scream for Titus. But at this rate, she might not have to do much more than kiss him.

"We have to talk if I'm going to…"

Now on her hands and knees, she slid one hand down his chest all the way to his waistband. He grabbed her hand before she could stroke his cock. She glanced up at him. Was he going to play coy now? How tedious.

"You misunderstand me, Maggie."

"Fallon," she said, sitting up.

"Fallon. I came to ask you—"

"I told you, no talking." She leaned forward and brushed her lips over his. She felt him go rigid immediately. Was he really surprised she had kissed him? Wasn't that what he had come for? She ran her tongue lightly over his lips and felt him relax slightly. His hands had gripped her shoulders at her first touch, but they loosened now.

She tasted his mouth, tried not to notice the flavor of champagne on his lips. Tried not to notice how warm his lips were, how pliable. Most men mashed their mouths to hers and took, took, took. This one didn't seem to want anything from her. He allowed her to kiss him.

She opened his mouth with the gentle pressure of her tongue and teased him with the promise of a deeper kiss. When his tongue met hers, she felt a spark of heat that shocked her. She hadn't expected to feel anything and was still puzzling over it when he dug his hand into her hair and pulled her closer.

She was losing control, she realized, and had to gain it back or she would be forced to actually go through with this seduction. She ran her hand down his chest again—why did it have to be so deliciously muscled and hard?—and forced herself not to be distracted. When she reached his trousers, she wrapped her fingers around the hardening length she found there.

"Stop." He was up and out of her bed before she could even catch herself. She all but fell on her face in the spot he had occupied. "This isn't what I came for. I have nothing against you or your profession."

She frowned. What exactly was that supposed to mean?

"But I don't pay women for their services. I'm not that desperate."

She stared at him. Desperate? Did he think she allowed any man into her bed? Did he think she allowed any man to kiss her?

She tugged at the bodice of her dress and squared her shoulders. "I don't mean to dispute you, sir, but you were the one waiting in my bed. And when I refused you, you threatened to blackmail me." She gave him a tight smile. "It smacks a little of"—she lowered her voice to a whisper—"*desperation*."

"That's because you misunderstood." He paced away from her, running a hand through his hair. With the lamps lit, she could get a good look at him. She knew who he was, of course. She'd seen him before.

"I misunderstood?" She watched him pace across her bedroom then turn back. "You were lying in my bed, and when I asked you to leave, you said you would not depart until you had what you wanted. How did I misunderstand?"

He raked that hand through his thick hair again. "Yes, I can see how that might confuse you." He paused and faced her. He was definitely not a handsome man. His face was too asymmetrical for handsomeness. His nose was slightly crooked, which suggested it had been broken at one time, and he had a scar near his right eye. His brown hair was short and not at all fashionably styled. He was medium height but had a breadth of chest and shoulders that made him seem less than elegant.

And yet she believed he'd never had to pay for a woman. There was something about his eyes that made him seem dangerous and mysterious and desirable. Her gaze dropped to his hands, now flat on her coverlet. They were large and dark, and she had an image of one of them cupping her breast. She closed her eyes and attempted to gather her wits.

"Perhaps we should begin again," he was saying. "I came to question you and to ask you for a favor."

She studied him, not knowing quite what to think. Was he lying? Telling the truth? "If you wanted to ask me a question, you could have done so on any number of occasions."

"That's what I thought." He slapped the bed with a hand. "But you're a damned hard woman to get alone. And my business is of a private nature."

Despite herself, she was intrigued. "Go on."

"I don't know how much you know about me," he began. She noted the subtle shift in his demeanor, from flustered to authoritative.

"Not as much as you know about me, apparently."

He grinned at her, and in that moment, she forgot to breathe. With that grin, he'd looked so much like a mischievous boy that she'd wanted to gather him in her arms and kiss him again. His smile was completely out of character. It almost made him look handsome.

"I used to work for the Foreign Office," he was saying, when she could focus her attention again. "I played a part in the wars against Napoleon."

She nodded, her mind racing ahead to try and determine where this was going. She had nothing to do with France, Napoleon, or the governmental offices and failed to see how any of this related to her.

"Over the years, I developed certain skills. One of those was to ferret out information."

"So you were a spy."

He made a sound of distaste in the back of his throat. "I gathered information."

"And now you are gathering information about me." Things were beginning to take shape.

"I didn't set out to do so, but the more I learned about you, the more… captivated I became. You were smart to keep your true identity hidden."

"Apparently it's not hidden well enough."

"I don't think there's anyone who could hide something so well I couldn't uncover it," he said without any trace of conceit. She almost wanted to laugh at his boast. She had a feeling there were still a few things he hadn't uncovered.

"You knew Lucifer."

She felt a frisson of fear streak up her spine, and tried to control her reaction. But he'd taken her so off guard, she was too late. He was watching her with those sharp, enigmatic eyes. "Tell me, Mag—Fallon. Was he ever a victim of your considerable talent for theft?"

Three

"WHAT IS WRONG WITH YOU, FALLON?" LILY ASKED the next evening at a soirée hosted by Mr. Heyward, who was the son of a baron and known for his lavish social functions.

"Nothing. Why?"

"You haven't listened to a word I've said for the past quarter hour. *And* you have been sitting with me for that quarter of an hour when Mr. Heyward has been smiling at you and making every effort to garner your attention."

Fallon glanced about the drawing room until she spotted Heyward. He toasted her and raised his brows meaningfully. Fallon looked back at Lily. "I'd much rather talk to you than Mr. Heyward."

"Oh, really? Then what have we—rather, I—been speaking of?"

Fallon had absolutely no idea. "Very well. I'll tell you what's bothering me. Take a turn with me about the room."

Lily raised her eyebrows but didn't object. They linked arms and began to stroll. Fallon imagined they made a lovely picture. They were both dressed in green—Lily's gown was green with pink trim and Fallon's green with russet trim. Lily's pale skin and auburn hair was offset nicely by the sapphires she wore at her neck and throat, and Fallon had donned her rubies.

But she couldn't concern herself too much with appearances at the moment. Lily was correct in that she should have been courting the attention of Heyward. A few months ago he'd given her a gold ring, which she'd sold for enough to pay her rent for two months. Undoubtedly he hoped the gifts would persuade her to allow him into her bed. They wouldn't, but even though she tried to refuse the gifts, men gave them to her anyway.

She considered them payment for services rendered, even if those services were only making an appearance at a social function like this one. Even the whisper that one of The Three Diamonds—well, Two Diamonds now that Juliette had married—would attend a function made the invitations highly sought after.

At least by the gentlemen of the *ton*.

Although Fallon noted several ladies, who would never so much as deign to step over her were she lying in the street bleeding to death, watching her and Lily surreptitiously. No doubt the courtesans' dresses would be copied and worn by several of the women in the weeks to come.

"We're walking," Lily said. "And I'm listening."

"Someone has found out about me."

Lily frowned, a delicate gesture that formed a small crease between her emerald green eyes. "What do you mean? Someone found out about Sinclair?"

"No. At least, I don't think he knows that much. But he knows about my past."

"What about your past?" Lily nodded to the son of the Marquess of Ainsall, who had been sending her poetry of late. "*I* don't even know about your past."

"Exactly. No one knows except Lady Sin, but this man works—or worked—for the Foreign Office. He found out about me, and now he's blackmailing me."

Lily stiffened. "What does he want?"

"Not what you're thinking." They paused by the hearth and pretended to study the Sèvres porcelain pieces on the mantel. "He wants me to help him find Lucifer's Diamonds."

"The same diamonds—"

"Yes."

"But why would he ask *you* to help him?"

"Because once upon a time I knew Lucifer."

Lily gaped at her.

"And once upon a time, I was very, very good at stealing."

Now Lily laughed. "Fallon, I don't think this is at all amusing."

"You don't believe me?"

"Of course I don't believe you. Is this some sort of game you're playing?"

Fallon held out a gloved hand and opened the closed fingers. Lying in her palm was a sapphire necklace. A distinctive sapphire necklace. Small, square-cut sapphires comprised the chain and a large, heart-shaped sapphire was situated so that it would nestle in the hollow of a lady's throat. Usually Lily's throat.

Lily gasped and put her hand to her bare neck. "How did you do that?"

"I told you. I'm a very good thief."

Lily shook her head. "It came undone, and you picked it up off the floor."

Fallon rolled her eyes. She adored Lily, really she did, but sometimes the girl was too willing to believe only good about others. She motioned for Lily to turn and fastened the necklace on her friend once again. "I am distracted tonight because I have to meet him later—the man blackmailing me."

Lily glanced over her shoulder. "Are you going to have to steal for him?"

"I have to help him find the diamonds. If I don't, he'll reveal all of my secrets. I think we both know the disastrous consequences if he does so."

Lily's silence spoke volumes. As courtesans, even the most fashionable courtesans in the *demimonde*, their status relied on their reputation and, to some extent, their beauty. A vibrant personality that attracted men could overcome a homely appearance—as Harriette Wilson had proved—but part of Fallon's charm was her mystery. When men conversed with her, they wanted to believe they were speaking with a fallen queen or a foreign princess. She could be anyone from anywhere, and the speculation about her added to her appeal.

But if they knew she was born right here in London, the daughter of a pickpocket and a whore...well, that would lessen her appeal considerably.

"Do you know where the diamonds are?" Lily asked.

"No. But I suppose I had better find out." She gave

Lily a little push. "Go, speak with Ainsell's son before he begins drooling. The poor boy is mad for you."

"Yes." Lily frowned. "Too bad I'm not mad for him."

Before Fallon could ask who she *was* mad for, Lily was gliding across the room and capturing the gazes of most of, if not all, the men in attendance.

Fallon slipped out a quarter hour later, wrapped herself in a black mantle and instructed her coachman to drive her to St. James Street. She was well aware no lady would ever deign to be seen in St. James at night, and many of them would not venture into this exclusive male preserve during the day.

But Fallon was no lady.

"Shall I accompany you, madam?" the coachman asked as he handed her down from the gleaming black carriage. It was still early, barely midnight, and only a few young bucks strolled together, stopping into gambling hells and clubs. A few paused to catch a glimpse of her, but none dared approach.

Yet.

"No, I'm fine. Go on home."

He looked somewhat dubious. "But madam—"

"I said I was fine. Go home and see to the horses. I'll find my own way back later tonight."

"Yes, madam."

He watched her stroll away. She pulled the hood of the mantle over her dark hair and wove through the gentlemen, most of whom paused to blatantly stare at her. They might not know who she was, but they did know any woman on St. James Street at midnight was no lady. And she was dressed far better than the prostitutes crowding every corner and alleyway.

Fallon could well remember the last time she had walked this path at night. It had been years ago, when she was not yet sixteen. Then she'd had her father with her, though that was scant protection. He was prone to whimsy, and he'd been speaking of selling her to the highest bidder. She was half afraid that was his plan that night. She couldn't think why else they would walk among so many well-dressed gentlemen of the *ton*. The other night she'd overheard her father whispering to some man or other about how much he could earn for Maggie's virginity. She did not think her father would be pleased to know it was long gone.

Fallon shook off the memory of her father and the girl she'd been and stopped in front of a nondescript building. There was no sign proclaiming this Lucifer's Lair, but she knew it well. This was the place, and Fitzhugh would be inside waiting for her. The gambling hell was closed now. Lucifer had fled to the Continent after he'd been linked to the murder of Lady Elizabeth, daughter of the Marquess of Nowlund. There were signs the building had been looted, but Fallon wasn't certain if Scotland Yard or local vagrants were responsible.

She continued walking, turning down the next alley in order to circle around to the back entrance. It wouldn't do to be seen entering the abandoned gaming hell, especially if she had to break in. She walked quickly through the alley, wishing she'd thought to bring a lamp with her. The alley was dark and wet, as it had rained earlier that day. She sloshed through a particularly deep puddle and winced, knowing her slippers would be ruined. The damp seeped through, and she curled her toes against the cold.

Behind her, she heard another splash.

Fallon was mid-alley, in the darkest recesses, and she kept walking. It was probably Fitzhugh behind her. He was supposed to meet her here.

She heard another splash.

But why would Fitzhugh walk through the same puddle twice? And why wouldn't he call out to her?

Bloody hell. She sighed. She really did not have time for this.

Fallon whirled and narrowed her eyes at the two large shadows moving toward her.

"Ah, there she is, Tom," one of the men said. Upper-class accent, Fallon noted. Words a bit slurred.

"What are you doing down here alone, sweetheart?" Tom asked, still moving toward her.

Wonderful. She'd managed to attract two "gentlemen" out on the Town and looking for amusement. Perhaps she could dissuade them with mere words. "Gentlemen," she began, "I am not a prostitute. If you're looking for that sort of entertainment, you should seek it elsewhere."

"Ooh! She speaks like a lady, James," Tom said. They were directly in front of her now, and their watery shadows fell over her.

"Come here, lady." James made a grab for her. She jumped back and threw her mantle over her shoulders, freeing her arms. Obviously the time for words was past. She was not thrilled about having to fight two men twice her size, but they were foxed, and that worked to her advantage.

Tom, who was on her right, charged her first. She easily sidestepped and thrust her foot out to trip him. But in the darkness, she misjudged the distance, and he merely stumbled past her. This, of course, did not better her position as now she had James in front of her and Tom behind.

"I think you missed her, old boy," James said. "Let me show you how it's done." He charged. At the same time, Tom—obviously not content to wait for his turn—reached for her. Tom caught her first about the waist. She used his weight and solidity as a lever and kicked up, landing one foot squarely in James's face. She knew it had hurt him because it hurt her foot.

That, and he bent over and screamed like a little girl. Not that Fallon had ever screamed like that when she'd been in pinafores.

"What the devil—" Tom began before she rammed her head back and collided with his face. He released her, and she whirled around, backing away while keeping the men in her sights. They were injured but far from disabled. If anything, an injured man was more dangerous than one who was unhurt, because the pain made him angry.

And sobered him up.

She knew this from very personal experience.

Tom was the first to recover. She saw him searching the shadows and pinpointed the moment he spotted her. His body went rigid. "You're going to pay for that, bitch," he seethed. "I'm going to make sure you don't walk right for the next month."

"You're welcome to try," she murmured, still backing away. At the end of the alley stood a short staircase that led down into Lucifer's Lair. She could run for it, but if it was locked, it would do her no good. She'd be trapped and cornered.

She could try to escape the alley the way she'd come, but she didn't think she could outrun the men, and even if she did, there was no guarantee of safety on the other side.

Her last option was to stand and fight. She wouldn't have minded the last option if she had any sort of weapon, but all she had was her reticule, and she'd dropped that sometime between James's grab for her and Tom's first charge.

Her best hope appeared to be to try for Lucifer's Lair and hope Fitzhugh was already there and the door was unlocked. Certainly she could find something in the building to use in her defense. She clenched her fists, trying to decide the best time to move, when James shook his head and started for her. Now both men advanced. Steadily.

Now was as good as any time. Without warning, she turned and ran toward the end of the alley.

"She's getting away!" one of the men called.

"She won't go far," the other answered. Fallon heard the echo of their rapid footsteps as they followed her. Her breath came quickly by the time she reached the stairs, drowning out the sound of the men's approach, and she wasn't certain how close they were. She didn't have time to look, either. She vaulted down the four steps, slammed against the door, and tried the handle.

Locked.

Bloody goddamn hell!

She hit it with her fist then glanced quickly about for some sort of weapon. A rotting board had come loose from the side of the building, and she grabbed it, working it back and forth to try and pry it off. Thank God for her gloves, but the thin kid leather was no match for the splinters in the rough wood. She heard one of the men say, "There she is," and Fallon jerked at the wood in desperation.

It stubbornly held on. "Come on," she muttered. "Come on." She leaned back and pulled on the wood with all her weight. Just as the men's shadows crept over her, the board came off in her hands.

She whirled, held it in front of her, and waved it at Tom, who was advancing down the stairs. "And what do you think you're going to do with that?"

She didn't know. Her arms ached, and she was still trying to catch her breath. If she didn't strike decisively, Tom would merely grab the board away and use it against her. She bit her lip as he came down another step. He was higher than she was and moving downward, whereas she was low and looking up. He had every advantage. If she attempted to swing the board at him, he would grab it for certain.

And so Fallon did the only thing she could—though it would doom her when James came for her. She raised the board and hurled it at Tom.

It struck true, knocking him squarely between the eyes. He hadn't been expecting that and lost his balance, tumbling down the remaining steps, clutching his face. Fallon jumped out of the way, but the space was cramped and he fell against her legs. She needed maneuverability if she were to fight James, but Tom grabbed at one of her ankles and she couldn't shake him off. James was already on the stairs, and their gazes met.

"Get her," Tom said, his voice wracked with pain.

At least she had caused some damage, she thought, as James reached for her.

ॐ

Warrick unbolted the door, opened it, then jumped back as Fallon and two men tumbled inside. He'd been on one of the upper floors when Fallon approached and had seen the beginning of the confrontation. He'd been about to rush to her defense when she kicked one of the men in the face and slammed the back of her head into the other one.

Warrick had been rendered completely immobile and utterly stunned. He watched as she deftly defended herself, two against one, and only when he finally realized she was in trouble did he snap to attention and sprint down to open the door.

Now he lifted Fallon from among the tangle of arms and legs and quickly scanned her face and arms for injury. She looked to be all in one piece.

"What…" She paused to catch her breath. "Took you…" She gasped in another breath. "So long?"

"It didn't appear that you needed my assistance. Someone has taught you how to defend yourself."

She glared at him. "And here I thought… you knew everything about me."

So had he. But she'd managed to surprise him—surprise and impress him—and that was not easily done.

"What the devil is going on?" one of the men

demanded, crawling to his hands and knees. Blood poured from a gash above his nose. "That little bitch cut me."

"You're lucky that's all that happened." Warrick set Fallon down and pushed her behind him. "Now get out of here before I have you charged for attacking a lady."

"And who the hell are you?" the other man asked. He was in considerably better condition.

Warrick disliked questions. He disliked answering them even more. He reached in his pocket and pulled out his pistol. He leveled the weapon at the men. "Any further questions?"

The men scrambled to their feet and backed away. When they were in the doorway, Warrick closed it, bolted the lock, and turned to Fallon. "Good of you to come." He checked his pocket watch. "You're late."

"I was detained," she said, her eyebrows coming together.

"Excuses, excuses." He lifted the lamp he'd hung on a nail next to the door and began to make his way back into the club proper. He scanned what appeared to be a parlor or study. Bow Street had been here. He could see their handiwork everywhere—overturned tables, drawers standing open, papers scattered on the floors. They were clumsy and overlooked more than they found.

"If you had that pistol with you, why didn't you threaten those men with it to begin with?"

He turned to see Fallon standing in the parlor's doorway. Warrick shrugged. "You seemed to have matters well in hand."

She shook her head. "That is no way to treat a lady."

"That's because most ladies are skittish ninnies who faint if a man utters the word *damn* in their presence. You should hope I don't treat you like a lady. I have no use for ladies." He turned back to the room and began conducting his own far more delicate search. He didn't know what he was looking for—something to do with the Diamonds in the Rough. Something to give him insight into Lucifer.

But, of course, that's why Fallon was here.

He glanced at her and saw she was shaking her head. "*This* sentiment on the topic of ladies comes from the son of Lord and Lady Winthorpe?"

He turned back to the task at hand, lifting a stack of papers and flipping through them. "I take it you know my mother."

"I know *of* your mother. She's one of the most persistent, scheming, marriage-minded mamas I have ever encountered. I apologize if that offends you."

He righted an overturned desk. "Why would it offend me? If you ever do meet her, tell her those words exactly. She'll be flattered."

"I seriously doubt it."

He glanced at her. "You shouldn't doubt me. After all, it takes a man with considerable convictions and impressive fortitude to resist the manipulations of a mother like mine. I tell you truly, I don't care for ladies." He rolled onto his back and peered under the desk he'd set on its feet.

"What are you doing?"

"Shine the lamp so I can see." Though her steps were light, he heard her cross the room. A moment later, the lamp's light illuminated the bottom of the desk. "Nothing," he muttered.

"Did you expect to find the diamonds? He won't have them here."

He stilled, willing her to go on. He could ask her about her association with Lucifer directly, but he knew she would not be forthcoming. Information she volunteered on her own was worth far more.

"If he has them at all, they're somewhere well protected. He's done with this place. He won't come back. It's been violated. At least in his mind."

"You knew him well," Warrick said, pretending to study the underside of the desk.

"No. Thank God. The man was diabolical."

"As the name would indicate."

"Yes, well the accounts I heard of him were terrifying. Even at fifteen I was not so much a fool as to believe he snacked on young virgins, but I knew something horrible went on here."

"So it wasn't only gambling?" Warrick sat. In his research he'd come across several interesting accusations against Lucifer of Lucifer's Lair. Now he wondered if Fallon would confirm them. He could hear traces of the lower-class accent creeping into her speech. She must have worked very hard to rid herself of it to become one of The Three Diamonds.

"My father wasn't a gambler," she said looking around. "He drank too much and he stole and he occasionally engaged in blackmail. He never gambled. Why would he when he couldn't be sure of making money? I don't know what his association with Lucifer involved. I was present at several of their meetings, but they didn't speak freely in front of me. All I can tell you is it wasn't gambling."

Warrick rested his arms on his knees. "And why do you think your father brought you to these meetings with Lucifer? He brought you here, I assume."

"Yes." She shivered almost imperceptibly. "I've been here before." She looked at him and even in the dim light he could feel the power of her gaze. "Why do you think a man brings a young girl to a meeting with another man?"

"You weren't just a young girl. You were his daughter."

"The daughter of a pickpocket and a whore. Trust me, he didn't have many tender feelings. He sold my mother until she was too ill to work any longer."

"And did he sell you to Lucifer?"

"No. That's when I left."

"And came under the protection of Sinclair."

She looked away. "As warm and cozy as all of this reminiscing makes me feel, I cannot help but ask what it is you want from me?"

"Tonight? Tonight I want you to look around Lucifer's Lair with me. I could use another set of eyes. And you've been here before. Perhaps you have some insight."

"That was ten years ago."

He rose to his feet. "Humor me."

"Fine. And after this our *friendship* is over. I've kept my end of the bargain."

"I don't recall us making a bargain." He took the lamp from her and started for the door on the far side of the room.

"Yes, we did. You said if I helped you, then you wouldn't reveal my past."

"That does sound familiar." He could hear her scampering behind him, and he walked all the more quickly to keep her hurrying after him.

"I've told you what I know. I don't know where the diamonds are. I'd never heard of them until Juliette mentioned them. I hadn't thought of Lucifer for years until he accosted her. I've held up my part of the bargain."

Warrick spun round and grabbed her arm. This was life and death—to him, if not her. "I'll decide when you've done your part. I decide what's involved in our bargain and what's not, and I'll say when you've fulfilled your part. Is that clear?"

She looked down at his hand. "You're hurting my arm."

He released her. "Forgive me." He turned left toward the thick wooden door he remembered from his surveillance earlier that night. When he heard her behind him, he turned the handle and pushed the door open to reveal the scarlet and black bedroom. "Now, tell me what the hell went on in here."

Four

FALLON STEPPED INTO THE ROOM AFTER FITZHUGH, keeping close to him. Not because she wanted to be close to him. He was holding the lamp, and she didn't relish the thought of standing in the dark, empty building by herself.

The walls of the room were black silk, as were the draperies and all of the furnishings. Except the bed. That was covered in a blood-red silk coverlet. Or at least it had been. Someone had ransacked the room and overturned the bed. It appeared the coverlet had been thrown over the bed as an afterthought. It looked very much like a splash of blood.

"I've never been here before," she said. And she didn't want to come back. "I assume it's Lucifer's private room."

"Not exactly to your taste," Fitzhugh said, strolling about, lifting objects here and there as though he was unaffected by the eerie style of furnishing. Perhaps he wasn't. She knew very little about him. If Juliette and Pelham hadn't been away from Town, she would have gone to her friend's husband immediately and asked him for more information on Fitzhugh. The two were said to be friends.

But Fallon wondered if a man like Fitzhugh—a man who stole others' secrets—didn't have a few of his own. And as she well knew, when one had secrets, it was next to impossible to have any close friends. Juliette and Lily had their own secrets, and they never questioned Fallon about her past. But most people were hopelessly nosy.

"You've been inside my bedchamber." He'd been in her bed. "You know my taste." She watched him move about the room. He moved easily, comfortable in his skin and with who he was. He was unself-conscious, which made her all the more fascinated by him. She was always conscious of her every move, of her every word. She often felt she didn't know who she was—Margaret, Maggie, Fallon, the Marchioness of Mystery? She could be all of them or none of them on any given day.

Fallon had spent a great deal of time watching others. She'd been trained from an early age to observe others. One didn't prosper as a pickpocket if one didn't learn to pick out the best marks and find their weaknesses. As she grew older, she watched people for other reasons. One could tell so much about the interior lives of others by observing how they behaved, how they interacted with others, how they acted when they didn't know they were being watched.

Sometimes she even made up stories about the people she saw—that woman was rushing to meet a lover. That man was angry with his solicitor. That little girl wanted a new hat but was too polite to say so.

She couldn't read Warrick Fitzhugh quite so easily. He had thoughts and emotions—of that she was certain—but he didn't betray them by his actions. The one trait she could identify was confidence. He spoke, moved, and acted confidently. He was a man who expected to be followed and obeyed. She wouldn't have expected so much certainty from him. After all, he wasn't his father's heir. He wasn't even the second son. He had a domineering mother, who'd bullied her other children into prestigious matches. She knew at least one of the matches was not a happy one. The husband of one of Fitzhugh's sisters had sent Fallon jewelry and gifts aplenty last year in an effort to woo her.

Most interesting, Fitzhugh was not handsome. Handsome men—men like Kwirley—were always confident. It was probably bred into them from an early age. She knew from experience that attractive people often got what they wanted. She couldn't count the number of times she'd used her looks to achieve some aim or other. But Fitzhugh was an exception. He wasn't ugly. His face was interesting—the broken nose, the scar near his eye…

The eyes. When he'd pulled her close a moment ago, she'd gotten a clear view of them. They were brown with gold flecks. They'd been smoldering when he'd hauled her against him, but she hadn't been afraid. In fact, she'd been aroused.

Of course, that might have been more the result of being thrust against his hard chest. She disliked tall, skinny men. This was a man who had strength and substance. He'd easily lifted her into his arms when she'd crashed through the door with those two idiots on top of her. She wondered what his chest looked like without his shirt.

"Are you going to stand there all evening?"

She blinked. "What would you have me do?" Oh, dear. Had he heard the sultry tone of her voice? She had to stop picturing him naked—or herself naked with him touching her. He was her enemy. He was blackmailing her. She didn't like him.

Fallon cleared her throat. "What I mean is, what am I supposed to do?"

"Look around." He gestured to the room.

Fallon frowned at the overturned desk and the broken table. "For what, exactly?"

He sighed impatiently. "I don't know. You'll know it when you see it."

"Of course. That helps." She made her way to the desk because Fitzhugh was on the other side of the room and she thought a bit of distance might be for the best. She was not a tidy person, but she could at least straighten the spray of papers and quills. There wasn't much she could do about the dried ink on the floor. She glanced at Fitzhugh, who was holding a parchment toward the lamp and reading. At least she looked busy.

She lifted papers and stacked them neatly, covering a yawn with her hand. She was weary and would much rather be sleeping than digging through Lucifer's forgotten papers. A five pound note fell out of an envelope, and she picked it up to stuff it back where it had come from. Even if she'd been poor, she would never be so poor as to take Lucifer's blunt. She opened the envelope and caught sight of a familiar emblem. She pulled the paper out, noting it was a receipt for a deposit box at Lloyd's Bank. This was not unusual. She imagined Lucifer had quite a few things hidden away in boxes all over London as well as abroad.

What interested her was that the box had been opened by a man listed as Gabriel. No surname, no other identification. Simply Gabriel.

Fallon remembered Gabriel. He looked every bit the angel he had been named for. He had golden blond hair he wore long around a narrow, defined face. His movements, his voice, his hands were smooth and soft. He'd touched her once, when he was leading her to her father, and she'd been shocked at how soft his hands were.

Hers had never been so soft.

She glanced at Fitzhugh. This was probably the sort of thing he would want to know about. She sighed. And if she told him, it would only prolong their association. And if she didn't tell him, she'd probably end up telling him later, and then he'd accuse her of keeping more secrets.

She sighed again. "Here." She held out the receipt. "This is probably what you're looking for."

"What is it?" he came toward her, took the paper, and walked back to the lamp. He scanned it. "Who is Gabriel?"

Fallon nodded. He'd cut quickly to the meat. Fitzhugh was no fool. "Lucifer's majordomo. He ran the club when Lucifer was away and obviously took care of some of Lucifer's financial dealings."

Fitzhugh glanced at her. "You met him?"

She wanted to lie, but he was looking at her with those eyes. Why did those eyes have to be so compelling? Why did they make her want him to keep looking at her?

"Yes. On several occasions."

"And?"

She struggled for the words to describe Gabriel and settled on, "I didn't like him."

"Why?"

"He was scary, but in a different way than Lucifer was scary."

He frowned at her. "Scary? The same way those two men you beat the hell out of in the alley were scary?"

"I was fourteen or fifteen when I met him." She stood and dusted off her gown. "That's the impression I carry."

"Fair enough."

"Good. Can we leave now?"

"Yes."

She started for the door and was pleased when he followed. She could not wait to go home and go to sleep. Perhaps she'd take a warm bath first.

"Let's find this Gabriel."

Fallon blew out a breath and felt her shoulders slump. "I *knew* you were going to say that."

He hailed a hackney cab once they reached St. James again and climbed in after her. "Now where?" she demanded. "Surely you don't propose we search every gambling hell in the city for him."

He actually seemed to consider the idea.

"*Fitzhugh*," she warned.

"Coachman, take us to Monmouth Street."

Fallon's jaw dropped. "*Seven Dials*? I'm not going to Seven Dials. Do you want to get us killed?"

"'Ave to agree with the lady, guv," the jarvey added. "Monmouth is a wee bit unsavory this 'our of the night."

"I'll pay you double," Fitzhugh stated and pressed the coins into the man's hand.

The jarvey released the brake. "Monmouth Street!" he called.

"No!" Fallon had half a mind to jump from the vehicle, but that was a venture almost as dangerous as Seven Dials. "I'll pay you triple to turn back!" she called to the coachman, but either he didn't hear or he had decided money in the hand was worth more than promises.

Fallon blew out a breath. "What on earth is in Seven Dials? Other than pickpockets, cutthroats, and gin?"

"The Merry Widow."

Fallon gripped the edge of the seat to keep from falling. "A brothel? I don't know what sort of arrangement you think we have—"

Fitzhugh held up a hand. "A business arrangement." He leaned across the coach and looked her in the eye. "Trust me, Fallon, if I wanted you, I wouldn't have to take you to an accommodation house. I could have you right here and right now."

Angry words of denial rose to her lips, but somehow she couldn't utter them. He was ridiculous. She wouldn't allow him to so much as touch her.

Would she?

His dark eyes seemed to challenge her, and she shivered. Perhaps it would be best not to test his assertions. She looked away—anything to avoid those eyes. "What is at The Merry Widow?"

"An old friend. If she doesn't know where this Gabriel is, no one does."

Fallon had a thousand questions, but she clamped her mouth shut and refrained from asking. He was a spy. Such men probably had unlikely acquaintances in every city. And she supposed if this woman helped them find Gabriel then she couldn't complain. Fallon wanted out of this partnership, and the sooner the better.

The coach passed the sundial at the junction of the seven streets that made up the area of Seven Dials, and Fallon pulled the hood of her mantle around her face and burrowed into the soft material. She could take care of herself, but that didn't mean she looked for trouble. It was a short jaunt down Monmouth and then the hackney slowed and stopped in front of a dilapidated building. Fallon wondered if a building existed in Seven Dials that didn't look as though it had been lifted by some giant hand, spun around, and dropped back down again.

"'Ere ye are, guv. Quick as can be."

Fitzhugh climbed out of the coach and held out his hand for Fallon. She pushed it away and climbed out on her own, ignoring the amused look in his eyes. She wasn't going to allow him to pick and choose times to play the gentleman, and she wouldn't be fooled. He might be the son of an earl—she looked up at the lurid sign proclaiming The Merry Widow with a lascivious looking woman on it—but he was no gentleman.

"Let's be done with this." She swept past him and pushed through the bawdy house's red door. Really, did the owner not realize a little subtlety could go a long way?

Inside was precisely what she had expected. A drab common room with threadbare chairs and couches hunched around a dying fire boasted two or three downtrodden men, standing with hands shoved in pockets. The place smelled stale and vaguely as though something had died. Fallon put a scented handkerchief to her nose partly to disguise the smell and partly to hide her face. As soon as they'd entered, the men had glanced her way. Two of them looked right back down again, but one stared at her with undisguised interest. She certainly hoped he didn't write for *The Morning Post*. The last thing she needed was this latest escapade tidbit making the rounds of the press.

"You need a room?" a hard high voice asked from a dark corner. Fallon jumped and whirled in the direction of the sound. She hadn't seen the small, dark...person standing there. She squinted and studied the...was it a man or a woman? His or her clothes hung limply around an indiscernible figure that was reed thin. The face was hairless and ugly—too ugly for a woman but far too delicate for a man. The dun-colored hair was cropped in no particular style and hung in shaggy clumps around the small face, which was thin and narrow. It could have been the face of a young man or an old woman.

"Get your abbess," Fitzhugh directed, using the slang for the proprietor of a bawdy house.

"And who should I say is calling?" the person said with something of a sneer in its voice.

"Warrick," he answered.

The person nodded and melted into another dark corner and then was gone.

"Warrick?" Fallon whispered. "I thought you were going to give her—him some sort of code name. You know, Jackal or Raven or Fluffy Bunny." She detected the ghost of a smile on his lips.

"I don't have a code name. I wasn't that sort of operative."

"You mean to say Fluffy Bunny was taken?" She knew she must be extremely tired to jest with him so. She should be annoyed that she was standing in a rotting brothel in Seven Dials at—she squinted at the tall case clock on the wall—half past three in the morning. Oh, she did hope that clock was not accurate.

"Precisely. And pray you never meet the man. Fluffy Bunny is terribly dangerous."

"Why else would he be called *Fluffy*?"

"This way, sir. Madam," the little person said from behind them. Fallon shuddered. How had it gotten behind them? It gestured to a door at the far end of the room and Fitzhugh motioned for her to go first.

She shook her head. "Oh, no. This is not the time for chivalry. You go first."

"There's nothing to be worried about."

"So says the man who's failed to earn a code name. Why, even I have a sobriquet."

"Yes, and we all enjoy conjecturing on how you earned it."

"The same way as Fluffy Bunny, I imagine." She followed Fitzhugh across the room, feeling the eyes of the men loitering there on her. She was almost relieved when he opened the door and she was away from that depressing place.

Except this room was far worse.

❧

Warrick knew the onslaught of roses was coming, and he tried to take a last breath of flowerless air to compensate, but it didn't help. He didn't understand Daisy's need to be surrounded by the flowers, but he could overlook the peculiarity because she was so valuable. He knew the moment Fallon entered because he could hear her gag quietly. He thought she'd looked rather ill in the common room. She hadn't known what was coming.

"Warrick!" A tall, handsome woman rose from a settee and walked gracefully to greet him. Her too-red hair had been twisted into a sophisticated style and her green gown was cut low enough to intrigue but was modest enough to keep a man wondering. He didn't think she was for sale any longer. She'd begun her career on the streets and had fought her way to a position where she now owned a section of those streets. He didn't agree with her business, but who was he to judge? She might sell young women, but she had more morals and scruples than many of the so-called paragons of the nation.

"Daisy." He gave her a genuine smile and met her halfway, taking her in his arms for a long embrace.

When he released her, she swatted his arm. "You should come by more often. We don't get many men like you in here." Her accent was pure London streets, though she'd managed to refine it slightly, probably aping her betters as best she could. And yet it was as familiar to him as his own mother's clipped consonants.

"You flatter me."

"Of course. And who is this mysterious lady? Your sister, I presume?"

Daisy was diplomatic, if nothing else. Warrick turned to observe Fallon, her hood still over her head and shrouding her face. The mantle enveloped her small, rounded figure and only her dark eyes peered out. He wondered if she realized for all the effort she made to conceal herself, it only made her that much more intriguing. She couldn't hide her beauty, no matter how she tried. The glimpse of sun-kissed skin and the flash of those impossibly dark eyes drew a man.

"No. She's not my sister. She's..." What the hell was she? He shook his head. "It's complicated."

Fallon lowered her hood and stepped forward with her gloved hand outstretched. He saw Daisy's gaze flick to the soiled glove. It wasn't in keeping with the rest of her appearance and gave a good indication of the night she'd had thus far. But then the abbess's gaze roved to Fallon's face, and she took a step back. "Gawd's nightgown!"

One of Fallon's dark brows arched slightly. She gave him a questioning look, but he wasn't going to intervene. Daisy stepped closer to Fallon, all but towering over the courtesan. To Fallon's credit, she didn't move back or cower. She stood where she was and endured the scrutiny. She was probably used to it.

"You're one of them. The Three Diamonds."

Fallon gave a slight nod of her head, and Warrick wondered if she encountered this sort of reaction often. To a woman like Daisy, The Three Diamonds were celebrities the way Sarah Siddons or John Philip Kemble were to those who enjoyed the theater.

"Don't tell me," Daisy insisted. "You're not the Countess of Charm. She's got red hair." She indicated her own hair, and Warrick wondered if the woman was attempting to emulate the third Diamond with her hair color. Having seen the countess up close, he had to say she was not succeeding. Lily's hair color was all too real and vibrant. "You're the Marchioness of Mystery. You're Fallon!" She said the last reverently then hurried to turn a chair toward Fallon. "You should sit down. Gawd, I'm beside meself!" Her accent pushed through the more agitated she became. "I have a genuine celebrity in my establishment!"

Warrick didn't have the heart to tell her Fallon was no celebrity, and he could read in the courtesan's tight expression the last thing she wanted was to have her virtues extolled and praised within these sullied walls. But she was nothing if not magnanimous, and she took a seat on the chair upholstered in a rose-patterned cloth.

"It's a pleasure to meet you," Fallon said, her smoky, cultured voice a sharp contrast to Daisy's. She glanced about, fumbling for some sort of compliment to make. Warrick could have told her Daisy was too awe-struck to hear anyway, but he was an observer at heart and liked nothing better than to watch a scene play out. He moved a vase of blackened roses aside and settled one hip on the edge of a desk. At least he assumed there was a desk under all of the foliage.

"You must enjoy roses," Fallon said.

Warrick coughed to cover his laugh. Trust Fallon to be understated. The room was smothered in roses in various stages of life. Rotting roses, blooming roses, drooping roses; roses in red, yellow, pink, white, and every mixture in between vied for space in the overcrowded room.

"They're my signature flower," Daisy said, her voice cracking as she spoke.

Fallon's brows came together. "And yet your name is Daisy."

Daisy nodded. "Iconic, isn't it?"

Fallon opened her mouth to correct the woman then closed it again and turned her gaze on Warrick. Apparently, she was handing the field back to him. He was ready to take it. Too much longer amid the stench of roses and he would be forced to stick his head out a window. He stood. "Daisy, I have an inquiry for you."

The abbess didn't take her eyes from Fallon. "What's that, luv?"

"I need to know the whereabouts of a man named Gabriel."

Now Daisy looked at him. "I hope you don't mean the Gabriel I think you mean."

"You know the man then?"

"I know *of* him, and that's all I want to know. If you want my advice, which you don't because you never do," she groused, "stay away from the likes of that one. His employer too."

"My information indicates Lucifer is on the Continent."

She snorted. "My information indicates Lucifer is wherever the devil—pardon my language, my lady—he wants to be."

Warrick tilted his head. He had been prepared to settle for seeking out Gabriel, but if he could find Lucifer...

"And I know that look in your eyes," Daisy said, pointing a jeweled finger in his direction. "I don't know where Lucifer is, and if I did, I'd forget about it right quick."

"What about Gabriel?"

She shook her head. "You don't want to see him, Warrick. I thought you had left this work. I keep telling you to find a lady and marry. Have a passel of brats. That's your lot, not this drudgery."

"And I have told you I will take all of that under advisement. But right now, men's lives are at stake. I need to find Gabriel, and I need to find him quickly."

Daisy held up her hands. "All right. I'll help you, though I don't think I'm doing you any favors."

"I don't expect a favor. I'm prepared to pay—"

She thrust her palm up. "Stubble it. I won't hear a word about payment. You don't owe me anything. Not after what you done."

Out of the corner of his eye, he saw Fallon's brows rise. He could imagine the train of her thoughts, and he rather thought he liked to keep her guessing.

"You'll find him at The Grotto. He won't be visible. He stays out of sight. But he's there most nights, running things from the back, so to speak."

"Sounds like someone else I know."

"Humph. I'm nothing like him."

"No, you're not." He went to Fallon and offered his arm.

"You're not taking her to The Grotto?"

"Why not?" he asked, amused at her protectiveness.

She huffed out a breath. "It's no place for her sort. Leave her here. I'll take care of her."

"Yes, I'm sure you will."

Daisy thrust her hands on her hips. "Not that sort of care, though if she wanted to bed a man or two, I wouldn't object. It would raise my standing considerably." She looked hopefully at Fallon, who simply drew her mantle around her face again.

"Thank you, Daisy. Come and see me if you need anything."

She shook her head. "As though I'd darken your door."

He escorted Fallon to the exit. "Good night."

"Thank you," Fallon said.

"You're always welcome. Take care of her, Warrick."

"I will." And, to his surprise, he meant it.

Five

OF COURSE THE HACKNEY WASN'T WAITING WHEN they emerged. Fallon didn't think Fitzhugh had really believed it would be. She had to stand about on her tired feet for a quarter of an hour while he arranged alternate transportation. In the end, the eager-to-please Daisy provided it. Fallon was beginning to wonder just what her relationship with Fitzhugh entailed. She seemed almost desperate to be of service to him.

Finally, they climbed into the coach and Fitzhugh gave the coachman directions to The Grotto. Fallon sighed. "Can this not wait until tomorrow evening? It will be after four by the time we arrive."

Fitzhugh gave her a veiled look. "The Grotto is not located in Seven Dials."

"Thank God for small mercies."

"Do you? I don't believe in God."

"That's not a surprise," she muttered. The man probably thought of himself as God. He certainly enjoyed impersonating a deity and ordering her about.

He lifted the carriage lamp and tilted it so the

light shone in her eyes. Fallon shielded her face and scowled at him.

"Remove your mantle."

"Excuse me?"

"I want to see what you're wearing underneath."

"Why?"

"Remove it or I'll do it for you. I will enjoy the latter option immensely, I assure you."

She was afraid she might enjoy it too, which was why she yanked at the braided cords fastened at her neck and allowed the mantle to slip from her shoulders. She watched his gaze trail over the green gown she'd been wearing for what seemed like days and felt her skin tingle where his glance touched it. She gripped her hands on the squabs and forced herself not to cross her arms over her chest. Why did he have to affect her like this? She had long ago become immune to the wiles of men. At one point in her life, she could have been easily seduced by Fitzhugh's look and his erotic threats. Now she should have been unmoved.

But she wasn't.

Fallon couldn't understand what was so different about this man, what made him stoke a fire inside her, but she knew she could not allow him to see the effect he had. He would use it against her. He was a man who used everything and anything to his advantage.

He frowned and shook his head. "I should have instructed you to wear red," he said finally.

Fallon felt her jaw drop. He was criticizing her wardrobe choice? She was one of The Three Diamonds. She was one of the most sought-after women in the country, and this man in... in—she made a quick study of his appearance—a wrinkled cravat, scuffed boots, and dirty trousers thought to critique her?

"And your hem has mud on it. I can only imagine the state of your slippers." He gestured with one hand, and Fallon reached forward and snatched it.

"If you speak one more word, you are taking your life in your hands, sir." She could have sworn his eyes glittered with amusement. It must have been a trick of the lamp. "If you recall, I was accosted by two rather inebriated *gentlemen* of your *ton*."

"It's not my—"

"Tsk!" She raised a finger. "My mantle is undoubtedly ruined, and if by some chance my gown survived the scuffle and can be salvaged, it will be a miracle. You should be offering to recompense me for the damage to my wardrobe, not evaluating it."

"And you"—somehow he had reversed their grips and was now clutching her hand—"should be thanking me for not telling every man, woman, and child in the city who you really are, *Maggie*."

"Oh, really? At this point, I almost wish you would so I could be rid of you."

"You wouldn't get rid of me that easily."

"Yes, I would. I…"

His mouth closed over hers in a hot, possessive kiss that caused the world to tumble and twirl. For a moment she was afraid the carriage had rolled over, and then she realized it was her head spinning. His mouth claimed hers so completely she was kissing him back before she knew what had happened. He didn't ask. He didn't request. He demanded her response.

And when his tongue slipped between her lips and she

tasted him, she heard herself groan. Shock and mortification blazed through her, but when she tried to pull away, his hands fisted in her hair and he pulled her closer. She was practically on his lap, and she had no idea how that had happened. All she knew was that his mouth slanted over hers again and again until she could think of nothing but his lips and the heat spiraling through her.

Some part of her was vaguely aware her hair had come undone as his hands threaded through it. Some part of her was aware she was kissing him back with far too much fervor and intensity if she intended to convince him she was not attracted to him in the least. And some part of her was aware that she didn't care one whit and she would be quite content if the kiss never ended and she stayed in his arms.

The next thing she knew she was thrown backward, her head hitting the side of the carriage before she tumbled to the floor with a hard jolt. It took Fallon a moment to realize this was not part of the effect of Fitzhugh's kiss and to register that the horses were screaming and Fitzhugh was shouting.

"What…?" She managed before the carriage rocked again and she was slammed first into Fitzhugh's knees and then back again so her head hit the seat.

Daisy's squabs were not as soft as they looked.

Fitzhugh's arms closed around her, and he lifted her up beside him. "Are you all right?"

She couldn't seem to manage any words, so she nodded her head.

"Good. Hold on." He reached into his coat and pulled a pistol out. Fallon shook her head to clear it. This was obviously the part of the evening where he shot her. Somehow it made sense that he would kiss her and then kill her.

But instead of shooting her, he pushed her back against those really-not-very-soft squabs and jammed the window of the carriage open. And then to her horror, he primed the pistol with a speed and efficiency she had never before witnessed—though to be honest she had little experience with pistols—leaned out the window, and fired.

"What in the devil's name are you doing?" she screamed.

"Stubble it," he muttered and attended to his pistol again.

"You can't shoot a pistol out the window! This isn't a fox hunt!"

"Oh, yes, it is," he said, finishing with the pistol. "And if we're not careful, we'll turn out to be the foxes."

The carriage rocked again, and the window opposite her shattered. She screamed and covered her face to ward off the shards of glass. Fitzhugh seemed unperturbed. He calmly stuck his head and arms out the opposite window and fired again.

When he was back inside, she grabbed his cravat and forced him to look at her. "*What* is going on?"

He gave her an incredulous look, as though she should understand any of this, as though one moment he wasn't kissing her and the next she was being tossed about the carriage like a piece of unsecured luggage.

"We're being chased."

"Why?"

He detached her hands from his neck cloth and looked to his pistol again. Good Lord, was he going to shoot *more*? How many pistol balls did he have?

"Good question," he said, pouring gunpowder down the pistol's barrel and then ramming a lead ball on top. "I didn't think to stop and ask our pursuers questions."

He leaned over her again, and this time she had the presence of mind to cover her ears before he cocked the hammer and pulled the trigger. She was probably going to be deaf anyway, but she might salvage some functionality in at least one of her ears. "Is this something to do with Lucifer?"

"That would be my guess." He glanced out the window again, then jerked his head in as something screeched past. Fallon closed her eyes, fearing the thing that had screeched past had been a ball from their opponent's pistol.

"Why do I have the feeling there is something you are not telling me?"

He grinned at her. How could the man smile when they were being shot at? He was mad. Absolutely daft. That was the only explanation. "Sweetheart," he said, "there's a hell of a lot I'm not telling you."

The carriage jolted again, and she clutched his arm to keep her balance. "This cannot be happening," she muttered as they careened around a corner. She'd been done with adventure in her life. She'd had more than she ever wanted before the age of six. And then Fitzhugh had to show up in her bed, and she was once again being chased, shot at, and blackmailed. Her life could not get any worse.

"We're going to have to jump," Fitzhugh said.

"What did you say?" Fallon asked. She almost laughed. "I thought you said *jump*."

"I did."

Something hit the carriage, rocking it to one side.

"Daisy's coachman is a superb driver, but we can't continue at this pace. All we need is one vegetable cart blocking our path, and we're done for."

"Fine. You jump. I'll take my chances with whoever is in the other carriage."

Fitzhugh shrugged. "That's your choice. They're not after you, but that doesn't mean they won't kill you. Or use you to get to me."

"You don't care about me."

"They don't know that." He peered out the window again. "There's a park coming up on your right. I'll bang on the hatch to let the coachman know to slow. As soon as we near the grass, we jump."

"I'm not jumping!" What was wrong with him?

"Have it your way." He peered out the window again, judging the distance. He was really going to jump from a moving carriage. The man was either a complete idiot or had his back up against a wall.

Another shot rang out. Probably not a complete idiot, but she was not jumping. That was suicide. She'd done a lot of foolish things in her life—stolen her father's money bag, slept with that fop Lord Durleigh, and once drank too much champagne in the company of the Prince Regent and had to be saved from his nefarious attentions by Juliette and Lily. She did not claim to be the cleverest girl in London. But she was not so foolish as to jump from a moving carriage.

Fitzhugh banged on the carriage roof and moved to a crouch. He was really going to do it. The carriage slowed, and everything happened as if in a dream. One moment she was shaking her head at him, thinking,

What a poor clodpole. The next moment, the carriage door was open, she was wrenched from her seat, and she was flying through the air. Fallon could have sworn she screamed, but there was no sound—only the rushing of the wind in her ears and the dull, ominous thud when she hit the grass.

She had enough presence of mind to roll and to tuck her head and legs. That didn't mean every inch of her wasn't jolted by the impact. The grass was undeniably hard. Was there nothing soft in London tonight? She tumbled slowly to a stop and lay, breathing heavily, staring stupidly at the sky above her. She blinked. Were those stars or simply lights dancing before her eyes? She closed her eyes, deciding at this point, she didn't really care.

"Fallon." Something was shaking her. She tried to push it aside, but it shook her harder. "Fallon, get up. They're coming for us."

She forced her eyes open. The task felt monumental. She could have sworn something was holding her eyelids down. "Wha…"

Fitzhugh was staring down at her. He had a leaf in his hair and a smear of dirt on one cheek. The dirt looked pretty good on him. She reached up, and he caught her hands, pulling her upward. She resisted. She didn't want to stand. She wanted to continue to lie here in the cool night and sleep. She was so weary.

"Fallon." His voice had an edge of concern now that pricked her and made her open her eyes again. It was slightly easier this time. "Can you rise? If not, I shall have to carry you, and that will slow us considerably." He looked over his shoulder, and she glanced that way as well. In the distance, she heard the clatter of approaching horses.

"You *pushed* me."

"I was trying to save you."

"And now?"

"I'm still trying. They're coming for us. We must go or we'll be killed. Or worse."

Worse. She had lived enough life to know there were many things worse than death. She tried to sit, found the task all but impossible, and grudgingly accepted Fitzhugh's aid. She wobbled to her feet and felt like retching. The world was spinning and tumbling.

"Let's go." Fitzhugh took her hand and pulled her behind him. She stumbled after him, not because she wanted to but because he really gave her no choice. She was vaguely aware that she was in pain. She couldn't quite pinpoint where the pain was localized—everything seemed to hurt—but she knew it wasn't good. She finally had the wherewithal to look about and saw Fitzhugh was pulling her toward a copse of trees. She didn't recognize the park, but at least the trees were close together, making them inaccessible to a carriage and providing the two of them some darkness in which to hide.

Fitzhugh glanced over his shoulder again, and she made the mistake of glancing too. The carriage was bearing down on them, its four horses foaming at the mouth from their exertions and the coachman whipping them all the harder. Fallon cursed Fitzhugh and then pushed her leaden legs faster. She was running beside him now.

"There," he said, pointing to a dark opening between two large trees. "Head for those trees." He didn't even sound winded. Fallon's breath came short and shallow, and she felt as though her lungs would explode. Meanwhile, the man beside her was sprinting along as though he did this nightly.

Fallon could feel the ground shaking beneath her feet, and the roar of the horses' hooves all but deafened her. She was too afraid to look over her shoulder and she could not run any faster. Something warm tickled her neck as the horses gained on them. And then, at the last moment, when she was certain she would be trampled, Fitzhugh gave her a hard shove, sending her flying into the safety of the darkness.

❧

Warrick rolled to a stop, lifted his head, and watched as the coachman did his best to control the horses. The turn was steep, and the horses screamed in protest. As it was, the carriage bounced against one of the trees, rocking it and sending a shower of leaves and branches on his head.

The carriage flew away, but he knew it would be back. He and Fallon had to get out of here. Under the canopy of trees, the night was dark and he had not seen where she landed. "Fallon?" he hissed.

No answer.

"Fallon!" he called louder. It would take a moment for the carriage to return, and until then, its occupants could not hear him.

Still nothing. Where the devil was she? He stood and surveyed the darkness around him, his eyes gradually adjusting. She couldn't be far. He would find her if he did a quick perimeter search, but he really didn't believe he even had the time for that much.

"Fallon, goddamn it! Where are you?"

He heard a moan and raced toward the sound. His boot thumped something hard, and the thing moaned again. He bent and cleared leaves off her fallen figure. This time he didn't even ask if she could rise. He lifted her and carried her deeper into the woods. She was lighter than she looked. All those curves made her seem more substantial, but she was a petite thing and fit easily into his arms.

He could hear the carriage returning now, and he scanned the darkness for somewhere to hide. The men would be as blind as he, and by the time they returned with dogs, he and Fallon would be gone. He spotted a fallen tree trunk a few feet away and arrowed for it. He could set her down on the other side and keep them both hidden from view. When he rounded it, he saw the ground beneath had been excavated by some creature or another, making just enough room to slide both of them inside. He set Fallon down, and she groaned again. It was a groan of pain, which concerned him, but he didn't have time to do much more than frown for the moment. Instead, he reached into the small cave and felt for occupants.

It was empty, and he lowered himself in then dragged Fallon in beside him. The space was small and cramped, and her body pressed against him. She was warm and solid. He had the faintest sense of the scent of something musky and exotic and knew it was her scent. Fitzhugh leaned his head back and closed his eyes.

For some reason, he was strangely content.

Six

FALLON OPENED HER EYES AND GROANED. SHE HURT...
everywhere.

"Here, madam, drink some of this."

Fallon did as she was bid, swallowing the tepid tea
then glanced at her server. It was Anne, her lady's
maid. Thank God. She looked about and noted she
was in her own room, in her own bed, and in her
own nightshift. Perhaps she had dreamed last night?
Although, she supposed she should classify it as more
of a nightmare.

But if it was a dream, why did it hurt every time she
breathed in? And if it was a dream, why was Fitzhugh
sleeping in the chair across from her bed?

"I'm sorry, madam," Anne said hurriedly. "I tried
to convince him to leave."

"What is he doing here?" Fallon hissed, not
wanting to wake him. "Where is Titus?" Titus could
throw him out.

"The gentleman brought you home, madam, and
wouldn't allow anyone but himself to carry you
up to your room. He seemed so tender about it,

I supposed we all assumed…" She trailed off, and Fallon knew what the staff had assumed. They knew they worked for a courtesan, even if they never saw her allow a man into her boudoir. She supposed they had their own notions about where her romantic liaisons occurred.

"Well, perhaps you could assume that he's the one responsible for putting me in this condition! He pushed me out of a moving carriage!"

"Madam!" Anne felt Fallon's head for fever. "Should I call for a physician?"

Fallon closed her eyes in frustration. The man had thrown her out of a moving conveyance, and she was the one everyone assumed was daft.

"No. Just leave me now. Thank you."

"Are you certain, madam? Would you like some refreshment? Cook prepared a small meal for Mr. Fitzhugh. I am certain she has more."

Fallon's gaze flicked to the tray on the table beside Fitzhugh. The plates were completely bare. So not only was he sleeping in her chair, he was eating her food! "I'm fine, Anne. That will be all."

Anne bobbed and closed the door quietly behind her. With only the crackle of the fire, Fallon could hear Fitzhugh's snoring. She lifted a pillow from the bed and threw it at him. Without even opening his eyes, he reached up, snatched the pillow in midair, and stuffed it behind his head.

"Oh!" Fallon was seething. "You're not asleep at all!" Wretched man.

"How can anyone sleep with all the noise you are making? I must say you make a very poor hostess, Fallon."

She jumped up, winced at the pain in her side, and eased back onto her pillows. "I don't recall inviting you."

"Exactly!" he said, opening his eyes. "A good hostess would not have commented—what's wrong?" He was up and beside her in a matter of seconds. He put his hand on her shoulder, and she shrugged it off then winced in pain again.

"Nothing."

He knelt beside her. "Where does it hurt?"

"Nowhere. Everywhere. It's not your concern."

"You've got quite a few bruises," he said, inspecting her. He took her arms in his hands and turned them this way and that. "But I don't see anything…"

"Stop touching me."

His fingers were light on her arms, tender, and she didn't want tenderness from him. He rose and began to feel her head. "A few bumps and bruises. Does this one hurt?"

"Yes! Ow! Stop touching me."

"What about your legs?" He bent, lifted the hem of her nightshift, and began to poke at her calves. Fallon kicked him away and lowered the gown.

"What are you doing?"

"For a courtesan, you're rather modest. Don't you dance naked at the Cyprians' balls or some such thing?"

Courtesans did dance naked at some of the debauched balls held by the Fashionable Impures like the Wilson sisters and Julia Johnstone, but Fallon had never participated. She wasn't all that modest, either, but she didn't like the effect his touch had on her.

Or perhaps she liked it too much.

"I said I was fine. I don't want to be poked and prodded."

"If you tell me where you hurt, I won't have to poke and prod. And stop denying it. I can see in your face, you're in pain."

"Fine." He was not going to let it go until she told him. She glanced up at him. He was barefoot, and his shirt hung loose over the waist of his trousers. He wore no cravat or coat, and his shirt was open at the throat. His hair was mussed but his eyes were clear. "If I tell you, will you leave?" she asked.

"No."

She let out an exasperated sigh. "If I tell you, will you—"

He bent and lifted her hem again.

"Fine. It hurts when I breathe!" she conceded. "My side hurts. Here." She pointed to the spot on her side, below her breast, where the pain seemed to coalesce.

He nodded. "Broken rib. How much pain are you having?"

"Enough." She didn't like his questions, but he'd put his hands on his hips and wasn't touching her any longer. Broken rib. No, she couldn't have a broken rib. Surely, if she'd broken anything she'd be in more pain.

"What about your breathing? Can you breathe deeply?"

"My rib isn't broken."

"Breathe deeply."

"Stop ordering me about!"

"I will if you just goddamn do what I say!" he roared. "Bloody hell, woman, do you have to be obstinate about everything?"

She narrowed her eyes at him. She would have stood and roared back at him if she wasn't certain it would cause her more pain. "I don't want your help."

"I don't care. Now breathe or I'll do it for you."

She frowned, and he waved his hand in dismissal. "You know what I mean."

"Not really," she muttered, but she did as he asked. The pain was there, but it wasn't overwhelming.

After he made her breathe several more times, he said, "I don't think it's punctured your lung. That's a good sign, but I'd like to examine you."

"Absolutely not! You are not a doctor, and you are not touching me."

His look was granite, and she knew he'd be just as immovable. "I can fetch a physician, if that's what you wish, but I don't know how you're going to explain this to him—or to the *ton* when word leaks that you've been injured and I was tending you."

Fallon opened her mouth to argue then shut it again. He was right. The speculation about an affair between them would run rampant. She didn't mind speculation about her liaisons, but only if it served her purposes. A connection with Fitzhugh was counter to her purposes. He was not a social sort of man and would gain her little, if any, press other than the rumors about their liaison. Added to that, there was that niggling little fact that he had men chasing him and shooting at him last night. She really did not want her name linked with his publicly.

"Am I fetching the doctor or are you taking off your nightshift?"

"I am *not* taking off my nightshift!"

"You really needn't be so modest. I haven't seen you naked, but some of your gowns leave little to the imagination. I've no doubt you have a lovely body."

She did not know why this statement should both infuriate her and send a shot of arousal through her.

"Of course, I won't be looking at it. This is purely a medical examination."

She rolled her eyes. "No, I'm sure you won't look. And this is quite the medical examination, considering you are not a doctor."

He shrugged. "I have hidden talents and skills, including some medical training. Unless you need me to deliver a child, I can probably tend you as well as, if not better than, any surgeon."

"Fine." Argument seemed futile. "But I am not removing my shift." She climbed back under the covers, then wriggled—a painful motion but necessary to raise her hem—and then lifted the material so he could see the inflamed area. Throughout it all, he wore a bemused look, but once he bent to examine her, his face grew grave and serious. He touched her very lightly, so lightly, her skin rose with gooseflesh at the stroke of his fingers. He bent close, and she felt his warm breath on her skin. He touched her hand where she held the material.

"Lay your arm down flat." His hand grasped the material of her shift, giving her no ability to protest. She lowered her arm, feeling incredibly vulnerable. She tried to stare at the ceiling, but her gaze was repeatedly drawn to his face. In that moment, it was completely unguarded, and there was a softness about his mouth, despite the intensity of his expression.

"Does this hurt?" He touched her ribs lightly.

"No," she said, feeling only the warmth of his hand on her bare skin.

He frowned slightly, and a small crease formed between his eyes. She studied the crease and her gaze followed the slope of his nose down and over the bump indicating it had been broken. "How did you break your nose?" she asked.

"I jumped from a carriage."

She wanted to believe he was hoaxing her, but his expression remained serious.

"What about when I touch here?" he asked. She jumped, and he nodded. "That's where it is. Hmm. I already see some bruising." He leaned closer, moving his arm and sliding the hand holding her hem upward slightly so that his knuckles caressed the curve of her breast. Fallon almost leaped again, but this time it was not from pain. The jolt of arousal from his touch on the tender skin of her breast was enough to force her to bite her cheek to keep from moaning.

He poked her rib again, and pain flared. "Ouch."

"My apologies. Breathe again."

She did so, and the movement caused the hand on her breast to slide farther up the curve. His gaze flicked to hers, and she could see in the way his eyes darkened that he'd realized where he was touching her. She expected him to draw his hand back quickly, to act ashamed or repentant.

He did neither. Instead, he slid her hem down slowly, dragging his fingers with the material until he'd covered her completely. She wanted to speak, but her mouth was too dry.

"The good news is I do not think your rib is broken."

"No?" she rasped. Absently, he handed her the cup of tea on the bedside table.

"I think it's merely cracked. I can wrap it for you, but I'll need some strips of old linen."

"I'll have my lady's maid fetch them." She rang for Anne and made the request. She would think about how she would feel when he touched her again later. He was a man, she reminded herself. He was the same as any man. There was no reason he should make her skin burn or her breath hitch. There was no reason she should imagine his fingers walking up the bare skin of her breast, sliding over her hard nipple…

"And when you've finished the binding," she said to break the silence and divert her thoughts from the path they seemed hell-bent on traveling, "then you shall go home."

"No."

She blinked and waited for an explanation. When none seemed forthcoming, she added, "What do you mean, *no*? You can't think to stay here."

He paced to her window, parted the draperies, and peered out before shutting them again. Fallon had a brief glimpse of bright sunlight before gray descended. "That was my thought, actually," he said, turning to face her. "Unless you'd prefer to come to my residence. But I assure you, yours is more comfortable at the moment, though mine is undoubtedly safer. Of course, you do have that ox of a man—"

"Why would I want to go to your residence?" she demanded, sitting forward. How she hated the persistent jab of pain in her side. If not for it, she would be on her feet and challenging him. He seemed to know she was slightly incapacitated because he gave her a sympathetic look. Pity—the last thing she wanted from the likes of him.

"You and I will stay close together from now on," he said.

"No, we won't." Damn this pain. She was standing. She winced as she slid off the bed, and he moved to assist her. She pushed his arm away. "Don't help me. It's your fault my rib is cracked."

"I'm prepared to accept the blame for your injury."

"Good!"

"In return, I don't believe a little gratitude for saving your life would be too far amiss."

"Saving my life? You all but killed me!" She liked this much better. Standing toe-to-toe with him, she felt much more in control. Why, the tingles of arousal had all but faded.

"The men who were after us might have killed you."

"After *us*? They were after you." She poked him in the chest. Unfortunately, she had forgotten his shirt buttons were undone, and she touched warm, bare flesh. She drew her hand back quickly.

"They were, but they would have taken you in my stead. I can't say they would have killed you. They might have taken you to their leader. He's the one who wants me dead."

"And who is that? Lucifer?"

He shook his head. "No. Your father."

⤝⤞

Warrick watched as all of the steam whooshed out of her. She deflated like one of those new balloons people were using to fly. So she hadn't known. He hadn't thought she did, but he couldn't be certain. He still wasn't certain. Courtesans were known to be excellent actresses, and she was no exception.

Of course, she was no courtesan—and that only proved her acting abilities were exceptional.

"What are you talking about?" she said coldly, backing away from him.

"Those were your father's men after Daisy's carriage last night. Well," he conceded, going to the window again and peering out, "I cannot be certain until we speak to Gabriel, but all of the information I have points to Joseph Bayley."

"He's dead," she said, but her eyes slid away and wouldn't meet his.

"And how do you know that? You haven't seen him since you were fifteen."

She took a deep breath and ran a hand though her long, thick, dark hair. "I know because I killed him."

"Here we are then!" the lady's maid said cheerfully, opening the door. Fallon moved away from him quickly, and he saw her wince. The pain on her face probably hurt him more than her. She was right about that at least—her injury was his fault.

"Thank you," Fallon said, cheerfully. "Put them on the chair, Anne."

The maid did so then moved about, straightening this and that, seemingly unaware that she was not wanted. Warrick was grateful for the moment to gather his thoughts. He'd done enough interrogations to have heard and seen just about everything. Nothing surprised him anymore, but Fallon's admission all but knocked him over. He had a thousand questions and couldn't even think where to begin.

"Is there anything else, madam?" the lady's maid asked.

"Yes, I—"

"No. You may go," Warrick answered.

Fallon shot him a look sharp with daggers. "My house. I give the orders."

"Then give them or I will."

The maid looked uncertain, her gaze darting to Fallon as though she was waiting for some sort of signal. He hoped she wasn't stupid enough to give one. "Shall I send for Titus, madam?"

Fallon glanced at him then shook her head. "No. We're not quite done here. You may go, Anne."

"Yes, madam." She left slowly, keeping her gaze on her mistress.

"Loyal servants," he remarked when the door finally closed.

"Yes, they are, and they won't hesitate to throw you out. If I were you, I'd leave on my own."

"Oh, I don't think so. First of all, you've piqued my interest with your confession of murder. Second, though you've proved yourself quite capable of defending yourself, I intend to stay nearby, just in case I am needed." He parted the drapes again.

"There's no one but you I need defend myself from!" she all but shouted. "You're the only one putting me in danger. And why do you keep looking out that window?"

"Because I want to be certain our friends from last night haven't found us."

"Why would they come here?"

He shook his head. "You're smarter than that, Fallon." He dropped the drapes closed and crossed to her. "You'd never have made it this far in life if you weren't."

"Are you saying they might have tracked us here?"

He tapped her nose. "I knew you were a smart girl. Now, take off your shift."

The look on her face was enough to send him into a fit of laughter if he'd been a man of less restraint. She looked absolutely appalled and horrified. He might as well have asked her to eat a spider or a wriggling rat.

"Go on." He gestured for her to lift the garment over her head. "How else am I going to bind you? And I promise I won't look." Well, that was dishonest, now wasn't it? "Very well, I won't look much."

"But I thought you were going to bind me over my shift," she all but sputtered.

"This isn't a pair of stays, Fallon. This is to secure your rib and keep it from any further harm."

"I think I shall be safe enough if you refrain from shoving me out of any more moving conveyances."

"I shall take that under advisement. Now, take off your clothes."

She glared at him. "I hate you."

He grinned. "No you don't."

"Excuse me." She walked to the door on the far side of the room and stepped inside. Warrick assumed it was her dressing room, an assumption that proved correct when she emerged wearing a pink silk robe. For some reason, the sight of her in pale pink made him feel a little guilty about all the lustful thoughts he'd been having. She looked so young and sweet in pink. He would not have thought the color suited her, and it did not suit the courtesan, but it suited the woman.

He held up the strips of linen. "I am ready to begin, madam."

"You're enjoying this."

"What man wouldn't?" He schooled his features into a sober expression. "All right. I assure you from this moment on, I will treat this as a purely medical task. I have to admit, though, I've only ever worked on men."

"I feel infinitely more relieved." She sighed and without further preamble slid the robe off her shoulders. He'd expected her to argue further, so he was not prepared for the sight of her ripe breasts revealed by the cascade of pink silk over flesh.

His mouth went dry. She was exquisite. Good God, but he'd never seen breasts like hers before. They were heavy and round, the aureoles tinged a dusky rose. Her nipples were large, round, and puckering in the slight chill. They practically begged him to kiss them, lick them, roll them over his tongue...

"Have you ogled enough, sir, or would you like me to turn from side to side?"

Warrick quickly flicked his glance away. He really had intended to attempt to maintain some semblance of professionalism about this task. Obviously his initial attempt had failed this completely, but perhaps he could salvage the rest of the procedure. "I apologize. You took me unawares."

"Yes, I'm certain after half a dozen orders to remove my clothing, it surprised you when I complied. I am cold, sir. Do your worst."

Good God, he was going to have to touch her. How was he going to touch her without *touching* her? He had always thought of himself as a man with substantial willpower. Now he knew he was far weaker than he had ever known. He cleared his throat, kept his gaze on the part of her still clothed, and moved closer. Immediately his gaze was drawn to those ripe breasts and he looked away again. He hadn't even touched her yet, and he could sense the heat of her. He could smell the exotic fragrance of her skin. He could all but feel the silkiness of her flesh under his fingertips.

He wanted her. He could not remember ever wanting a woman this much, and all she'd done was show him her breasts. He'd seen breasts before; he was no inexperienced lad. And she hadn't even disrobed seductively. Not to mention, she'd as much as told him she hated him. Was he reduced to lusting after women who could barely stand him? Perhaps it was time he found himself a woman.

He took a fortifying breath and lifted one of the linen strips to her rib cage. She shivered slightly. "Did I hurt you?" he asked.

"No." Her voice was ragged. She didn't hate him nearly as much as she claimed.

He began to wrap one of the bandages around her ribs, but he made such an effort to avoid touching her breasts, he dropped the fabric. "Sorry." He bent to retrieve it then tried another angle. But this one required him to bend, practically burying his face in those ample breasts. Perhaps if they were not quite so lush, he could have better ignored them. Perhaps if her nipple wasn't half an inch from his lips…

He tried to position the linen, tried to position his head, rubbed her breast with his wrist, and jumped back. "I apologize again."

She sighed. "Just get it over with."

Right. She had the idea. He would do it quickly. "I think this might work better if I kneel," he said. "You're on the short side."

"I'm petite."

He knelt and had to hastily lower his gaze again. Why had he thought this vantage point would be any better? She was *not* petite everywhere. Keeping his eyes averted, he wrapped the first strip of linen around her. He brushed the fullness of her breast twice, but he tried to ignore the heat the sensation shot through him.

"How do you know Daisy?" Fallon asked.

"Who?"

"Daisy? The woman whose brothel we visited last night?" She sounded bemused, but he understood what she was doing. They should speak of something. It would keep both of their minds off fantasies of nuzzling her breasts with his lips, swirling those hard, hard nipples with his tongue, and then taking them into his mouth and sucking.

Of course, that might not have been the exact direction of her thoughts.

"Daisy. Yes." He wrapped another strip around Fallon, trying to make sure it was tight and secure, and attempted to remember who Daisy was. For the moment, he could only picture Fallon's dark eyes, full lips, and... other attributes.

"She seemed rather grateful to you. Why is that?"

"Ah." He wrapped another strip of linen about her.

He didn't want to discuss this, but he couldn't think of another topic at the moment—at least not one that didn't involve erotic language and several questionable suggestions. "I saved her brother. I suppose she feels indebted to me for that, though I told her she owes me nothing."

"How did you save her brother?"

He tightened another linen strip around her as he contemplated how much of the story he could reveal. Fallon had a small frame, and he would have thought this task would go quickly, but it seemed interminable. "We both fought on the Continent in the Peninsular Wars. I didn't know him, but I happened to be nearby when he was wounded during battle."

Warrick saw in his mind the muddy, blood-soaked battlefield in what had once been a peaceful cornfield in Portugal. He could hear the screams of the men and, worse, the screams of the wounded horses. Cannonballs exploded before and behind him, and he reined his own horse in and patted the animal's neck. "I don't want to be here either," he had muttered. But the documents secreted in his satchel contained vital information, and he must get them to Wellington posthaste.

He tried to steer the animal around the clumps of fallen men, but it was inevitable they would trod on some of the dead. There were simply too many to avoid all of the bodies. Another cannonball exploded nearby, and Warrick heard the screech of shrapnel as it tore through the air. He kicked his mount, urging him through the smoke. A few more yards, and they'd be clear. But when the smoke cleared, they all but ran down a young man wandering about the field. Warrick turned the horse sharply. The animal, already spooked, reared. The young British soldier—at least Warrick thought he was British; it was difficult to tell from the soiled uniform—fell to his knees. Warrick tensed, prepared to kick the horse back into a trot, and then he swore. He cursed his goddamn conscience and jumped off the beast.

"Where's your commanding officer?" he asked the soldier, yelling to be heard over the battle raging somewhat to their east now.

The man looked up at him, his face impossibly youthful, his eyes clouded with pain. He grabbed Warrick's lapels, streaking them with blood. "Help me."

Warrick hadn't been able to refuse.

"You saved his life," Fallon said, sounding surprised.

"I did what any soldier would have done."

"And that's not the whole story. You did more than that or Daisy wouldn't feel so indebted."

He wrapped another strip of linen and realized it was the last. He tied the end and tucked it into the bindings.

"I didn't know you fought in the wars."

"I told you, there's a lot you don't know about me. I'm finished." He stood and dusted his trousers off. "Cover yourself."

She did so. "Thank you." She moved from side to side. "It feels better."

"Don't thank me yet. You're not the only one with questions."

Her dark eyes rose to meet his.

"Tell me how you murdered your father."

Seven

FALLON COULDN'T HAVE BEEN MORE RELIEVED WHEN A
quiet knock sounded and Anne opened the door.
"Madam, I'm sorry to interrupt. Cook would like
to know if you intend to dine in, and if so, will the
gentleman be joining you?"

Fallon glanced at Fitzhugh. He gave her a slow
smile. "I never turn down a free meal—unless it is at
my parents' house."

She didn't know why that should make her
want to smile. She wanted him to leave—and take
all of his soft caresses and warm stares with him.
She didn't want to like him, but she found it was
difficult not to.

"Anne, tell Cook the gentleman and I will dine in,
and could you speak with the housekeeper and have a
room prepared for Mr. Fitzhugh?"

Anne's brows rose, but she bobbed her acquies-
cence. "Yes, madam."

When they were alone again, Fallon said, "What
are your plans for this evening?"

Fitzhugh sat in one of her silk chairs, upholstered

in emerald green. "Perhaps after dinner we might play charades. Or I could read the *Times*, and you could play the piano and serenade me."

"It sounds remarkably domestic," she drawled. "Not the sort of thing either of us would enjoy."

He looked away. "No, not at all."

"I have an engagement," she said.

Fitzhugh raised his brows. "Don't tell me it's a gentleman caller. I know you're not really a courtesan."

She frowned at him. "And how do you know that?"

"I told you—"

She sighed. "Yes, I know. There's a hell of a lot you're not telling me. And since we are sharing confidences—"

"Are we sharing confidences?" he asked, setting his ankle on top of his knee. "I don't recall you answering my question."

She ignored him. "There is one comment you made that has made me curious."

"By all means, let me ease your curiosity. But Fallon…"

There was something in his tone that made her meet his gaze.

"Nothing is free."

Oh, she knew that well enough.

"Last night at Lucifer's Lair, you said, this search was a matter of life and death. You used those words exactly. *Life and death*. Are these diamonds really that valuable?"

He studied her. She couldn't have said why, but she felt more naked now under his gaze than she had when she'd been undressed. "They're not diamonds," he said finally. "Lucifer's Diamonds aren't jewels at all."

She frowned. "Juliette said he came to her looking for diamonds."

"It's a code name, rather like you are one of The Three Diamonds. The diamonds Lucifer wants are a small band of elite British operatives who fought against Napoleon and orchestrated his defeat during the Peninsular Wars. In some circles, these men are referred to as Diamonds in the Rough."

Fallon shook her head. "So there are no diamonds."

"Not in the sense Juliette and Pelham assumed. But I assure you these men's identities are as valuable, if not more so, than a handful of diamonds."

Fallon raised a skeptical brow.

"You don't believe me?"

"I think you might be exaggerating slightly."

He looked amused by that statement.

Fallon paced the room, trying to untangle the various threads in her mind. "Last night, we weren't actually searching for information about diamonds but about spies?"

"Actually, I was hoping to discover to whom Lucifer sold my friends' identities."

"How do you know he sold their identities?"

"Because one man is dead already, and another has been targeted."

Fallon opened her mouth to speak and then took a step back. "Wait a moment. Are you telling me *you* are one of these Diamonds in the Rough?"

"I don't recall divulging that information."

"And that is why we were being chased last night. Someone is trying to kill you!"

"I suppose that's not entirely inaccurate."

"And you dragged *me* into this?" She grabbed the first thing she could reach and thrust an amethyst-colored pillow at him.

He caught it, stood, and tossed it on the chair. "I had little choice. I needed someone who knew the enemy."

Fallon shook her head. "I don't know who or what you think I am, but I have nothing to do with spies or Bonaparte or the French. I know we won the war and Bonaparte is exiled, and that is the extent of my knowledge. I can't help you."

"That's where you're wrong, Fallon." He strode directly to her, and she had the urge to back away. But she was no coward, and she wasn't going to allow him to push her into a corner. Especially not in her own home. In her own *room*, nonetheless. Those gold-flecked eyes of his were hard and serious. He was so close she could almost count each and every one of those flecks.

"How is that?" She hadn't meant it to come out as a whisper, but she couldn't seem to find her voice or enough breath to breathe, much less speak.

"Because the enemy, in my case, is not the French."

"It's not?" she rasped.

"No." The word was practically a caress, and he was standing so near she could not help but think how easy it would be for him to take her in his arms, press her against him, and kiss her until she gasped for breath. He could kiss her that way. She had no doubt of it.

"My enemy is your father."

The world seemed to spin, and Fallon clenched her fists to keep from spinning with it. Her father was dead. How could Fitzhugh think Joseph Bayley was his enemy? "I thought I already explained that my father is dead."

"Are you certain?"

"Yes." But as soon as the word was out of her mouth, the niggling doubts began. *Was* her father dead? There had been so much blood. She hadn't thought anyone could survive after losing that much blood. But what if she'd been wrong? She had been fifteen years old, terrified, and eager to be away. She'd fled, thrown the knife in the Thames, and run until her legs could no longer carry her. She hadn't looked back.

"I can see you're doubting yourself."

"I'm not. He has to be dead." Why else would he have completely disappeared? No one saw him after she'd plunged that knife into him. She hadn't heard so much as a whisper of his doings. And he would have come looking for her. If he'd still been alive, he would have come for his revenge.

"Because you killed him."

She looked down. She had never told anyone she'd killed her father, except the Countess of Sinclair. The countess had a way of making people tell her things, whether they wanted to or not. But that was all right with Fallon because she knew the countess would take her secret to the grave. She knew the countess loved her no matter what she had done—and she had done some rather unlovable things.

She did not want to confide in Fitzhugh. It wasn't that she didn't trust him. He was a spy, for God's sake. He could probably keep her secret better than she could. But there was a sense of intimacy formed when one shared one's secrets. Fallon avoided that sort of intimacy. She had no use for intimacy, no use for the vulnerability that came with it.

Added to those reasons, she didn't want to relive her father's death. She sometimes managed not to think of it for days or even weeks. If she spoke of it now, if she confided in Fitzhugh, she knew it would haunt her again daily, hourly. She could not face that. She was too tired right now. Too weary.

"I think I'll go find your housekeeper," Fitzhugh said, stepping back. Fallon was surprised to see him capitulate so easily. "I'd like a few moments to ready myself before dinner."

"Of course." She wanted the same.

"And where did you say we were going after dinner?"

She hadn't. "You are not going," she said. "You don't have an invitation."

"Sweetheart," he said, going to her door and opening it. "You're my invitation."

Dinner was a tense affair, punctuated by the clink of silver on china. Fallon was vaguely aware Cook had prepared a delicious meal with fowl, fish, and a variety of soups and vegetables—a mountain of food for only two people, though Fitzhugh was making an effort to scale the mountain—but she didn't taste any of it. Fallon couldn't help but feel she didn't belong.

It was absurd. This was her home, her dining room, and her servants. But she felt like some sort of invader. All this talk of her past with Fitzhugh was making her remember it, making her doubt who she was now.

Nagging thoughts invaded where they were not

welcome—she didn't belong at this table with its crystal goblets and delicate china. She didn't belong in this lovely town house with its silks, satins, and velvets. And who was she to tell a servant to fetch this or carry that? She was no better than they were and probably born far lower.

She was even looking down at her coppery dress of shimmering silk and wondering if everyone at Alvanley's ball was going to look at her and wonder just who she thought she was, dressing up like someone of quality.

Not that she'd ever pretended to be quality.

She'd masqueraded as a courtesan for years. No one thought courtesans respectable enough to be quality. She glanced down the table at Fitzhugh, who was nodding to the footman refilling his glass, and scowled. Fitzhugh raised his brows at her, and she didn't mistake the twinkle in his eyes. He thought all of this amusing.

"Why the pretty moue?" he asked.

"It's not a… whatever you said. It's a scowl."

He narrowed his eyes and shrugged. "If you say so."

She wanted to throw her plate at him, but it would be a waste of good china. Instead, she glanced at the footman. "Please leave us. That is if Mr. Fitzhugh doesn't want to drink yet another glass of my wine."

"I believe I finished the bottle," Fitzhugh said with absolutely no sense of remorse whatsoever.

When the footman was gone, Fallon said, "How do you know I'm not really a courtesan? And don't give me one of your enigmatic answers."

"Enigmatic." He lifted his goblet and studied the

wine. "I like that word." His eyes met hers. "You're described that way, aren't you?"

She was. That was how she'd first learned the word. The countess had made Fallon read and study for hours and hours when she first went to live with the Sinclairs. The countess said that no one would ever take her seriously or consider her anyone or anything if she didn't learn to speak and write correctly. And so Fallon had learned, but there were still words that were unfamiliar. Words like *moue*. She didn't know what the hell it was, but she was pretty sure she didn't do it.

"Answer the question, Fitzhugh."

He sipped his wine. "Are you ever going to call me Warrick?"

"No. Now answer the question."

"I think we should make a wager."

"I think you should answer the question." She traced the edge of her plate and wondered how much it would cost to replace. It might be worth the expense to smash it over his head.

"Here's the wager. If I can persuade you to call me Warrick tonight, then you tell me about your father."

She was never going to tell him about her father, and she was never going to call him by his Christian name. "Fine."

He raised his brows. "You agree? That easily?"

"Yes, that easily. Now—"

"And you won't renege?" He set his glass on the table.

She let out a puff of outrage. "I cannot even believe you would suggest such a thing. I honor my bets."

"Good. In answer to your question, I couldn't find any of your lovers."

She blinked, at a loss momentarily.

"You asked how I knew you were not really a courtesan. I tried to find one of your former lovers—or protectors, is that correct? The papers had you paired with all sorts of gentlemen, but when I approached them, none had any real intimate knowledge of you."

"I am discreet."

"You are the soul of discretion, my dear Fallon, but men, especially when they're a bit in their cups, are not. They often talk, and that talk often turns to women. When I brought up your name, there was a lot of speculation but no real firsthand knowledge."

"That's because the Earl of Sinclair—"

"Is lying for you as well. I know the Sinclairs, Fallon. My mother and the countess went to school together. There is absolutely no way the Iron Countess, which is what I called her growing up, would allow the earl to bed you or any of the other diamonds under her own roof. I never believed that for a moment."

Fallon felt her mouth go dry, and she groped blindly for her untouched goblet of wine. She drank a sip and then another. "Well, you don't know the countess as well as you think then."

She drank another swallow of wine. Hell, she might as well just drain the glass. Fitzhugh watched her unladylike behavior without reaction. "I'm not going to reveal your secret, Fallon," he said.

"No, you're just going to blackmail me with it."

He shrugged. "I thought we were past that."

"Oh, you think I *want* you in my house, eating my food and drinking my wine? You think I want to help you? You think I want you sleeping in one of my beds?"

"Maybe you want me sleeping in your bed." He was across the bloody room and she still felt a flash of heat when he said it. It was the way he looked at her, as though he knew just how she liked to be kissed and where she wanted most to be touched.

"No, I don't. What I want is for you to go away."

"And I will. After I find your father."

"What are you going to do with him when you find him?"

He lifted his own glass and toasted. "I'm going to finish what you started."

❦

Lord Alvanley's ball was a tedious affair. Warrick hadn't expected anything different. The same people were there as were at all the other events of the Season he avoided, though, to be fair, most of the stodgy ones had stayed away. That was probably because Alvanley had invited the entire demimonde. It wasn't unusual for courtesans to attend Society events, but they weren't usually present in such large numbers. He saw why Fallon felt the need to attend, and he glanced across the room to where she stood, surrounded by about half a dozen young men.

He noticed she spoke very little and smiled even less. But she gave such sultry looks from those warm brown eyes and licked her plump red lips so seductively that the men probably did the talking and smiling for her. He watched her touch one of the men—a puppy of about twenty—on the arm and waited to feel some sense of jealousy. But none was forthcoming. Warrick knew he wasn't immune to the emotion. And he knew he wanted her enough to envy any man who garnered her attention.

But none of these men captured her attention—not really. This was all a play, and she was the actress on center stage. She flirted and lowered her lashes and swayed her hips, and she went home alone.

That wasn't entirely true. There had been one and possibly two men she'd bedded. He was nothing if not thorough, and he couldn't find that they'd paid her in any way for these encounters. In both cases, there had seemed to be real affection between the two. Which only made her human, and far more restrained than he, since he had certainly had years where he bedded far more than one or two women.

And there hadn't always been much affection.

But he did feel affection for Fallon. She was refreshingly honest and quite clever and could throw a hell of a punch. And she was beautiful, too. He couldn't forget her looks, but those weren't why he liked her, why he wanted her. He liked her because he respected her. She could hold her own, far better than many of the men he'd worked with. She might grouse and complain, but she was no wilting flower. For that alone, he might have forgotten the blackmailing and let her go on her way.

Except he didn't want her to go on her way. Not without him. They were going to bed together. He didn't know when and he didn't know where, but he knew they shared an uncommonly powerful attraction, and there was only one place for an attraction like that to lead.

Unfortunately, tonight he was taking her to The Grotto to meet Gabriel. He glanced at his pocket watch. They'd spent an hour at Alvanley's. Her time was up.

He started across the room. She must have seen him coming because her eyes widened, and she shook her head slightly. He kept walking, forcing several couples who were loitering in his path out of his way.

She shook her head more vigorously, causing the men surrounding her to look about for the cause of her distress.

He kept walking.

And when one of her suitors blocked his path, he gave the man a slight arch of the brow and that was all it took to convince the clodpole he should move. Not all of her suitors were so intelligent. A few stood their ground.

"Sir," one pup said, his voice all but breaking. "I don't believe the lady wishes to make your acquaintance."

"The lady already knows me. Fallon, we're leaving."

"You may go at any time you like," she told him from between the shoulders of her entourage. "I'm staying."

"No, you're not. Come with me now, or else I'll be forced to take more drastic measures."

"Sir," another puppy said. "The lady has refused you. Please take your leave. Don't worry, Marchioness. I will protect you."

Warrick all but rolled his eyes. He didn't know whether to be amused or annoyed. He settled on annoyed. "Last chance, Fallon."

"No," the first pup said. "It's *your* last chance." And the idiot tried to punch him. Warrick easily caught the boy's fist and pinned his arm behind his back. "Ow, ow, ow!"

"Fallon, your lapdog is in distress," Warrick said. "Are you coming with me, or need I make more of a scene?"

"I'm coming," she said, pushing through the men still surrounding her. "Let him go. Mr. Dunsyre, are you all right?" she asked, stooping to look in his face.

"Ow!"

She glared at Warrick. "Release him."

Warrick opened his hand, and Dunsyre fell to his knees and cradled the arm. "You almost broke my arm."

Warrick raised a brow. "If I'd wanted to break it, you'd be doing more than fighting tears right now, boy."

Something poked him in the chest and he looked down to see Fallon's finger poking him again. "Stop harassing people and leave. I'm not going with you."

She turned away from him, and he grabbed her elbow and bent his mouth to her ear. Several of her admirers moved as though to protect her, but Warrick gave them warning glances and they paused. "Come with me now, or I will really make a scene," he murmured.

"You have already made a scene," she hissed. "I don't think you can do any worse."

He shook his head. "Fallon, I thought you knew better. I can always make it worse." And in one swoop, he caught her about the waist, tossed her over his shoulder, and marched across the dance floor, interrupting the quadrille.

Shocked gasps and murmurs and an angry scream from Fallon herself reverberated in place of the orchestra, who had gone suddenly silent, but no one tried to stop him. Her friend, the red-haired Countess of Charm, did run alongside him. "Fallon, are you all right? Mr. Fitzhugh, what is happening?"

"She's fine, Countess," he told her because she looked genuinely concerned. "I'm not going to hurt her. We have a small errand together. That is all."

"I see." She scampered ahead of him. "I am not certain Fallon has agreed to this errand."

"I haven't, Lily," Fallon called from over his shoulder. "Make him stop."

Lily gave him a plaintive look, and he shook his head. "My apologies, Countess."

"Oh, dear." She moved aside, and he could feel Fallon struggling to lift her head to see her friend as they passed.

"Lily, help me! This is an abduction! Help!"

And then he was out of the ballroom and taking the steps two at a time to reach the vestibule. She really was quite a light little thing. He wasn't winded at all. The footman at the bottom of the steps did not so much as raise an eyebrow when Warrick asked for Fallon's carriage, and to avoid the crowds congregating at the top of the staircase, he decided to await the carriage's arrival outside.

When he stepped outside, Fallon made a real attempt to free herself. She'd pounded his back before, but clearly she had not wanted to make the incident more than it was. And she probably truly believed someone would come to her aid. Now she struggled and fought and clawed at him. He adjusted her slightly and bore the brunt of her kicks and punches. In her current position, she couldn't do him much harm.

"Do you want me to put you down?" he asked when she paused to catch her breath.

"Yes!"

"Then say my name."

"You ass! Put me down!"

"Wrong answer. My name is Warrick."

"And you are an ass! Put me down!" And she was back to punching and screaming again.

Finally the carriage arrived, and he deposited her inside, closing the door before she could escape. She tried anyway, and he had to restrain her. He didn't mind all that much because it meant he wrapped his arms around her and held her still against him. He could smell the clean fragrance of her hair as she whipped her head to and fro in front of his nose. "You're going to hurt yourself further if you don't stop," he said. "Your rib, remember?"

"You weren't thinking of my rib when you slung me over your shoulder."

"Yes, I was. I would have carried you under my arm if I hadn't been protecting your rib."

"Ooh, I *hate* you! Let me go."

"Will you stop trying to escape?"

"Yes, damn it! The bloody carriage is moving now."

He released her and she jumped away from him, tumbling into the seat across from him. With a wince she clutched her ribs. "I told you to be careful," he said. She threw her reticule at him, but he ducked.

There was a long silence, in which he assumed she was thinking of all that had happened. He, in turn, rolled his neck and shoulders to loosen them.

Finally, she exploded. "What is wrong with you?" she all but screamed. "Are you trying to ruin me?"

"I asked you to come with me nicely," he pointed out. She muttered something he didn't really want to hear, so he parted the drapes to check their location. A few more minutes and they would reach The Grotto. He glanced at her. She looked disheveled, but it would have to do. He supposed Gabriel knew they were looking for him by now. At any rate, they'd lost the element of surprise.

The carriage slowed, and Fallon said, "Where are we now? I'm not getting out. I look a fright."

"You look wonderfully tousled," he told her. "Anyone would think we just had a tryst in the carriage."

"I don't want anyone to think that. I don't want to tryst with you."

"You flatter me," he said. The worried-looking coachman opened the door, and Warrick jumped out. He held out his hand, and when Fallon gave him a mutinous look, he said calmly, "Come out, or I'll have to—"

"All right! I'm coming." She descended without his assistance then stood peering up at a dark building in the heart of Chelsea. "Where are we?"

"The Grotto."

"And what is The Grotto?"

He shook his head. "And you call yourself a courtesan. Come on and find out." He took her hand and she promptly snatched it away. "Stay close to me," he warned.

"I'd rather lie in bed with a snake," she retorted.

He pulled open the black door of The Grotto. "You may just get your chance."

Eight

FALLON HAD ALWAYS THOUGHT OF HERSELF AS A woman of the world, by which she meant very little shocked her. Her father had been a thief. She'd practically learned to steal in her crib—not that she had a crib. Her mother had been a whore. Fallon had seen men and women copulating from a very early age. And now she'd lived seven years as a courtesan. Even if Fitzhugh was correct, and she wasn't really a courtesan, she played the part well. She went to the Cyprians' balls, graced Harriette Wilson's salons, and had wandered once or twice into the darker recesses of Vauxhall Gardens. She had seen depravity and lust and debauchery.

But she had never seen anything like The Grotto.

Upon entering, Fitzhugh led her down what appeared to be a dark tunnel. It was dank and stuffy and seemed to slope downward, almost as though they were traveling into a real grotto. At some point, possibly midway, a naked woman stepped into their path. It was so dark, Fallon could only see her because the woman held a lamp. Fitzhugh immediately reached into a pocket and gave her a couple of coins. Obviously, this was the entrance fee.

Fallon didn't particularly want to go any farther, but she wasn't going back alone. She had heard something rustling back there, and she was pretty sure it had been rats. If it wasn't rats, she didn't want to know what it was.

When the light from the naked woman's lamp faded, Fallon said, "Are all the women naked?" At the courtesans' balls, women often danced in various states of undress, so nudity was no shock to her. But she liked to know what was expected, and she wanted Fitzhugh to know she was not disrobing.

"No," Fitzhugh answered. "She's nude to ensure she doesn't steal the entrance fee."

"Couldn't they just search her before she went home? She must get cold."

Fitzhugh chuckled. "I think you're missing the point."

She was treated to a display of the point of The Grotto a few moments later when they entered the main room. It was circular in design and dimly lit by sconces that cast a flickering shadowy light. On one side was a bar with a large man pouring spirits. Scantily dressed serving wenches brought the men and women—mostly men—glasses and tankards as the men watched the show on the stage across the room. Fallon took one look at the stage and turned away. A shirtless man was being whipped raw by a woman dressed in executioner's garb.

Fallon looked elsewhere and noted the main room branched off into various caverns, and each was labeled with words and illustrations. There appeared to be some sort of spanking room, an orgy room, a self-pleasuring room…

Fallon cut her eyes away. She really didn't think she wanted to know the purpose of the other rooms. "Let's find Gabriel and get out," she said.

"Uncomfortable?" Fitzhugh asked.

She debated lying. She was supposed to be worldly after all, but this place was not so much worldly as frightening. "Yes, actually," she answered.

"Me too."

Fallon blinked in surprise. "Really?"

"You think because I'm a man I like this sort of thing?" He indicated the whipping on the stage. "It's not to my taste any more than it is to yours."

She thought about asking him what his taste was but wisely decided otherwise. He might just tell her.

Fitzhugh approached the man at the bar and put a fiver on the scarred wood.

"What are you drinking?" the man asked.

"I need information," Fitzhugh said.

"I supply gin, not information."

"Fine. I'll have a glass of gin and one for the lady."

"How chivalrous," Fallon muttered. No lady drank gin. Of course, no lady frequented a place like this. But when the man on stage began whimpering, she thought perhaps a sip of gin wouldn't be amiss.

Fitzhugh handed her a glass, and Fallon drank. It was horrible stuff, but it gave her something to do and somewhere to look besides the man, who had resorted to begging.

"I need to speak to Gabriel," Fitzhugh said.

"Don't care," the barkeep answered and moved away.

Fitzhugh gave her a shrug. "That didn't go as planned."

"Ask one of the serving wenches," she told him. "They're probably not immune to your charms."

He grinned. "I have charms?"

She shook her head, refusing to answer. Fitzhugh smiled at the next wench who passed him, and she paused, keeping a safe distance away. Fallon thought the poor girl had probably been pinched and grabbed more times than she could count. "I need to speak to Gabriel," he told her.

The girl, who was probably all of seventeen but who looked thirty, glanced over her shoulder. "He's busy."

Fitzhugh withdrew another fiver and put it on her tray. "Could you show us somewhere we could wait for him?"

The girl glanced down at the fiver then at Fitzhugh. The blunt disappeared, and she nodded at him to follow her. "Private rooms are this way."

They entered another dark corridor, and Fallon was glad to be away from the main room and the man being whipped. This corridor was quiet. On each side were closed doors. Fallon could hear groans of pleasure and the slap of bodies through the thin wood.

"Here." The serving girl indicated an empty room. A stained bed, listing to one side, had been tossed in the corner.

"Thank you." Fitzhugh gave her another fiver. "Send Gabriel to us when he's done."

The girl looked at the fiver then at Fitzhugh. She opened her mouth as though to say something, perhaps give a warning, but then she took the fiver and nodded. "It will be a few moments."

"We'll wait."

When she was gone, Fitzhugh closed the door, and Fallon was relieved to note the room was actually relatively quiet. She wouldn't have minded sitting down, but she wasn't going near that bed.

"Now what?" she asked.

"Now we wait. When he arrives, let me talk."

"Fine. I don't know what I'm doing here anyway." The shadows in the dim light became clearer and she realized the frescoes she had initially thought were abstract depictions were actually cavorting couples. She tilted her head at the angle of one couple. She couldn't imagine that would work in reality.

"See anything you'd like to try?"

"With you? Never."

Fitzhugh pointed to a depiction of a man kneeling before a woman, his face buried between her legs. "I'd like to try this."

Fallon looked away, but it was too late. Heat had shot from her belly to the apex of her thighs. She shifted uncomfortably. "Perhaps that serving wench will oblige you."

"I'm not interested in her." He moved closer, making it more difficult to ignore him. "I'm interested in you. I can't help but wonder…"

She knew he'd left off so she would ask him what he wondered. It was a trick, and she wasn't going to fall for it. But, damn it, what did he wonder? She glared at him. "You wonder?"

"What you taste like."

The wave of arousal hit her so hard she all but crumpled. The room seemed to spin, and her belly tightened.

"I know you want me, Fallon." He moved closer, leaned in, and whispered in her ear. "Let me taste you. Let me touch you."

She shook her head.

"All you have to do"—he nibbled the spot just behind her neck with his lips—"is lift your skirts. I'll do the rest."

No.

But she already knew she'd give in. She was allowing him to kiss her neck, allowing him to whisper in her ear. He was right. She did want him. She glanced at the fresco again. She wanted that.

"Why?" she asked when his hand groped for her hem and began to inch her skirts up. "What is in this for you?"

"I get to feel you come," he said. "I get to make you come."

His hand inched down her bodice. Since he'd dragged her out of Alvanley's ball without giving her the opportunity to fetch her pelisse, he could easily skate his fingers over the half-moons of her breasts. Her skin immediately prickled with awareness, and her breath caught in her throat. His hand dipped inside her bodice, and she could not help but arch for him.

She felt the buttons at the back of her gown loosen, and then the bodice dipped down, exposing the top of her stays and sheer chemise. Those deft fingers pushed the material down and freed her from its confines.

The cool air in the room caressed her bare skin while his fingers hovered above her. "Have I told you," he began, circling her, "that I adore your breasts?"

"No." She was surprised at how level her voice

sounded. Inside she was burning, aching for him to touch her with more than his eyes.

"They're exquisite. Perfect."

Fallon didn't understand why he was talking so much. Why didn't he just touch her? Was he trying to drive her mad? Knowing him, she rather thought he was.

"May I?" he reached one hand out, stopping just short of cupping her.

"Why stop now?" she murmured.

"Why indeed?" His warm hand smoothed over her flesh, sending heat shooting through her. He cupped her, caressed her, then lightly brushed his fingertips along the slope of her breast. When his fingers reached her nipples, he lightened the pressure, making her moan. She could hardly feel his touch, and it made her yearn for it all the more. Her nipples puckered, and it took all her willpower not to thrust herself into his hand out of desperation.

"Do you like that?"

"Harder," she said.

"Oh, no." He shook his head. "You want light and teasing." His fingers mimicked his words. "You only think you want it hard and fast."

"You don't know what I like," she protested, but he was rapidly proving that he did. She could feel the wetness between her legs, could feel her body tingling, throbbing for him. For more of his touch. His fingers, his hands.

His mouth.

As though reading her mind, he dipped his head to her breast and flicked his tongue across her nipple.

Again, his touch was so light, so teasing, she barely felt it. She was almost in pain with wanting him now, and she did push toward him. "Put your mouth on me."

"I don't think so." His tongue flicked out again, swirling around her hard flesh, tasting her, tickling her, making her flesh swell and pulse. She was hot and cold, wet and then dry when he blew on her moist nipple.

And then he repeated his actions on her other breast, and Fallon was all but panting. How was he doing this to her? She was no virgin, but her body had never reacted like this. She'd never wanted a man so much, never craved release so much. She needed him. She felt she would go mad if he didn't take her soon.

He pushed her back against the wall, and she all but wept with joy. He was going to take her, hard and fast. But no. He knelt before her and raised her skirts. She wanted him inside her, but this would do. Without any protest or pretension, she spread her legs. He pushed her skirts up and secured them between her back and the wall. For a long moment, he just looked at her. She felt she'd never been gazed at for so long and so thoroughly.

And then his hands inched up her thighs, and his fingers spread her. Just the gentle touch of his hand made her buck with pleasure. But when he leaned forward and touched his mouth to her, she could not help but cry out. She dug her fingers in his hair and pressed him hard against her.

But damn the man! He would not give her what she wanted. His tongue traced and laved and flicked, and her hips moved with his rhythm. Her body screamed for release. She was so close and then so far.

So close, so close, and then he withdrew, teased, and she had to build up to it all over again.

"Make me come," she demanded. "I need you."

His tongue did something unexplainable that made her cry out. "Please," she begged.

"What will you give me?"

"Anything. You can have anything. Take me. Just make me come." At the moment, she meant it. She couldn't think, couldn't comprehend her words. She'd never felt like this before. Never felt so out of control, so desperate, so achingly aroused.

"Say my name," he murmured against her most intimate folds. "Say it."

Deep in the recesses of her hazy mind, she knew what he was doing. Deep down, she resisted his will. But the baser part of her cried for release. "Warrick," she said in a harsh whisper. "Warrick."

He licked her long and deliberately, his touch still gentle, but it was enough. Pleasure spiraled through her like long wisps of smoke, exploding into fireworks as he continued to lick her. She arched, bucked, screamed, and came. And came.

She couldn't seem to stop. Just when she thought she had reached the apex of pleasure, he touched her again, and she was spiraling and spiraling. Finally, when she could take no more, when another climax would surely shatter her completely, he pulled away.

She collapsed into his arms, and he held her. She didn't know how long she lay in his embrace. He held her so tenderly, his hands smoothing back her hair, and wiping the tears from her cheeks. She looked up at him, and he kissed her with such sweetness.

"Why are you doing this to me?" she asked.

"I told you—"

"No." She shook her head. "Why are you treating me like this? Like I'm someone special?"

"Because you deserve it, and because, Fallon, you are special."

❧

He could see her debating his words. Did she truly not realize how extraordinary she was? How beautiful? How captivating? How clever? How utterly irresistible?

He'd never been with a woman who reacted the way she did to his touch. She was so passionate. He wanted to touch her again, just to watch her reaction.

"I suppose I have to tell you about my father now," she murmured. She was righting her bodice and her face was cast downward so he could not see her expression. Warrick didn't like to admit it, but he had manipulated her so that she would say his name. He'd wanted to hear the word in her husky voice. But now he regretted doing so. He wanted her to say his name voluntarily and without remorse. He wanted her to *want* to say his name.

And the devil take him if he should know why he cared if she said it at all.

She glanced up at him, the last remaining traces of passion clearing from her eyes. He cleared his throat. "That was the wager."

"And you won."

"It wasn't entirely fair…" he began.

She shook her skirts out. "We didn't place stipulations. I honor my bets, and I'll tell you."

He stepped closer, longed to take her in his arms again. "Fallon, you do not have—"

A quick rap sounded on the door, and it opened to reveal a tall, blond man. Warrick could tell from Fallon's reaction that she recognized him. Warrick was no judge of male beauty, but this man appeared to be the sort that ladies tended to swoon over. He had thick golden hair, clear blue eyes, a straight nose, prominent cheekbones, height, breadth, and all the rest. "I'm told you want to speak with me. Is there a problem with the services you received?" His voice was low and melodious, and Warrick got a sense this was a man who did not enjoy being summoned.

"We need a moment of your time," he said, but Gabriel was looking at Fallon. Fallon noted his interest as well and moved closer to Warrick. He shouldn't have brought her, he thought, belatedly. He should have left her safe at the ball.

"Do I know you?" Gabriel asked her, his look positively predatory. "You seem familiar."

"I'm the Marchioness of Mystery, one of The Three Diamonds," she said, sounding remarkably confident, despite what he knew to the contrary. "You might have read of me in the papers."

Warrick rather doubted this was the sort of man reading the *Morning Chronicle*. More likely, he remembered Fallon from an earlier time. A time when she'd been called Maggie.

Gabriel was already shaking his head. "No. That's not it."

"We've actually come to ask you about Lucifer," Warrick interrupted.

Gabriel raised an amused eyebrow. "Are you with Bow Street? I already told them I don't know where he is."

"I'm certain you were extraordinarily helpful, but I'm not with Bow Street, and I'm rather more interested in Lucifer's Diamonds. I want to know to whom he sold them."

Gabriel looked bored. "I know nothing about any diamonds. I merely managed Lucifer's establishment. I didn't involve myself in his personal affairs. Now, if that is all—"

"No, that's not all," Warrick said, "because you haven't answered my question."

Gabriel spread his hands. "Because I don't know the answer."

"Let me see if this reminds you." He pulled a pistol from his great coat and leveled it at Gabriel. "Remember anything yet?"

Gabriel's face turned ugly. "You're going to pay for this insolence. I'll see you flayed alive."

"Promises, promises. Now answer the question."

Gabriel crossed his arms over his broad chest. "I don't think so, and if you kill me, you'll never get the answer you seek."

Warrick pulled the hammer back. "I don't have to shoot to kill." He lowered the pistol and aimed it at Gabriel's knees. "What do you think, Fallon? Right or left?"

"Leave me out of this."

"Too late for that. I think... left."

"Wait!" Gabriel took a step back.

Warrick raised a brow. "Remember something?"

"I have heard of the diamonds, but I don't know how Lucifer received the spies' names or whom he sold them to. I suspect he blackmailed some official who owed him money for losses incurred at the tables."

"Tell me something I don't know."

"Would you have me concoct lies? That's as much as I know. Lucifer's mistress stole the information before I saw it."

Warrick sighed, narrowed his eyes at his target, and shot Gabriel in the foot. Fallon screamed, and Gabriel swore and fell to the floor clutching his bloody boot. "Fallon," Warrick said calmly. "Lock the door."

She gave him a wild-eyed look. "What?"

"Lock the door before someone comes to investigate."

She moved to do so, skirting around Gabriel, and slid the bolt into place. "You're mad," she said. "You are completely mad."

"That's right," he said, keeping his gaze on Gabriel. "Now are you going to cooperate or do I shoot the other foot as well?"

"You shot one of my toes off," Gabriel seethed.

"Only one? I'm a better shot than I thought. Tell me about Joseph Bayley."

"Who?"

Warrick sighed again, and Gabriel held his hands up in surrender. "All right! All right! Bayley bought one of the diamonds."

"Why?"

"How the bloody hell do I know? Gah, this hurts like the devil."

"Speculate, Gabriel. Why would a crime lord like

Bayley turn to international espionage? Why would he want one of the Diamonds in the Rough dead?"

"Because he could collect a sizable bounty for killing the spy."

"That's right. Who is offering the bounty?"

"That I do not know. You can shoot me a dozen times, and I couldn't tell you. I don't think even Lucifer knew."

Warrick considered this. "Where can I find Bayley?"

Gabriel snorted. "Do you think he advertises his whereabouts? I'm sure he has a hole somewhere, but even if you find it, you won't get in. Now she... wait a moment. Bayley."

Fallon shrank back from Gabriel's keen gaze, but it was too late. He'd recognized her.

"I knew I'd seen you before. You were with him. This was... years ago. You were his daughter, and he was trying to sell you to Lucifer."

Fallon was shaking her head. "I don't know what you're talking about."

"Oh, I never forget a face or a name. But your name wasn't Fallon back then, it was Margie. No, Melanie. Wait, I'll think of it."

"Gabriel, stay focused," Warrick said. "I want to know where Bayley is."

"Why? So she can have another go at killing him? Maggie! That's it. You were Maggie Bayley. You tried to kill him. You'd better stay away from him, little girl, or you might just get a spanking you'll never forget."

"Fitzhugh," she said, her voice full of warning. "I'm ready to leave."

"Very well. And if Gabriel doesn't know where I can find Bayley, I suppose there's nothing to stop me from killing him." He reached in his pocket and took out another pistol. Always handy to have two so he didn't have to waste time priming a second.

"I can send him a message!" Gabriel said quickly. "Some of his men frequent the club."

"Now that's cooperation," Warrick said nodding. "I knew you could be reasonable. Tell Bayley if he wants to find Warrick Fitzhugh, to come to The Merry Widow in Seven Dials tomorrow at midnight."

Gabriel was shaking his head. "That's too soon. Give me two nights."

"Very well." He took Fallon's hand, edged toward the door, and pulled the bolt. "And Gabriel, if I have to come back…" He opened the door and pushed Fallon out. "You'll lose a body part far more vital than your toe before I kill you." He stepped out the door, closed it, then grabbed Fallon's arm, and started to run. "Hurry. I don't relish being flayed alive."

"Why did you shoot him?" she cried as they burst into the main room. He arrowed for the tunnel through which they'd entered.

"Because he didn't think I would."

"And now he's going to kill us!"

"He has to catch us first." He heard shouts behind him and the sounds of pursuit. "Run!"

Fallon fell twice in the tunnel, but he hauled her back to her feet and pulled her along. The darkness made it difficult to navigate but also concealed them from their pursuers. Unfortunately, the pursuers had lamps with them, and when Warrick made a check of their progress, he saw the light bouncing off the wall just behind him. "Damn it!"

"What now?" Fallon asked, her voice full of exasperation.

"They're gaining." He saw a fork ahead and angled for it. "This way."

"This isn't the way out," she argued, pointing to the clearly worn tunnel path they'd been following.

He pushed her into the smaller tunnel ahead of him and hissed, "When are you going to trust me?"

"Oh, I don't know," she said, working to keep up with him. "When you cease putting my life in danger. Ouch!" She bent, panting. "My rib. I don't think I can go much farther."

"You don't have a choice." He pulled her along, deeper into the darkness as the sounds of pursuit faded. But Gabriel's men would double back, and he needed to find somewhere to hide when they came looking. The tunnel was manmade, but this fork was obviously an afterthought. It was rough and damp, crudely carved out of rock and soil. But it was very dark and one of several forks he'd seen as they made their way into The Grotto. It would buy them time. Warrick stumbled over something and thrust his hands out, touching rock. He felt the wall before him and realized he'd reached the end of the tunnel. Fallon stumbled after him, and when he bent to help her to her feet, he felt metal. A chain. He tugged it and felt a door in the floor open. So this was the purpose of the tunnel. A hiding place for God knew what.

"What is it?" Fallon asked. "Why aren't we running?"

"Because I found where we're going to hide."

He felt around the area and found several digging implements. He could pile those on top of the door, concealing it. He just needed to get the tools arranged, then get inside the door, before reaching up to pull the tools into place.

"There's a trapdoor here," he told Fallon. "We're going down through it."

"A door in the ground?"

"Don't argue, and don't ask questions. Just trust me." He guided her to the door and said, "I felt a ladder. Hold my hand until you have your footing."

"I don't want to do this," she said tightly.

"Just trust me."

"As if I have a choice." And then she was in the hole, and a moment later she released his hand. Warrick arranged the tools then lowered himself into the hole. He opened the door a sliver and pulled some sort of mallet over the top. And then he allowed the door to shut and descended into the black.

Nine

FALLON STOOD IN THE UTTER BLACKNESS AND SEETHED. How were they going to get out of this? She really did not want to spend the rest of her certain to be short life alone in a hole with Fitzhugh.

Something rustled somewhere behind her, and little feet scampered along the ground. She clenched her fists and glared silently at God. *That did not mean I wanted a mouse companion!*

Fitzhugh jumped down beside her and grasped her arm to steady himself. She shook him off. "Do not touch me. I hate you."

"No you don't."

If there was one thing she hated, it was being contradicted.

"Yes I do. Look at us! We're in a hole in a… hole! I could be at Alvanley's ball right now. I could be drinking champagne and eating his famous apricot tarts. As it is, I'm in mouse-infested hole with *you*."

"You were bored at Alvanley's."

He was doing something. She could hear him moving about.

"I was content. There is a difference. Not everyone needs to be chased every moment of the day. And now I shall spend the next several weeks trying to control the damage you did to my reputation when you carried me off over your shoulder."

He didn't respond, and she heard something scrape over the floor. It was too big and heavy to be a mouse.

"I was happy with my life," she moaned, doubting he was even listening now. "It was a nice life."

"You weren't happy," he muttered.

"Yes, I—"

She heard a thudding sound, and his arm came about her waist clumsily. He got his bearings and covered her mouth then bent close to her ear. "Not a word. Not a sound. They're coming this way."

She glared at him in the darkness. How she hated this! She hated the unsettled feeling in her rolling belly. She hated the tightness in her chest. She hated the way her hands shook slightly.

She hated the way her heart thrummed in anticipation. Damn him! He was right. She had been bored. She hadn't been happy. Not really happy. But she didn't love this life either. It was too familiar, and the memories it conjured were not pleasant.

The thudding sharpened into footsteps and grew nearer. The men were searching the passage. If she and Fitzhugh were found, they'd be killed or worse. Fitzhugh was probably going to be killed anyway. There was a price on his head, and for some reason he thought her father—her dead father—was the one who hoped to claim the reward.

The small room where they crouched shook as the

men clomped directly above them. Small rivulets of soil trickled down over her face and onto her lips. She brushed it away and held her breath. She could hear the murmur of voices, the rattle of coins in someone's pocket, and Fitzhugh's breathing. It was slow and steady, unlike her own fast and uneven gulps.

Gabriel's men stood directly above them, and Fallon clasped her hands together in prayer. *Please don't let them find us. Please.*

The men above them shuffled, and one of the implements Fitzhugh had laid over the door clattered. She could hear the sound of it being righted. And now the man who lifted it would see the door, pull the chain, shine a light into the hole…

She closed her eyes tightly. This was it. She should have drunk more champagne. She should have eaten all those slices of cake she refused so her gowns would fit. She should have allowed herself to fall in love.

The footsteps thumped again and then withdrew. Fallon's breath leaked out slowly. They were retreating! They hadn't seen the door! Fitzhugh gave her a squeeze to remind her to stay silent. Finally, after what seemed an hour of silence, he whispered, "We're safe for the moment."

For the moment. What were they going to do now? They couldn't stay here indefinitely.

"I found a lamp and a tinderbox." He was rummaging about again, and a moment later light flared and then went out again. It was enough for her to get a sense of the space they occupied. It was rough and small, a little room fashioned of wooden boards and housing several crates. Light flared again, and this time Fitzhugh managed to harness it and light the lamp.

The room glowed, and Fallon counted over ten crates stacked on one side. "What are those?"

"Something Gabriel doesn't want anyone to know about," Fitzhugh said, turning to her. "If the men knew about this room, they would have searched it and found us." His dark hair was dusty with soil and a streak of grime ran across one cheek. His clothes were wrinkled and dirty, and the sleeve of his coat was torn. She looked down at her own gown. It was ruined. Yet another gown he'd ruined.

"So what now?"

Fitzhugh eased himself onto one of the crates. "I knew you were going to ask that."

"Then you should have a ready answer."

"Give me a few moments to think." He glanced up at her, and for a moment the look reminded her of the way he'd looked at her when he'd been touching her and kissing her in Gabriel's room. She felt the shiver of anticipation and looked away. She didn't want to remember what had happened between them. She didn't want this attraction to him.

"Unless you have an idea you'd like to share," he said.

She scowled at him. "Very funny."

"I'm not being facetious. You have quite a bit of experience getting yourself out of dangerous situations. I'm open to suggestions."

She shook her head. "That was years ago." But it was all coming back now. It had been slowly coming back since she walked into her bedroom and found him lying on her bed. The edges of her awareness prickled and came alive. A part of her mind she hadn't relied on in years began to search and strategize. If this room really was Gabriel's secret, then he would want to have a way to access it without anyone seeing him. She couldn't see him getting down on hands and knees to jump into a dark hole. As her own clothing and that of Fitzhugh's attested, that was dirty work. Gabriel was fastidious about his appearance. "There has to be another entrance," she said slowly. "I don't think he'd come in the way we did. That's the escape hatch."

Fitzhugh appeared to consider what she said. Fallon had to admit, it was nice to have a man actually think about one's words and ideas without dismissing them outright. At least Fitzhugh pretended to think about her suggestions before making his own supposedly better ones. "You're right." He jumped off the crate. "Let's look about for a concealed entrance or exit."

Fallon blinked at him. "I'm right?"

He was bending over, inspecting the wall behind the crates. "I don't know. Help me search."

When she simply stood there, he glanced over his shoulder at her. "Is there a problem?"

"I'm surprised you accepted my idea so quickly."

"Why? Because you're a woman?"

"No." But that was the reason exactly. She'd never known a man who took suggestions or advice offered by a woman so easily. "Well, yes, actually."

"When you've done the kind of work I've done and survived," he said, pushing one of the crates aside, "you learn to put aside societal prejudices. You're an intelligent woman who's had experience finding her way out of difficult situations. Your suggestion makes sense."

Fallon nodded. He was right. He was exactly right. Why didn't more men think like he did? Of course, if they did, she would still be relying on the Sinclairs to support her. Men wanted to save her and protect her. They paid her expenses and gave her lavish gifts to make themselves feel needed and wanted. She wouldn't be one of The Three Diamonds if there weren't societal prejudices. She began moving a stack of spades and other digging supplies from one corner in order to search behind it. It was slow work because she didn't want the metal to clang. Across the small room, Fitzhugh continued to move crates. "There's got to be a hidden door somewhere," he muttered.

She continued moving the spades, quietly and carefully. The rusty metal against the skin of her hand felt familiar. She could remember holding a spade much like the one in her hand now when she was little taller than the tool itself. She remembered shivering as she walked behind her father in the dark night with the fog swirling about the hem of the dress she'd outgrown and now showed her ankles. The bubble of fear lodged in her throat when she saw the graveyard, and she wanted to run away, run back home. But home wasn't any safe haven. She was better off with the dead than the likes of her brothers, who would just as soon cuff her or kick her than welcome her with open arms.

"What are you thinking about?"

Fitzhugh's voice shook her, and the fog cleared. She wasn't in a graveyard at all, and she wasn't certain if she might not have preferred it at the moment. "I was remembering carrying a spade like this," she told him.

He nodded. "One of your father's jobs?"

"He was a resurrection man."

"Of course. Dangerous business but profitable if you aren't caught."

She shuddered. "Gruesome. I'd rather steal off the living than the dead any day. But I was too young to make much as a pickpocket yet." She could see it in his face—the way his brows came together slightly and he swallowed. She knew that disapproving look. "You think to pass judgment on me?" she said quickly, going back to her work. "I'm not the one who put us here."

"It's not you I'm thinking of," he said quietly. "I'm wondering at the kind of father who brings a child with him to dig up dead men and steal from their graves."

"The kind of father who tries to sell his daughter to Lucifer a few years later."

"Is that why you tried to kill him?" The comment was made so offhandedly, in such a conversational tone that she might not have noted it. He was good. Fitzhugh was very good. There was no question he had made an excellent spy.

She set another spade down. "Is it time for me to tell the story? Is that what you want to hear right now?"

He shrugged. "It seems as good a time as any, seeing that we should soon meet with your father."

"I told you, my father is dead. And if he were alive, why would he want you? Killing a spy? An elite spy?" She leaned back against a stack of crates. "That wasn't his style. That wasn't the kind of job he took. He wasn't smart enough to be successful at something that requires that much planning."

"That's why he needed you."

She ran her hands over her eyes. They burned, and

she longed to close her heavy lids and sleep for days. She wanted to forget Fitzhugh and her father and the first fifteen years of her life. "Do you want to hear the story? It's nothing new, the same story every street urchin probably tells."

At his encouraging nod, she went on with a sigh. "I was a girl. Not only did I commit that sin, but I was an unwanted girl. My father had three boys, and those were his bread and butter. I don't know if they were really my brothers. I don't know if my mother bore them or some other woman. Perhaps they all had different mothers. He always liked women."

"But he didn't give you up, didn't throw you in the Thames or leave you on the step of a foundlings house."

"I suppose I should be grateful for small mercies, but if you think he kept me because my mother had some sympathy for me, think again." She ran the palms of her hands against the rough wood of the crate she leaned against, feeling the splinters prick her skin. "She didn't treat me any differently than she did the dog, and she generally kicked whatever mutt latched onto us out of her way."

"She was a prostitute."

Fallon nodded. "My father brought men home, and she serviced them. There was a thin curtain between her bedroom and the rest of our small house so I knew what was going on. And when I got a little older, my father started looking at me the way he looked at her. I knew what was coming."

"He was going to sell you too."

She nodded. "I didn't want that. Above all, I didn't want my mother's life. By the time I was eight or nine she was sick with the French disease. Horrible way to die." She shut her eyes, trying not to remember the sores on her mother's body, the mental confusion, the screams at night. "I'd already been stealing for my father, picking pockets, grabbing food from vendors' carts. Do you really want to hear this?"

"Yes."

She straightened at his empathetic tone. "I don't want your sympathy. If you're going to feel sorry for me, then I'll stop right now."

"I don't feel sorry for you."

She narrowed her eyes, studying him in the dim light. "No, I'm sure you're gloating over your perfect childhood." She didn't know where it came from, this defensiveness. She supposed it had lain latent for years as she moved through the *ton* and adopted their ways. But she'd never been one of them. Deep down, she'd always known that. Fitzhugh was going to make certain she didn't forget.

"I can't complain. I did have a rather idyllic childhood, but it was far from perfect and nothing to gloat over. I certainly haven't overcome what you have. I haven't made myself into the kind of person you have."

Fallon studied him for a long moment. Had that been respect in his tone? She could have heard him incorrectly... "In any case, I started taking more chances, stealing bigger items, going with my brothers—actually, by that point, one was in prison and one was dead, so it was *brother*—on his schemes. We made a good team."

And it had been through Arthur that she'd met Frankie. But Fitzhugh didn't need to know about Frankie. She didn't have to give him that.

"But it wasn't enough."

"No. My father was a greedy bastard. Sorry."

He held a hand up. "Don't apologize to me. I'm sure he deserves far worse."

He did, but Fallon could hear Lady Sinclair in the back of her mind saying, *Fallon, language!*

"He decided to sell me to the highest bidder. I overheard him talking about it with some of the other men from his gang. I don't know if Lucifer was going to buy me for himself or to sell my virginity to someone else, but when we went to Lucifer's Lair, I knew the reason. And I knew what would happen when I was bedded."

"You weren't a virgin." He said it matter-of-factly without any disgust.

"No, but my father didn't know that. He would have killed me. No." That wasn't right. He would have done far worse. "He would have passed me around to all his friends and then killed me."

"Fallon—"

"You need to understand why I did it, Fitzhugh. I didn't want to murder him, but I also wasn't going to be sold, especially when that sale meant the worst kind of death and torture. I tried to run away."

He was beside her now, his hands tender on her forearms. "You don't have to justify it to me. I'm not judging you. I've done far worse than anything you can even imagine."

"No, you haven't, and if you did commit murder, it was in the name of service to your country. That's honorable, not... not—" What was the word? She'd read it somewhere. "*Patricide*," she said finally.

"There's a fine line between duty and murder," he

said, looking away. "I promise you I'm no saint. Tell me the rest."

"He found me and brought me back. He beat me too, hurt me so badly I was in bed for a week. That delayed the transaction a bit, but it didn't deter him. He'd negotiated a high price for me. He came home drunk and boasting about it. He said... I won't repeat what he said. It wasn't the kind of thing a father says about a daughter."

She was far away now, present in the room with Fitzhugh and cognizant of his warm hands on her arms, but at the same time back in that filthy little hovel with her father. Arthur had been gone by then, she didn't know where, and it had been the two of them. And he'd been crowing about how smart he was, how much he'd get for her. He'd been so drunk, drunk enough that he made a grab for her, loosened the ties on her blouse. He only wanted to see the merchandise, he'd said.

She'd smacked his hand away in an effort to cover her breasts, and he'd fallen backward. She hadn't hit him hard, but he'd been foxed and unsteady. He fell, and when he rose again, there was murder in his eyes. The knife had been on the table. He'd been using it to carve the mutton he'd brought home for himself. None for her, of course. She'd been providing her own food for years now. Before she knew it, the knife was in her hand and she was slashing at him.

She was fighting for her life, fighting to keep the knife away from him, fighting to save her poor, miserable life.

And when all was said and done, she was covered in blood. His blood. And he lay motionless on the rough floor of their ugly house. She knew what came next.

Prison would be a blessing considering what Arthur or any one of her father's gang would do to her.

And so she'd run.

"And that was when Sinclair found you?"

She nodded. "I was shivering in a corner of Hyde Park in the early hours a few days later. I was hungry and tired and about to give up. Sinclair rode by on a gray horse, and at first I thought he was some kind of apparition. I thought I was imagining things. And then he reined the horse in, jumped down, and asked if I needed help." Fallon laughed a little at the memory. She could only imagine how she must have looked to the earl—a ragged, filthy, little beggar who would just as soon steal his purse as do him the same kindness.

"I said no, of course. But he said I was to come with him anyway. I was too tired to argue. I thought prostitution was pretty much inevitable at that point, and he seemed nice enough and as far removed from my father and his associates as I could get. He took me home with him, and that's when I met the countess."

It was also when she'd realized the huge disparity between the wealthy and titled and the world she'd grown up in. Fallon had stared in wonder at the enormous town house with its sunny rooms, high ceilings, and soft furnishings. She was ashamed to remember how the first few months of her stay all she'd thought about was what everything was worth and how easy it would be to steal it. Why, she could just walk out the door with a silver candelabra that would pay her rent for a year.

But she hadn't. Partly because she liked the countess and she liked Juliette, who had also been living under the Sinclairs' roof at that time. She liked having a clean, soft place to sleep. She liked being clean. She liked how Sinclair never expected anything of her. And, most surprisingly, she enjoyed her lessons.

She'd never learned to read or write, and her speech had been absolutely horrible. But the countess herself had sat with Fallon for hours and hours each day, teaching Fallon how to be a lady. And Fallon had wanted to be a lady.

Most of all, she wanted to stay with the Sinclairs, where she was safe and where she knew her father's men would never find her.

But as the years passed, she occasionally ventured back to her old haunts. No one recognized her, and there was no hint of her father, not even a whisper of his name. She began to feel bolder and braver. By then Lily had joined them, and the countess had come up with a plan to help the girls become self-sufficient.

"You became The Three Diamonds. It's a brilliant plan, and it has served you well."

"But there's one problem. My past is still my past. You discovered it."

"I'm a good researcher."

"Good enough to be certain my father is still alive?"

"Absolutely certain." His fingers trailed up and down her arms. "You didn't kill him that night. You may have gravely injured him, forced him underground for a time, but he's back. And he wants me dead."

Fallon closed her eyes. For so long she'd thought her nightmare was over, but it had just been in hiding. Her father wasn't really dead. If Fitzhugh could find her, so could Bayley, especially now that she'd told Gabriel her real identity.

"I'm not going to let him touch you," Fitzhugh said, grasping her arms. "I'm not going to let him hurt you."

"You can barely protect yourself right now." She indicated their present hiding place. "How can you protect me? And don't pretend you didn't involve me in all this to use me as bait. Don't forget where I came from. I know how to catch a fish."

Fitzhugh let her go and looked away. "I admit, that was my intention." He raked a hand through his hair. "I hoped I could find some clue as to the identity of the man paying your father. Who is he? Does your father work for him, or is he a man who prefers not to dirty his hands? It's someone wealthy, and if my instincts are correct, someone with a title or a place in the government."

"But so far we're at a dead end."

"Yes. The only lead I have is to your father, but I won't use you as bait."

She shook her head. "Why not? Don't tell me you care about me. I'm no naïve virgin. I know what happened between us back at The Grotto doesn't mean anything."

"Doesn't it?"

She frowned and studied him, confused. "Why are you always making cryptic statements like that? Are you trying to imply that what happened *did* mean something to you?"

"And what if it did? What if I told you I'm half in love with you, Fallon?"

Her heart kicked so hard, she had to sit on the edge of the crate to keep from falling. She did not understand this man. She thought she understood all men, knew what they wanted. But this man bewildered her. She looked up at him. He was watching her, waiting.

"I wouldn't believe you. I'd think it was some sort of trick or ploy."

He nodded. "Of course you would." He bent over, ostensibly searching for the exit again. "Men tell you that all the time."

"They do," she admitted. "But not... not like this." She couldn't explain exactly how Fitzhugh's admission was different. Was it because they were locked together in a hole in the ground? Was it because he could have already had her and didn't take the opportunity?

But he'd never been after her body. No, what he wanted from her was far more dangerous. And now he was playing with the hottest fire of all—love.

"You don't mean it, do you?" she asked, finally.

He glanced over his shoulder and gave her a sardonic look. "Are you going to help me look, or would you rather sleep here tonight?"

She stood and began moving spades again. She was almost at the end of the pile when Fitzhugh swore.

"What is it?" she turned quickly to find him smiling.

"I've got it." He grinned at her. "You're too smart for your own good, Fallon." He brushed the dust and dirt away from a door that matched the interior of the room quite well. But it was a door and big enough for even a tall man like Gabriel to use as an entrance and exit. "Ready to see where it leads?"

"Probably right into Gabriel's lair."

"Then I'll rescind my earlier compliment on your intelligence." He tugged the handle, and the door creaked open. "What do we have to lose?"

Fallon peered into the dark tunnel. *I've already lost it*, she thought, and crawled inside.

Ten

WARRICK STRIPPED OFF HIS SOILED COAT AND SHIRT and left them in a pile for his valet. He'd dismissed the man, wanting time alone now that he was finally in his own home, in his own bedchamber. He'd deemed it too dangerous to return to Fallon's residence, but his own was a bloody fortress. Neither Gabriel nor Joseph Bayley nor Lucifer himself was going to get in. If they made it past the guards patrolling the perimeter, they'd never make it past the locks, bars, and the four two-hundred-pound mastiffs that served as his intruder alerts.

The Grotto's hidden door had led to an alley a few blocks from Gabriel's establishment. Warrick and Fallon had emerged into the dark night, blinking like surprised owls. He'd expected her to argue about returning to his town house, but she was either too tired or finally resigned to trusting him because she followed without comment or protest.

And now she slept in a bed just a few doors away. At least he hoped she slept. He didn't sleep. He never slept anymore. It was too dangerous.

He paced his room, ignoring his untouched bed. Fallon was complicated. That shouldn't attract him, but for some reason it did. She hadn't believed him when he'd said he was half in love with her. He could have proposed marriage and she probably would have laughed. He imagined men proposed to her all the time. Conventional methods of wooing a woman were not going to succeed with Fallon. She was too jaded, too wary, too wise.

And that was all the more reason to treat her as a business associate and little else. He didn't need a complicated woman. He had enough of those in his life between his mother and sisters. And good God, he could only imagine the looks on their faces were he to be seen courting the Marchioness of Mystery. His mother would probably faint. Or at least pretend to faint.

He did not need another complicated woman.

So why couldn't he stop thinking about Fallon? Why couldn't he stop imagining what it would be like to have her here in his room, beside him in his bed? She'd be naked, that glorious honey-toned skin silvered by moonlight...

He glanced at his window, where the drapes were firmly closed. He'd have to open them before he carried her in here. And was there a full moon tonight?

He sat on his bed, put his head in his hands, and willed himself to stop thinking about her, stop planning her seduction, their lovemaking. This wasn't a mission. He had bigger, more important dilemmas at the moment than whether he or she should be on top. Besides, he would be on top the first time. He wanted to be able to look down at her face when she climaxed, and he wanted to control the penetration. He'd take her with agonizing slowness. She thought she liked it fast and hard, but he'd show her there was something to be said for torturously slow. He'd make her cry his name again. He'd make her cry it again and again.

And that would probably wake up the servants.

Damn it! He flopped onto his back. He didn't care about the servants—except they would likely report to his mother, and then she'd show up, wanting to know what was going on. She'd report back to his father, who was already not speaking with Warrick. Oh, the shame of having a son who insisted on pursuing a place in the Foreign Office. And the shame of the younger brother who followed him into battle. But just because the Earl of Winthorpe had disowned Warrick didn't mean the man didn't receive regular briefings about his wayward son.

And that didn't mean Warrick didn't hope his father would one day accept him again. Accept him for who he was—not who his father wanted him to be. And he was a man who would take great pleasure in making love to Fallon, whether she was the Marchioness of Mystery or not. And to hell with his mother and father.

He was a grown man and could do what he damned well pleased.

He lay on the bed for another quarter hour and unwillingly succumbed to a restless sleep. He dreamed he was on a battlefield. He couldn't say which one. It was gray and misted with fog. It looked like any of the dozens of battlefields he'd seen in his career—littered with the corpses of dead and dying men; reeking with the stench of blood, sweat, and excrement; and punctuated by the agonized groans of the wounded.

Warrick didn't want to be here. He was supposed to be somewhere else. He couldn't think where at the moment, but it was urgent. He felt for his satchel, where the documents he was ferrying would be stored, and his hand came away wet. He stared at it, at the bright crimson dripping from his fingers. Was it his blood or another's? Where was his horse? Had he lost him? Was that why he was walking?

He stumbled and fell to his knees, his face inches from the severed head of a man. Warrick tried to jump up, but he couldn't get his footing on the slippery, uneven ground. And then he looked down and realized he hadn't been walking on ground at all. He'd been walking over bodies—hundreds of them, thousands of them. He'd been stepping on their hands and chests and noses, trudging through their blood and waste, and he had to climb over thousands more to reach the edge of the battlefield.

That was if there was an edge. It seemed to go on and on, disappearing in the omnipresent fog. He wanted out of here, but he was seeking... something. Something vital. He called for help, hoping one of his countrymen would hear him. It was stupid to call out—the enemy could come just as easily as an ally, and he had those documents. Not that he cared about them anymore. There was something else.

He called out again, knowing he shouldn't but desperate now, his state verging on hysteria. The eyes of the corpses were looking at him, staring at him. "Don't look at me!" he yelled.

And that was when they opened their mouths, their yawning black mouths. "Fitzhugh," they chanted. "Fitzhugh." The gaping mouths mocked him. "Warrick!"

"No!" He shot straight up, clawing at the air around him, trying to free himself of the bodies and the dream. "No!"

"I'm sorry. I'm sorry."

It wasn't the voice of a dead soldier. It was the low voice of a woman. He closed his eyes, opened them again, and tried to focus. Fallon.

"I heard you calling out. I kept thinking one of your servants would come, but no one did. I wanted to make sure you were all right."

"Fallon," he croaked, sitting. Damn! How could he have allowed himself to sleep?

"I knocked." She indicated the open door. "But you didn't answer, and then I heard you yelling, 'Don't look at me.' I was afraid someone had attacked you."

"I'm not upset," he said, understanding immediately what had happened. "Thank you for coming. I'm fine."

"You're covered in perspiration and white as a sheet. I can see that even in this dim light." She gestured to the candle she'd brought with her. "You're not fine."

He ran a hand through his hair and scrubbed his eyes. The nightmare was fading but not quite fast enough. He could still feel the terror and the hands of the corpses pulling at him. "It was a nightmare. Nothing more."

"It sounded like a very serious nightmare. It woke me from a sound sleep."

He envied her that. He could not remember the last time he'd slept soundly. He raised his brows when she sat on the bed beside him. "Do you want to tell me about it?"

"No." He stood. He was still wearing his trousers, but he found his discarded shirt on the floor. He slipped it over his head, leaving it open at the throat.

Fallon rose as well. "I see, I'll go back to my room then."

He'd hurt her feelings. Damn it! He wasn't in the state of mind to deal with her—or anyone. He was still shaking, his mind sluggish and reluctant to return to reality. He couldn't think about etiquette right now. "Fallon," he said, making an attempt anyway.

She paused.

"It's not that I don't appreciate your concern, but I don't want to speak of it. To anyone." And especially not to her. It was his pain, his private torment. He didn't want to inflict it on others.

"I understand." She nodded and turned to go again. "But, if I may inquire, why didn't your valet or another one of your servants come? I'm certain you roused the entire house."

He blew out a breath. "I suppose they are used to it," he said.

"Used to it? Used to you calling out at night? You scared me half to death."

"I frequently have nightmares. My servants are accustomed to the interruption and do not trouble me."

She blinked at him. "You have nightmares like that often? Why?"

"I told you—"

She raised a hand. "Of course. You don't wish to

speak of it. It's fine for me to tell you my most intimate secrets, but you are not expected to reciprocate
and let me in."

"Fallon—"

"It's late, and I'm tired. I have *troubled* you more
than enough. Good night."

Warrick swore when she closed the door. This was
not how he had hoped things would go if he ever
managed to find her in his room. He thought about
going after her, but he was in no state to smooth
over roughened feelings. His own were too raw at
the moment.

He looked at his bed, the Gothic-style canopy an
unlikely enemy, and sat at his desk to work.

His mother always told him everything looked
better in the morning. Warrick thought that one of
her more sensible sayings, but it didn't prove true at
breakfast. Fallon looked exquisite. She wore a simple
day dress in white and rose with a gauze fichu tucked
in the bodice. Warrick couldn't help but notice it
was a low bodice, and it seemed to him the gauze
only served to tantalize, not conceal. Obviously the
clothing she had sent for had been delivered, and—he
studied her elaborate upsweep—perhaps her lady's
maid had come with it. Fallon looked fresh and pretty
in his bright dining room and gave no indication she
remembered anything of the night before.

She gave no indication she saw him at all.

She didn't acknowledge him when he walked in
and didn't return his greeting. So his punishment was
silence. Well, he knew how to deal with silence. He
went to the sideboard and filled his plate. He didn't

look at what he chose. He wasn't hungry and couldn't care less what he ate. He was considering his options. When he was younger, and far more naïve, he thought it a blessing when his mother or one of his sisters treated him to silence. But experience had taught him that accepting the silence was never a good idea. Unlike men, women really wanted to say what was on their minds. And if they didn't get it out, they'd explode or retaliate in other ways.

He set his plate on the table, nodded to the footman who poured him tea, and studied Fallon. He would pick a fight. That would do very well with her argumentative temperament.

"Thank you, George," he said to the footman. "That will be all."

Fallon watched George go, and Warrick could all but see her plotting how to make her own exit. *Don't be in such a hurry*, he thought as he opened the *Times*. "You'll stay here while I make the rendezvous at The Merry Widow tonight," he said, not looking at her.

Silence. She was debating. She wanted to speak but remembered that she wasn't speaking to him. He turned the page.

"Stay here?"

He smiled, gaze on the paper. "Of course. It's far too dangerous for you to come along."

"Too dangerous? You've dragged me to meet every other denizen of hell. If my father is alive, I want to see him."

Warrick perused the paper and leisurely turned another page. "I don't think that's wise."

The paper flew from before him, and he looked up

to see Fallon with hands on her hips, eyes blazing. "I don't care what *you* think. I can do as I like, and I'm not staying here."

"Fine."

"And don't tell me—fine?"

"Yes." He rose. "Fine. But you'll stay in Daisy's office. You can see the drawing room from her spy hole. I don't want to expose you to your father unless I have to."

"He'll want to see me."

"We don't always get what we want."

She shook her head. "So I'm to be some sort of bargaining chip."

He didn't argue. This was the reason he'd recruited her. He wished to God he hadn't, but there was no room for regrets now. It wasn't just his own life he was saving. He needed to know who Bayley was working for.

Fallon was shaking her head at him. "You really aren't a gentleman at all, are you?"

He couldn't say why the barb stung. He'd done things no gentleman of the *ton* would ever do, acted in ways even someone of the lower class might find distasteful. He did not particularly care if he was considered a gentleman or not.

So why was he suddenly infused with rage? Was it because he heard the echo of his father's words in Fallon's?

"I'm a soldier," he said through clenched jaw. "My duty is to my country, not Society."

"I would think protecting the weak a universal trait, not simply one of Society."

He laughed. "You, weak? Darling, I wouldn't want

to meet you in a dark alley. I'm not at all certain I would come away unscathed."

"And now you insult me!"

He almost laughed again. She really was incensed. "That's no insult. I admire a strong, fearless woman." He leaned close. "Especially in bed."

"Don't flatter me. It won't lure me into your bed."

"Then perhaps this will." He reached out and pulled her into his arms. She resisted, but he'd taken her off guard and her surprise was enough to give him the upper hand. He pulled her close, lowered his mouth to hers, and claimed it.

She tried to speak, to protest, to curse him or worse, but he was merciless. He slanted his mouth over hers, taking her with a wildness and abandon he had almost forgotten he possessed. Slowly, she stopped pounding his chest with her hands, stopped trying to pull away, and sank into him. Her body melted against his, her heavy breasts warm against his chest. Her arms wrapped around him, and her sweet mouth opened for him.

He was the one struggling for composure when her tongue met his. She stroked him, teased him, dueled with him until he was no longer certain who was kissing whom. He wedged her legs open with his knee and pushed his thigh between them. She was warm there, and he pressed intimately against her, eliciting a groan. He groaned himself when she took hold of him through his breeches.

"You're hard," she whispered against his mouth.

"I want you."

"I should say no."

He kissed her neck, and her head lolled back. His lips trailed to her shoulder, making their way to that plump, ripe flesh spilling out under her fichu. "You should," he agreed.

"This is a bad idea."

"The worst." He used his tongue to tease her skin through the gauzy material and pressed his thigh against her core. She shivered.

"I'm trying very hard to resist you," she said, her voice low and husky.

"Keep trying. In the meantime, I think I shall push you against that wall, toss your skirts up, and thrust into you."

She moaned. "I wish I didn't like that suggestion so very much."

"Me too." He began moving her backward when he heard a sharp tap on the door.

"Sir," his butler said. Warrick jumped away from Fallon and pushed her behind him.

"Get out, Pressly."

"I'm sorry for the interruption, sir, but..."

But Warrick had already seen her. "Never mind, Pressly. I understand."

The butler gave him an apologetic look and moved aside. Lady Winthorpe stepped into the doorway and raised a thin brow. "Having tart for breakfast, Warrick?"

He sighed. "Good morning to you too, Mother."

Eleven

HIS MOTHER WAS A SMALL WOMAN WITH A PREFERENCE for large hats that dwarfed her delicate features. This morning she wore a bluish green gown—he supposed the color had some other more sophisticated name, but he didn't know it—with a hat to match. The elaborate plumage, consisting of feathers and ribbons looked heavy enough to cause her to list to one side.

She took one step toward the table, and Pressly hurried to pull out a chair. "Tell the footman to bring me a cup of tea," she ordered as though she, not Warrick, owned the place. "You do still employ a footman?" she asked.

"Two, Mother. Thank you, Pressly, that will be all." He folded his arms across his chest. "Was I expecting you, Mother?"

"If you mean to inquire as to whether or not we had an appointment, the answer is no. But I do hope the world hasn't become such that a mother is now required to make an appointment to visit her son." She gave Fallon a long perusal. "Though I suppose I do see where it might avoid some unpleasantness."

Warrick watched as the footman entered with the tea and supposed there was nothing for it. She was settling in. Perhaps if he embarrassed her—well, embarrassed her further…

He moved aside, revealing Fallon. "Mother, might I introduce you to—"

She held up a hand. "No, you may not." She sipped her tea. "I know who that woman is, and I must say, Warrick, I am disappointed in you. A courtesan. Really!"

"Well, Mother, as you know, I live for your approval."

"No, that is not something I know, though I dearly wish it were true. Perhaps then your father would be able to speak of you without clutching his heart, as though in pain."

Warrick wanted to roll his eyes. His father was one of the healthiest men he knew. If he was suffering heart palpitations, Warrick would crawl back home on hands and knees.

"I should go," Fallon said quietly.

"No. Stay and finish your breakfast."

"I find I have lost my appetite."

"Ha!" His mother exploded. He knew she would not be able to ignore Fallon for long. "You had better watch your tongue, you strumpet. I am the Countess of Winthorpe."

"And I am the Marchioness of Mystery, as though anyone gives a fig!"

Warrick had the urge to flee and allow the women to work the matter out for themselves. But he had not fled the Battle of Valencia nor the Battle of the

Bidassoa. He supposed he could stay for this one, though he suspected the outcome would prove particularly bloody.

His mother was standing now, and Warrick made to step between the ladies. "Mother—"

"I don't care whom you have slept with," his mother was saying. "Whether it's the Prince Regent or the whole of the Shropshire countryside. You will not speak to me thus! And I demand you go upstairs, pack your tawdry things, and leave this house at once."

"Mother—"

"Do you think I have designs on your son? I'll have you know, our association is purely through his design. I don't want him."

Warrick gave Fallon a sideways look. "You don't have to go that far."

"Do not be ridiculous," his mother said. "I know your friend recently married the Duke of Pelham. You obviously hope to improve your situation in a similar manner. Well, choose someone other than my son."

Fallon pointed a finger at his mother. The two women were practically nose to nose. If it came to blows, Warrick wasn't certain whom he should champion. At the moment, neither seemed to deserve his support.

"I'll have you know Juliette loves Pelham, and he loves her. And I wouldn't marry your son for all the—"

Warrick cleared his throat. "You needn't complete that statement. I assure you my pride is already bruised. First my mother finds it necessary to defend me, as though I am once again a child of four, and then one of the most sought-after courtesans in the country cannot say vehemently enough how much she does not desire me."

"Warrick, really," his mother said. "Do stay out of this."

Warrick threw his hands up in frustration. Would leaving now really be so much a retreat as a calculated withdrawal?

"Listen, you little slut," his mother was saying. "I have tolerated the rumors about you and my son because I have been friends with the Countess of Sinclair for more years than I can count. I don't care what you do with her husband, and I don't want to know. But you will not do it with my son."

"No, I won't. Excuse me."

Warrick watched Fallon stomp out the door, head held high as she breezed past the footman, who was pretending not to listen, but who would certainly inform his whole staff of this incident at the first opportunity.

"There," his mother said. "Problem solved." She wiped her hands together and took her seat again.

Warrick glared at her. "Did it ever occur to you, Mother, that she and I are working together?"

"Oh, dear God. Do not mention that dreadful spy business to me. I do not want to hear about it."

"And I would prefer you do not meddle in my affairs. If I wanted your meddling, I would not have left Winthorpe House."

"Your father threw you out, if I remember correctly." She lifted a scone from his plate. "Are these freshly made?"

"I'm not going to quibble over details with you, Mother. Father is embarrassed that he has a son who has a vocation for which he is financially compensated."

"Nonsense." She nibbled on the scone. "I do believe this is freshly made," she said in surprise. "Your brother Anthony has a paid position, but he has chosen a respectable career. If you had only done the same—"

"Sadly, my talents do not lie in the clergy, Mother."

"Well, from the display I observed a few moments ago, I should say not! But why not buy a commission in the army? You could command a regiment."

"Because I don't want to. I want to work in espionage. And right now I need Fallon's help."

His mother sighed, loud and long. "I really do think this has gone on long enough, Warrick."

He frowned.

"I mean the feud between your father and you. I am not a young woman any longer, and I want peace in my household. All of my daughters and sons, save you, are wed and well situated. Is it too much to ask that you be similarly placed?"

"What are you proposing?"

"Keep your vocation, if that is what you love, but come home. Make amends with your father. I believe if you were to marry, he would accept you back with open arms. The promise of grandchildren tends to soften him, you see."

Warrick thought it was more she than his father who wanted grandchildren, but he did not comment.

"You remember Lady Edith?"

Of course he remembered her. She was the woman his parents had picked for him to marry. She was the daughter of a duke—wealthy, beautiful, and cold as ice. "As I recall, Mother, she is engaged to Lord Findley."

His mother shook her head. "That is not going to come off."

"It seemed rather fixed the last time I heard her spoken of."

His mother frowned at him. "Really, Warrick, are you going to trust some gossip you heard weeks ago or what I am telling you right now? The engagement is over."

He supposed if anyone knew when an engagement was at an end, it was his mother. "Why?" he asked.

"What does it matter? There's no scandal, I assure you. I suppose the two did not suit."

There was more to the story, but she wasn't telling.

"And you want me to give her another chance?"

"If she'll have you, yes. It would please your father and me and do a great deal toward mending broken fences."

Warrick nodded. He had no interest in Lady Edith, but he would admit there was a part of him that wanted to reconcile with his father. He missed their chats, the closeness they'd once shared, the easiness between them when walking in the country. And, truth be told, he missed his family. He'd been alone for a long time. Now he wanted to be part of something again.

"What are you proposing?"

"I am hosting a ball in a few days. Surely you received the invitation."

"Mama." He groaned. He detested balls.

"Just listen. I have invited Lady Edith. Come to the ball. Reconcile with your father. Dance with Lady Edith. Your father will be so pleased. He does not say it, but he misses you terribly."

Warrick nodded. How could he refuse?

৯৯৯

Fallon moved back toward the stairs and began the long walk to her room. She didn't know why hearing Lady Winthorpe discuss the woman she hoped Fitzhugh would marry disturbed her, but it did. Perhaps because she knew she would never be good enough. Perhaps because she knew his mother would never accept her.

And who cared? She didn't want to be accepted by his mother. She didn't want to have anything further to do with him. But though she'd stormed out and said she was leaving, she wasn't so much a fool as to actually go. She knew she was in a veritable fortress here, and she wasn't taking the chance that Gabriel or her father's men were waiting for her on the outside.

Still, she would have liked to go home. And she would have liked to get her hands on a copy of the *Morning Chronicle*. She imagined the Cytherian Intelligence column was rife with stories about Mr. F— carrying the Marchioness of Mystery out of Lord A—'s ball over his shoulder.

She reached her bedchamber and dismissed the maids straightening it. She was only going to climb back into bed anyway.

She could kill Fitzhugh. She really could. The problem was that she also wanted to kiss him. And at this point, why not? Everyone thought they were lovers anyway. It wasn't as though she had a reputation to protect. She pulled the covers up to her chin and closed her eyes.

She knew him now. He wouldn't reveal her past to the *ton*. He wasn't that kind of man. He might threaten it. He might even do his worst in order to get what he wanted. She understood this wasn't just about him. He was trying to save lives, trying to find a murderer. But she knew him well enough to know he was a rarity.

Fitzhugh was a true gentleman. She might accuse him of being otherwise, but he wasn't going to intentionally sully a lady's reputation. Even if the lady in question wasn't really a lady at all.

She closed her eyes, willing sleep to come. She was tired. His screams last night had woken her from a deep sleep, and after seeing him, she'd only snatched a few restless hours. What had he been dreaming about? He'd been drenched with sweat and white as a ghost. But that hadn't startled her as much as the trembling. She'd never seen a man shake like that. What had scared him so much?

Where had he been? What had he done?

And why did she want to hold him and find a way to make it all go away?

A knock sounded on her door, and she sighed. "Go away, Fitzhugh. I don't want to talk to you."

"It isn't Mr. Fitzhugh, miss," a female voice said. "It's Kitty, the maid."

Fallon frowned. "Come in."

Kitty poked her head in the door. "You have a visitor, miss. I told her you were indisposed, but she insisted I tell you she was here."

Fallon covered her face with the sheet. "Don't tell me it's Lady Sinclair."

"No, miss. It's another like you."

Fallon lowered the sheets. "Like me? You mean a courtesan?"

"She said she was the Countess of Charm."

Fallon laughed. "Lily. Yes, send her up."

"To your bedroom, miss?"

"Yes." Fallon supposed she was shocking the servants as well as Fitzhugh's family. Now they had not only one fallen woman but two in their hallowed halls. She sat and tried to do something with her hair and then abandoned the effort. This was Lily. They'd seen each other looking far worse.

The door opened and Lily popped in. Fallon had rarely seen her auburn-haired friend without a spring in her step. Lily wore an apple-green dress with cream stripes and a matching hat. Lily almost always wore green or blue. She said those colors complimented her eyes. "There you are!" She immediately engulfed Fallon in an embrace. As usual, Lily smelled like apples and something else clean and wholesome. Lily leaned back and looked into Fallon's eyes. "You poor darling. Tell me what's going on."

Fallon smiled. She had never known anyone as sweet-natured as Lily. With her freckles and dimples, she looked like she should be working on someone's farm. But Juliette had been the farmer's daughter. Lily, like Fallon, grew up in the city. Not London. Lily was from York, and Fallon could still hear a bit of the North in her speech. She wasn't conventionally beautiful. Her face was a bit too round, her hair a bit too bright, and her smile a bit too wide. But she was pretty. She was the kind of pretty that when she smiled men forgot she wasn't beautiful and fell in love with her anyway.

"How did you find me?" Fallon asked.

"I have my ways."

Fallon groaned. "Don't tell me my presence here is in the papers."

"Give me more credit than that!" She pulled off her gloves and reached into her reticule. "Here is a copy of the *Chronicle*."

Fallon turned right to the page and scanned the story. It was just as she expected. "I suppose it could be worse."

"I don't see how. The man literally carried you out of Alvanley's ball over his shoulder, as though you were a sack of potatoes. A well-dressed sack of potatoes, of course." She patted Fallon's hand. "I don't know Mr. Fitzhugh well."

"I wasn't aware you knew him at all."

Lily waved her hand, dismissing the statement much quicker than Fallon preferred. "But he isn't the type to make such displays. Fallon, are you in some sort of trouble?"

Fallon stared at Lily. "No. Well, perhaps. How do you know *anything* about Mr. Fitzhugh?"

"You're not the only one with secrets."

Fallon didn't doubt it. She'd once seen Lily staring at a miniature of a little boy and weeping. But that sort of secret was nothing like Fitzhugh's type of secret. "It's my father," Fallon said.

"I thought your parents were dead."

"My father is apparently alive."

"Is he trying to blackmail you?"

"No." Fitzhugh had taken care of that himself. "But he's not altogether a nice man, and Fitzhugh wanted to protect me." That wasn't exactly the truth, but it was close enough.

"Well, you're in good hands." Lily patted Fallon's arm.

"How do you know that? I fail to see how you can know so much about Mr. Fitzhugh."

"I like to know a little bit about everyone." This was true. Lily did seem to have a nose for all the best gossip and knew every scandal before the papers ever did. Sometimes before those involved even did! "What can I do? Are you comfortable here? Can I bring you anything?"

"No. I'm—actually I'd like another change of clothing."

Lily brightened. She loved being useful. "What sort?"

"Something dark."

"Something seductive?" Lily raised her brows.

"No." Fallon laughed. "It's not like that."

"Why not? Fitzhugh is just your type. He's not too pretty, and he scares me half to pieces. Never mind. I shall have something sent right over." She pulled her gloves on, and Fallon caught her wrist.

"Lily, don't go yourself. Send one of your servants or a note to one of mine."

She nodded. "I'll be careful. Now, I must be off!"

"Where are you going?"

"I'm meeting Lord Darlington in the park."

"Darlington? I thought he was away and in mourning for his mother."

"He's just back in Town, and I hope to cheer him up." Lily glanced at herself in the cheval mirror and righted her bonnet.

"How will you do that?"

"Why, remind him of the bet he and Juliette made,

of course. He promised to stand on his head if the Duke of Pelham attended Prinny's ball. I'm going to collect for Juliette."

"She'll be ever so appreciative."

Lily shrugged. "She may not care, but I do." She gave Fallon another hug. "Be careful, and don't hesitate to ask if there's anything else you need." With a quick kiss on the cheek, she was gone.

In Lily's haste, she hadn't closed the door completely. Fallon moved to do so, but a hand on the wood prevented it. She followed the hand to the arm and then to the man.

Fitzhugh smiled. "Good. You're alone." He stepped inside and closed the door. "There's something we need to discuss."

Twelve

THERE WAS SOMETHING ABOUT SEEING HER IN A bedchamber that fired his blood. Really, seeing her at any time and in any place fired his blood, but when she was standing directly in front of a rather large tester bed, he couldn't help but imagine her splayed on it, her hair fanned out in all its sable glory and her body gloriously naked.

"I didn't invite you in," she said. "I have nothing to discuss with you. And do not try to leave me behind when you travel to The Merry Widow tonight."

"Fine."

"Fine?" His agreement was too easily given.

"Fallon, trust me. I am amenable to taking you as long as you agree to stay out of sight." He stepped closer, and that was a mistake. He could reach out and touch her easily at this distance, and he couldn't quite stop imagining doing so.

"Why must I hide?"

"Because if Bayley gets the chance, he'll grab you. He can use you to get to me, and I can't give him any leverage. I need to know who is behind this assassination plot. I have to find the leader. That's the only chance I have of saving... the rest of the Diamonds in the Rough."

She narrowed her eyes. She was no fool, and she knew he'd almost slipped and given her a name. "All right. I understand that well enough, but how could my father use me to get to you?"

He shook his head. "Do you really still not know?" He did touch her now. He took her hands in his and raised one to his lips, brushing his mouth over her soft fingers.

She watched him, looking perplexed. "Know what?"

"That I'm in love with you, Fallon." He kissed her fingertips. "That I think about you all the time." He took one of her fingers in his mouth and sucked lightly. She took a quick, sharp breath. "That I want you."

"Why are you saying this?"

He laughed. Before Fallon, he had never been inept at making a woman know he wanted her. Of course, he'd never told a woman he was in love with her before. Perhaps that was the problem. Perhaps he was doing it wrong. "I'm saying it because it's what I feel." He cupped the back of her neck and drew her gently to him. "And I think you feel some of it as well. Am I mistaken?"

"No," she whispered.

"Do you want me?"

She hesitated. "Yes. I want you." She moved to kiss him, but he put a finger on her lips.

"How are your ribs?"

"What? Oh, they're fine."

"Are you still wearing the bindings?"

"Is this really what you wish to discuss at the moment?" A line had appeared between her eyebrows, and she looked slightly annoyed.

"Humor me."

"Yes, I'm still wearing the bindings. They help."

"Then we'll have to be careful."

"Careful? When?"

"When we do this." He scooped her into his arms and kissed her, moving toward the bed. She gasped in surprise and then kissed him back.

"Put me down," she murmured against his lips.

"Your wish is my command." He set her gently in the center of the bed and climbed in beside her, kissing her again, pressing his body to hers, careful not to put any pressure on her rib cage.

She kissed him back, her hands twining in his hair then moving to his shoulders to pull him harder against her. "I want to feel you," she whispered. "Skin on skin."

"We're both wearing too many clothes," he said.

She looked down and laughed. "You're still wearing your boots. Kitty will have my head if you spread dirt on the counterpane."

"Kitty is going to be too busy untangling these sheets and remaking the bed to worry about a small detail like that." He kissed her throat.

"Oh my," she murmured. "That sounds quite scandalous."

"Only if we do it right." He reached her gauze fichu and let his tongue trail over the soft material until he reached the swells of her breasts. Then he pulled the gauze out and watched it flutter to the floor. He kissed her skin, training his tongue over the soft flesh, already pebbling from arousal and the cool air. "I suppose this is one of those gowns with dozens of intricate fastenings."

"Just push up my skirts," she said.

He frowned down at her. "I don't think so. Now that I have you, I want to do this properly."

"Warrick." Her voice was breathless. "I don't want to wait."

"I'll make it worth the wait. I want to see you." He rolled off her and held out a hand to help her stand. With a huff, she rose and offered him her back. Why did these gowns have such dainty hooks and eyes? His fingers felt monstrous and clumsy beside them.

"You know, the more I stand here and think about this, the more I think it a bad idea."

"Then stop thinking," he said between clenched teeth as his hands fumbled with the fastenings. He got the dress open then sighed at the stays. Why did women have to wear so many layers?

"Perhaps we should keep a professional relationship."

"Our relationship was never professional. I wanted you the first time I saw you."

She turned to look at him. "You hid it well. I made quite the effort to seduce you."

"Turn back around." When she complied and he was unlacing her stays again, he said, "No, you didn't. You were seducing a man. Not me. You didn't know me at all."

"I feel I hardly know you now."

There! He pushed the gown down to her ankles and

tugged the stays off. She stood in only her chemise and petticoat. Those were easy garments of which to divest her. "Do you want to know me? Know my secrets?"

She looked as though she wasn't certain. "Yes," she whispered.

"Here's one secret." He undid her petticoat and let it fall to the floor. "I think you are the most beautiful woman I have ever seen."

She sighed. "Fitzhugh…"

He cupped her chin. "Call me Warrick." He kissed her softly. "And it's true." He kissed her soft cheek then moved to her neck, tracing a gentle path to her shoulder. There, he slipped the sleeve of her chemise off and let it fall down her arm.

"Tell me something about you. Something no one else knows," she said.

He paused and glanced up at her face. There were so many things no one knew about him. Things he didn't want anyone to know. Things he was not proud of.

"You know my real name. You know all about me." She began to undress him now, loosening his cravat and tugging his coat off his shoulders. "I think it's only fair."

"You're right, of course, but most of my secrets aren't the kind of thing one speaks of before going to bed. They'll give you nightmares or turn your stomach."

She nodded, unbuttoning his shirt and then pulling it over his head. "What about this scar here?" She touched a white gash that began in the center of his chest and continued to his flank, along his rib cage. It had long ago healed, but when she touched it, it felt hot once again.

"War wound," he said. "Bayonet."

"Bayonet?" She stood back and looked at him. His gaze traveled to the neck of her chemise. One sleeve was down to her elbow, and the curve of her creamy breasts was exposed. He wanted to slip the silk down farther and cup her. "Shouldn't you be dead?"

"It was a glancing blow, fortunately for me. I was on horseback and jogged at just the right time."

"Were you fighting? I thought you were a spy."

"Spies don't always sneak around behind the action. Sometimes we have to cross battle lines. I happened to be crossing at a particularly bad time."

"But you made it across."

"I did. Honestly, I didn't even feel the wound until I was off my mount. War is like that. The excitement numbs the pain."

"And what happened to the man who bayoneted you?"

He looked down, the image flashing across his mind as though it had happened mere moments ago.

"Warrick!" Suddenly, Fallon was beside him, and he realized he was on his knees on the floor. She knelt and cupped his face in her hands. "What is it? You were fine and then all of a sudden you sank to the floor." She rose hastily and poured water from the pitcher on the bedside table. "All the color has gone out of your face. Shall I call for your man?"

"No." He grabbed her arm and held tightly. "Just give me a moment." He sipped the water and took deep breaths. Gradually, his hands regained some feeling, and he noted the softness of her skin under his fingertips. He would concentrate on that, he thought. He would think of her silky skin and her low, husky voice, and he wouldn't be back on the battlefield. Fallon would keep him grounded.

"As I said, I chose to cross battle lines at an inopportune moment."

"Are there any good moments?"

He smiled at her and sipped the cool water. "Yes, when the two sides are sleeping. And, in fact, it was early morning, and I thought several hours until fighting would begin again. But I happened to cross at a spot close to where a small skirmish was taking place. As I was moving through a field, a flood of redcoats came running over the hills."

"Our men?" she asked.

He shook his head. "The papers never report on the cowardice of our men, only the bravery. Honestly, I can hardly call it cowardice. It was more like survival. In any case, the French came running after them, and I was stuck in the middle. One of their boys, and I say *boy* because I don't think he could have even been sixteen, came after me. I was on horseback. He was not. He wounded me, and in the heat of the moment, I drew my sword and went after him."

"The heat of the moment?" Fallon knelt beside him again. She tucked her legs under her, looking perfectly content to sit on the rug. His hands itched to take her hair down, to see how far down her back it would fall. "Surely you were trying to stay alive."

"I was on horseback, and he'd failed to mortally wound me. I could have kept going, but I turned my mount and went back for him."

"It was war, Warrick," she said quietly, looking him directly in the eyes.

"It was revenge, and he was a boy. I killed him." He put his head in his hands. "God, I can still hear the sound the blade made as it sliced through him—a sickening wet sound. His blood splattered everywhere. It ran down my sword, covering my hands. Do you know how many times I've read *Macbeth*?" He looked up at her now, found her eyes soft with compassion. She should be disgusted by him.

"How many and why? Shakespeare." She shuddered.

He almost smiled. No pretending to be better than she was for Fallon. "Dozens, and it's because I can relate to Lady Macbeth. I don't think I'll ever wash that soldier's blood off my hands. And the look on his face. It gives me nightmares."

"Is that what you were dreaming about the other night?"

"No. That was something else." He sipped the water again and struggled to keep his hold on Fallon's arm.

"You don't see yourself as a hero, do you?" she asked after he was breathing normally again.

"I did what any other soldier would do for the most part. I did worse than some."

"And you did much better. Look at Daisy's brother. You saved him. She's grateful. I'm sure you did even more than that for the country. If not, no one would want you dead."

"That's one way to look at it."

She took his hand. "It's not easy to forget killing a man. I know. I've done it—or at least I tried. But you have to stop thinking of yourself as the man who killed the French boy. You're so much more than that, Warrick."

"I killed others."

"And you saved others, I warrant. You're still saving others. You're trying to save the rest of the Diamonds in the Rough, and look how far you'll go to do so. You've all but kidnapped me."

He laughed. He wanted to believe her. He wanted to stop seeing himself as a murderer, as a monster. He wanted to be... not a hero. He wanted to simply be a man.

He set the glass on the table. "And now I'm going to complete my diabolical scheme and ravish you."

"Not if I ravish you first," she said and unfastened the fall on his trousers.

He was hard instantly, and when her mouth closed over his, he had to stop himself from taking her right there. She kissed him with a passion he hadn't expected. She kissed him to make him forget, he realized. And he knew, instinctively, in Fallon's arms, he would forget.

"Take your hair down," he murmured, running his hands up and down her body, learning her dips and curves.

She sat back, reached up, and began to pull the pins out. He imagined she'd remove one and shake it free, but obviously the style in which she wore it was more complicated than that. It fell down in sections, the long brown strands uncurling like apple peels as they tumbled to the floor. And then she swept it over her shoulder, and he could see the ends almost did brush the floor.

"Obviously you're not in favor of the current style of cropping one's hair," he said. His fingers itched to touch those silky tresses, to wind it around his hand, and bend her head back.

"Lady Sinclair said men like long hair. It's erotic."

"I can't argue with her there. What else does Lady Sinclair say?"

"What *doesn't* Lady Sinclair say? She has opinions on everything. I do seem to recall her once telling Juliette or Lily that seducing a man is a slow art. One does not hurry."

"One might hurry a little," he said. "Patience is not every man's virtue."

"Oh, but it is yours, else you would never have succeeded in espionage." As she spoke, she took the hem of her chemise, which had bunched at her knees, and worked it up her thighs, slowly revealing more and more of that honey-kissed skin. Her thighs were sleek and smooth, her hips flared and were the perfect shape for a man's hands. Her waist was small, perhaps it looked even smaller with the stark white bindings above it. And then there were her breasts. He had thought of those breasts countless times since he had last seen them fully bared. He was not disappointed. "Should I remove these bindings?" she asked.

His throat was so dry, he had to swallow before he could speak. "Leave them. I'll be gentle, but I don't want you hurt again."

"Oh, no." She leaned nearer to him, brushing her lips against his mouth and the tips of her breasts against his chest. "Don't be gentle." She pushed him back, kissing him as he fell on the soft carpet. Perhaps Kitty the maid would not have reason to be annoyed after all. It did not appear as though they would make it to the bed.

He allowed her to take control, allowed her to touch him and kiss him as she pleased. She was surprisingly tentative in her touches initially. He soon learned she was testing and teasing, learning what he liked and what drove him to madness. He refused to beg, but when she reached for his trousers, he all but thanked her. She withdrew them slowly, her fingers making lazy trails on flesh kissed by cool air. "There," she murmured in that low, husky voice he found arousing as hell. "Now I finally get to see you."

He didn't know why he had the sudden urge to cover himself. He wasn't overly modest or bashful. He had a body like any other man's; perhaps he had more scars than some. He had the sudden urge to cover some of the worst patches of white, knitted flesh, but she stayed his hands and gazed into his eyes. "Every one of these has a story, doesn't it?"

"I suppose."

"Are they all tragedies?"

He considered. "Not all, but more than I'd like to admit. Someday you'll know all the stories. I'd like to tell you. But not today."

She gave him a puzzled look, and he knew what she was thinking. There was no *someday* for them. They had this day, this moment. But he wasn't going to be content with that. He was keeping her. Of course, he had to stay alive first, but he'd managed it so far and against far more dangerous adversaries than Joseph Bayley. "Let me touch you," he said, sitting.

"Oh, no. I'm not quite finished with you yet."

Warrick didn't know how much more he could take. He had already exercised great restraint in not taking her hard and fast after several of her more inventive perusals of his body. And now she dipped her head, and he knew his task was about to become even more difficult.

"No, Fallon—"

She closed her mouth around him, and he all but bucked from the sheer heat of her. And when she began to tease him with her tongue, to suck him gently and then harder with that mouth, he had to grip the carpet to keep from calling out. The servants were undoubtedly aware of what was going on, but there was no need to make it patently obvious. And still, he could not help but allow a moan to escape.

"You like this?" she asked.

"*Like* is not a strong enough word for how I feel at the moment," he said between clenched teeth. "But I fear I won't be able to hold on much longer."

"Then let go," she said, taking him fully into her mouth.

As much as the idea appealed, he wanted to be inside her. He wanted to watch the pleasure sweep over her face as he found his own release. With regret—more than he could ever express—he nudged her up. "I want you, Fallon." He kissed her gently and began to lower her to the floor, but she resisted.

"You don't always give all the orders," she said, pushing him back on his elbows. "You should know by now I'm not very good at following them." She straddled him, then leaned over and pushed him to the floor. Her hair swept over his chest, teasing him, making him dig his hands into the carpet to hold on to the last vestiges of his self-control. He wanted to grab her, lower her onto his throbbing erection, but he couldn't touch her ribs for fear of hurting her.

And he knew the more he tried to dictate to her, the more she would resist. And he really couldn't take much more of this exquisite torment. Finally, finally, she guided him to her hot inner core. He could feel the heat of her, feel how wet she was for him. He forced his hips to remain still and not to buck into her as his body dictated. Slowly, with what seemed almost calculated cruelty, she took him inside her. She held him like that, clenched hot and hard within her, for a long moment, and then she moved. She rocked back and forth, testing, teasing, tempting. He wanted to cry out, plead with her to end the torment and ride him hard, but he gritted his teeth and fought for control.

And then she sighed. It was a small thing, but her head fell back, and with the sigh came the loss of her control. Her hips bucked, and she began to move quickly, taking him hard and fast. She fell forward, clenching his chest with her hands and meeting his gaze. Her eyes were hazy and cloudy, the brown of her irises seemingly endless.

Now was his moment. Warrick took her hips in his hands and took control, moving deeper, slower, longer. She sputtered a protest that ended on a moan, and then he felt the first waves of her climax.

Her eyes fluttered open to stare at him in wonder as she clenched around him. In that moment, she transcended beauty. She called out his name, again and again, and he felt her let go.

He wanted, more than anything, to come inside her. He knew the pleasure would be all he imagined and more. But he couldn't do that to her, couldn't put her at risk for a child.

Not yet. Not when so much was still uncertain.

As she collapsed with a small cry, he pulled away from her and spent his seed on the floor. When he opened his eyes again, she lay drowsily on the carpet, and her satisfied smile was enough to make him want her all over again.

Thirteen

FALLON NEVER WANTED TO RISE AGAIN. HER ENTIRE
body felt soft and boneless, warm and heavy. She was
vaguely aware of Warrick beside her. How could
she not be aware of all that hard, bronzed flesh? The
man was obviously used to working hard. Even the
memory of those muscles bunching and straining all
but made her throat go dry.

"I don't suppose Kitty will be all that happy with
us after all." He indicated the carpet and gave her a
sheepish smile. She smiled back because he looked so
much like a naughty schoolboy, she couldn't resist.

"You didn't have to do that," she said quietly. "But
thank you." She'd never met a man like Warrick.
He was so considerate. He treated her like she was
someone special. And the pleasure he gave her... She
didn't know what he did, how he managed it, but
somehow this time was even better than the last.

And she knew this was just the beginning. She
knew he could make her feel more.

But for that she would have to surrender to him,
she would have to believe him when he told her he

loved her. And she was not that big of a fool. No pleasure was worth the pain she would feel when this—whatever it was—ended.

And it *would* be over. He was going to marry Lady Edith—or one of her kind. He was one of *them*—the nobility. She was, and had always been, one of *us*—a street rat. Who was she to aspire to become the wife of the son of an earl? It would never happen. His mother would make certain it never happened.

And why had her mind jumped to marriage anyway? *She* wasn't in love with him. She'd long ago outgrown childish notions of true love. It might be true for others, like Lady Sinclair or even Juliette, but it would never be true for Fallon. She was too soiled, too undeserving. All her life, she'd done nothing but steal, lie, and cheat. And even if she didn't steal or cheat anymore, she was still lying. She was living a lie.

The Marchioness of Mystery. There was no mystery about her. She was a London gutter rat.

"I'd like to lie about with you like this all day," he said, reaching over to caress her thigh. For some ridiculous reason, his touch made heat shoot through her again. What was *wrong* with her? She was so sated she could barely move. "But I have other business."

Fallon rose on one elbow, grimaced at the pain that caused in her ribs, and struggled to a sitting position. "What business?"

He grinned and touched her cheek. "Afraid I'm leaving you out? Don't worry, this is mundane business. I have a meeting with my solicitor. It has nothing whatsoever to do with the Diamonds in the Rough."

He rose and began to dress. She watched him,

enjoying the view of his body. Even with all his scars, he was beautiful. It had been some time since she'd seen a man unclothed.

"Should I pose?" he asked, with a look over his shoulder.

She blinked. "I'm sorry. I didn't realize you were so modest."

"I'm not usually, but I don't have beautiful women ogling me very often. Especially not women who are not self-conscious themselves."

Fallon glanced down at her nakedness. She really wasn't self-conscious. Her body wasn't perfect, but what woman's was? Still, she spotted her shift among the discarded clothing and donned it. "I thought it wasn't safe to go out."

"It's not," he said, struggling with his boots. "You should stay here. I'll be back in time to fetch you for the rendezvous at The Merry Widow. In fact, I want to arrive early to be certain everything is in place."

She narrowed her eyes. "Is this your plan to get rid of me so you can go on your own?"

He took her chin between thumb and forefinger. "No. I will return for you." His eyes swept down her body. "Somehow this chemise makes you look more erotic than when you wore nothing at all." He bent and kissed her gently, and Fallon had a momentary flash of what her future might have been. She saw Warrick, her husband, kissing her tenderly before going about his work for the day. She saw herself with a house full of children. She saw mornings of slow, leisurely lovemaking, and nights spent asleep in his arms.

And none of it would ever come to pass because she was not good enough for the son of an earl. Even if she wasn't really a courtesan, she was still no one. She couldn't even claim her father was a respectable shopkeeper.

Warrick broke the kiss and touched his forehead to hers. "I'll see you soon."

She watched him go, pressing her hand to her belly as he walked out the door. Her heart felt as though it had plummeted a few inches. She couldn't let him do this to her. She couldn't let him give her false hope. She had to remember who she was and all the lessons she'd learned. She would not fall in love. Not with Warrick Fitzhugh, not with anyone.

An hour later, Fallon had just dozed off when a knock sounded on the door. "Kitty," she moaned pulling the pillow over her head. "Go away."

"I would, miss, but there's someone here to see you."

Fallon growled. "Who is it? The Countess of Charm again?"

"No, miss. This time it's the Countess of Sinclair."

Fallon's eyes flew open. "Devil take it!"

"Miss? What did you say?"

Fallon jumped to her feet and whirled around looking for a robe. But she had not ordered the valise with her things from the town house unpacked yet. And, of course, she couldn't get dressed on her own. "Put her in the drawing room, Kitty," she said, "and make sure she has tea and cakes. Then come help me dress."

"That won't be necessary," a voice Fallon knew well answered.

"My lady, you shouldn't be up here." Kitty sounded horrified.

"Bosh. You said the master was not at home, so unless that was code, Fallon should be alone. I'm coming in, my dear."

"Of course you are," Fallon muttered, sitting back on the bed.

The countess entered, looking every bit as regal as always. The silver handle of her ebony walking stick gleamed, as did the jewels at her neck. She wore an afternoon dress of blue trimmed with lavender that brought out her eyes, and her hat was elaborately plumed with at least a dozen feathers. She raised the netting covering her face and arranged it on the brim of the hat. "Oh my."

She closed the door on whatever Kitty's last words might have been and shook her head. Fallon rolled her eyes.

"Yes, you look quite debauched, my dear. I might even say *thoroughly* debauched."

"I was taking a nap."

"In that case, you are the most restless sleeper I have ever met, and I suspect you were having a rather wonderful dream. Your cheeks are glowing."

"How did you find me, or am I to assume you are omniscient?"

"Alas, I am not." She sat on the bed beside Fallon. "I saw Lily's man at your town house when I went to call on you."

"Of course. The *Morning Chronicle*." Fallon was happy to hear Lily's man was at her house. At least another change of clothes would be en route.

"Everyone is talking about it," the countess said.

"Don't they have anything better to talk about?"

Lady Sinclair raised her brows. "No, no they don't, and besides, I thought you liked when your name was mentioned in the press. I almost thought you staged the whole incident to make the top of the Cytherian Intelligence column."

"How do you know I didn't?"

"Oh, I know better than that." She stroked Fallon's hair in a gesture that made Fallon think of mothers and daughters. She had no memory of her mother ever stroking her hair, which was too bad. It was nice. "Fitzhugh isn't the kind of man to go along with a scheme of that sort."

"Oh, so it's because of Fitzhugh, not because I would never do something like that!"

"Darling," the countess said, squeezing her about the shoulders. "One never knows what you will do. You have no fear. Now, tell me what is going on. How long have you and Fitzhugh been lovers?"

"We're not lovers."

The countess looked pointedly at the rumpled bedclothes and Fallon's scattered clothing. "Really?"

"We may have been intimate, but that doesn't make us lovers."

"True enough, and I would believe you if you were more free with your favors. As it is, you bestow them quite stingily. But Fitzhugh, yes, I can see why he would turn your head."

"He hasn't turned my head." Fallon rose and paced. "He's just a man, like any other man." That was true. She had to believe it was true.

"Oh, no he's not." The countess shook her head, causing the plumage on her hat to wave gently about. "He's intense and dangerous and not at all handsome. I know how much you detest men who are prettier than you."

Fallon laughed. "You are impossible."

"But I'm not incorrect, and Fallon, while I will be the first to admit that what happens in your bedroom is your business, I will caution you against Fitzhugh."

Fallon bristled. "Why is that?"

"Watch your tone, young lady. I am not implying you are not good enough for the man, though I am certain you have already convinced yourself of that."

Fallon sighed and crossed her arms over her chest. Sometimes Lady Sinclair made her want to pull her hair out.

"It is only that I know he is the sort of man you could fall in love with, and I do not think that a good idea."

"I'm not in love with him!" Fallon sputtered.

Lady Sinclair studied her face and then said, "Hmmm. This is a lovely room, though, is it not?"

Fallon sighed. "Don't change the subject. Tell me. Why is it not a good idea for me to fall in love with him—not that I am going to."

"Because I know his mother, and she is a woman who gets what she wants."

"That sounds familiar," Fallon muttered.

"And she wants Lady Edith for her youngest son. Fitzhugh will have nothing to say about it."

Fallon thought about protesting that Fitzhugh seemed quite able to make his own decisions, but then she decided against it. After all, *she* was a woman who made her own decisions, but she could no longer count the number of times Lady Sinclair somehow convinced Fallon to do something other than what she wanted.

Lady Sinclair rose. "That is my advice. Do not, whatever you do, fall in love with Warrick Fitzhugh."

"Is that all you came to say?"

"No, but the more I think about the matter, the more I believe that should be sufficient."

Fallon shook her head. She was certain the countess had some ulterior motive, but she was too tired to try and untangle it. Lady Sinclair rose. "I bid you good day. I won't ask why you are not at home, but I will, of course, keep your secret."

"It's not much of a secret."

The countess prodded Fallon's leg with her walking stick. "What Lily and I know is not necessarily common knowledge. Now, whatever you are about, be careful."

"I will." Fallon rose and, surprising even herself, gave Lady Sinclair a hug. The woman who had always seemed like a mother to her embraced her back. She smelled like lavender and something else... something indefinable but that reminded Fallon of home. Wherever that was.

"Oh, my dear girl," Lady Sinclair said, patting Fallon's back. "How I do wish I could bundle all three of you up and tuck you safely away."

Fallon closed her eyes. "I think that sounds lovely."

"Ha!" Lady Sinclair shook with laughter. "You would hate me for it inside of a day. And I cannot blame you." She pulled back. "Who wants to be safe when they are young and invincible?" She put a warm hand on Fallon's cheek. "You do know I love you?"

Fallon lowered her eyes, feeling vaguely uncomfortable. She loved the countess too, but she wasn't used to such declarations. And now she'd had two in one day. At least she could believe the countess. "I know," she said.

"Good. Call on me soon." And the countess walked to the bedroom door. She had a hand on the handle and the door open before Fallon could summon the words she wanted.

"I love you too." Her voice was choked, but she'd said it. The countess, who had her back to Fallon, stiffened. And when she turned, Fallon could have sworn she had a tear in her eye. But that was ridiculous. The countess never cried.

"I know you do. But it's nice to hear it."

When Lady Sinclair was gone, Fallon sank back on the bed and closed her eyes. She hadn't realized how much saying that simple phrase to the countess would mean to the woman. Lily and Juliette said it all the time, but Fallon always assumed the countess knew how she felt—how grateful she was for all the Sinclairs had done for her and how much affection she had for both of them. But she supposed saying the words had its own meaning as well.

She must have drifted off because when she awoke, Kitty was moving about the room, tidying it. "I'm sorry to wake you, miss, but Mr. Fitzhugh is home and he says you're to be ready to depart in an hour."

Fallon covered her eyes as Kitty lit a lamp. "What time is it?"

"About nine o'clock, miss. Are you hungry? I brought up some bread and cheese."

"I'm famished, Kitty." Fallon reached eagerly for the tray and had to stop herself from stuffing bread and cheese into her mouth like some sort of starved street urchin. Sometimes it was the small habits that were the hardest to break. Instead, she sipped the tea and ate dainty bites of the food she, and her stomach, would have preferred to wolf down.

"A trunk with some of your things arrived this afternoon, miss." Kitty lifted Fallon's stays and petticoat off the floor. "Would you like to dress in one of the gowns it contains?"

Fallon nodded, remembering to swallow before she spoke. "Yes, preferably something dark."

"I shall look in the trunk, miss."

While Kitty and another maid moved the trunk into the room, Fallon finished her meal and went to observe Lily's choices. Two day dresses, a riding dress, a burgundy evening gown, and three very flimsy, very lacy nightrails. When Kitty lifted those, the poor girl blushed all the way to her toes. Fallon wanted to say they were not hers. They were Lily's addition and attempt at being *helpful*, but Fallon thought it might be better to simply ignore the garments. Instead, she studied the assortment of stays, shifts, and petticoats. Exactly how long did Lily think she would be here? She'd packed enough for a week.

"That one," Fallon said, pointing to the burgundy gown with jet beading. I'll wear that tonight." She lifted her ruby necklace from a box Lily had packed. "And this."

"Yes, miss."

Fallon was ready in an hour, but just barely. She wasn't entirely pleased with the way Kitty had styled her hair. It was swept up and coiled high on her head. She wasn't certain if she looked regal or like a lamp post. But Kitty was looking nervously at the clock, and so Fallon shrugged her shoulders, grabbed her wrap, and started downstairs. It wasn't as though she cared what her father thought of her. She hadn't seen him in years, and to say they parted on bad terms was an extreme understatement.

So why was she nervous? Why were her hands shaking? Why could she not seem to take a deep breath? She reached the ground floor of the town house and thought to check her hair once more in the gilded mirror hanging in the vestibule. Oh, it really was too high! She couldn't go like this.

"Bloody hell."

Fallon spun around and spotted Warrick lounging against the banister. She hadn't seen him a moment before. He was studying her and shaking his head. "I know," she said. "My hair isn't right. I'll fetch Kitty—"

"Don't move."

She raised a brow as he moved forward, coming closer. "There's no time for any alteration, and I wouldn't want one anyway. Good God."

Fallon sighed. "It's not *that* bad."

"No, it's not bad at all. In fact, I'm going to have a devil of a time keeping my hands off you and even more of a challenge keeping other men's hands off you. You're bloody radiant."

Fallon blinked. "Thank you. I think."

He bent over her gloved hand, kissing it lightly. "I wish we were going anywhere but where we must tonight. I'd like nothing more than to see that gown in the glitter of ballroom chandeliers."

"I thought you didn't dance."

"Tonight I could make an exception."

❦

Warrick had not intended to return home so late. He didn't like leaving Fallon, even though he knew she was completely protected in his home. Still, he felt the urge to hurry through his business with the solicitor and return to her.

Admittedly, his intentions might not have been purely protective.

And so when he stepped out of his solicitor's office and onto the street, he almost knocked over the woman waiting to enter. "Pardon me," he said perfunctorily. "I'm terribly sorry."

"Warrick? Is that you?"

He paused and studied the woman more closely. "Louisa?" He took her arms and smiled at her. "What are you doing here?"

"Apparently we have the same solicitor." She embraced him. "I've missed you." She pulled back, touched his cheek. "You look tired."

"You look lovely, as usual. You always were the best-looking of the Fitzhugh clan."

She gave him a sad smile. "And you were always the best liar. I know I don't look well."

She didn't. She looked thin and pale. He'd heard rumors her husband had recently acquired a new mistress. His neglect of his wife was obviously taking its toll. "Do you want me to speak to Hartford? I can be persuasive."

"Good Lord, no!" She shook her head emphatically. "I am pathetic enough without asking my little brother to confront my husband."

"I'm not so little anymore."

"No, you're not." She adjusted her hat. "I know Mother paid you a visit."

He rolled his eyes. "Do not tell me you are going to lecture me as well."

"At one time I would have. Now, I say happiness is fleeting. If you've found it, embrace it."

Warrick raised his brows. His oldest sister had always been something of a moral stickler.

"I see I've shocked you." A strand of her light brown hair blew across her cheek. "But you see, I like her."

"Her?" He moved aside to allow a clerk to pass. "Fallon?"

"Yes, your courtesan. Did you not know she rejected Hartford? He offered her carte blanche, and she said no. She didn't want him."

Warrick was not surprised.

A woman with a yapping terrier passed them, and Warrick nodded politely. Louisa waited until she was out of earshot to continue. "And so my point, dear brother, is that you should not allow Mother to arrange your life. Not all of her efforts are successful."

"Point taken." He moved to open the solicitor's door for her, but she put her hand on his arm.

"I know you have your pride, but so does Papa. If you go to him—"

Warrick stiffened. "I have tried to speak to him."

"I know. He didn't mean what he said. He was stricken with grief and not himself. He loves you. He doesn't blame you for Edward."

Warrick shook his head. He wished that were true.

"We all loved Edward," Louisa was saying, "but he is dead, and you are alive. We miss you."

"And I miss you." That much was true, at least.

"I should go in." But she did not release his arm. "Will I see you at the ball?"

"Louisa." He shook his head.

"Come, Warrick. Papa wants to see you. He loves you." The bell on the solicitor's door tinkled faintly as she disappeared inside. Warrick stood on the street, watching a steady stream of horses and carriages pass by.

You killed him. His father's voice rang in his ears. *You murdered my son.*

Warrick loved Louisa, and as much as it pained him to admit it, she was wrong about their father. His love for Warrick had died with Edward.

Several hours later, Fallon served as the perfect distraction from the meeting with his sister. Warrick followed Fallon to the carriage, trying very hard not to stare at the creamy skin of her back. Where in God's name had she unearthed that gown? It was the most seductive thing he had ever seen. Somehow she managed to wear it without looking the least bit tawdry. It dipped low in the back, showing an appalling amount of flesh, and hugged her curves when she moved. The dark red color made her skin look warm and creamy. He wanted to kiss her, run his hands over that skin to feel for himself.

But this would not do. He had more important matters to think of at the moment. Matters of life and death. It would be better if he put Fallon out of his mind. He would find somewhere to hide her until he had Bayley where he wanted him.

Tonight Warrick intended to find out who had ordered his termination.

The Merry Widow was all but empty when they arrived. It was still early, and Warrick knew it would not stay so for long. This time, when he and Fallon entered, the clerk showed them directly back to Daisy's chambers. She was sitting at her desk, spectacles on her nose, looking at a ledger. She looked up when they entered. "Finally! I received your note and didn't know what to make of it." She stood and crossed the room to stand opposite Warrick. "I don't know who Joseph Bayley is, but I'm not going to leave my own establishment." She looked at Fallon. "I shouldn't have to leave, should I?" And then as though really seeing Fallon, she reached out and touched the glittering beads on her gown. "Marchioness, do you think you could stand in the common room for just a few moments? Or, better yet, stand outside—"

"Daisy, she's not here to bring you more business. I'm afraid tonight I have to ask you to repay a favor."

"You know I am more than happy to do anything you ask, Warrick, but why do I have to leave?"

Fallon put her hand on Daisy's arm. "Warrick just wants to protect you, Daisy. The men who are coming here tonight are dangerous."

"As though I don't know how to deal with dangerous men." She puffed her chest out.

"Daisy, I have no doubt of your capabilities, but I'd feel better if you were safely away. If you were here, I'd spend the entire time worrying about you and not thinking about what I should."

Daisy blinked. "Oh, well, if you put it that way I suppose I could find somewhere else to go for a few hours."

"Thank you, Daisy." He leaned forward and kissed her cheek. "Now I owe you a favor."

"Rubbish." She waved her hand. "I still owe you at least a dozen."

"Daisy," Fallon said, "what is it Warrick did for you that you are so indebted to him?"

Warrick opened his mouth to change the subject, but then he reconsidered. Perhaps he should allow Daisy to sing his praises. It might make Fallon see him in a different light.

"I know he saved your brother," Fallon added.

"That he did," Daisy said. "But then, when he brought my Robbie home, he also helped him find a place. It's not many who want to hire a man with a deformity, even if it was from the war. Now Robbie works as a groom for Lord Darlington, and it's perfect because Robbie has always loved horses."

"Lord Darlington?" Fallon glanced at Warrick. "I see."

Warrick shrugged. "Darlington needed a groom."

"But that's not all he did," Daisy said. "When Robbie was gone in the war, I didn't have any means of income. I'd been a dressmaker, but the shop I worked at had to close when the lady what ran it fell ill. I ended up on the streets."

"Oh." Fallon put her hand on Daisy's arm.

"Don't pity me, my lady. It was good money, and I didn't mind the work. I like a handsome gentleman, I do." She winked at Warrick, and he shook his head and laughed. "But some of the other girls couldn't stand on their own, and there are some bad men…what you'd call…" She put a finger to her lips.

"Unscrupulous?" Warrick suggested.

"Yes! That's it. They were unscrupulous, and the girls didn't have anywhere else to go. So Warrick helped me open this place. Now there's a safe place for girls to ply their trade." She grinned. "I make a bit of money myself."

Fallon looked about the room, and Warrick wondered if she saw what he saw—the trappings of a woman who had come from nothing and made her way in the world. That was, if anyone could see past the mounds of roses.

"And I can buy as many roses as I please!"

"That must be lovely. Was Warrick a client of yours?"

Daisy looked horrified. "Oh, no! I mean, I wouldn't mind giving him a tumble, but he's always been all business." She narrowed her eyes at Fallon. "But I expect that might not be the case with you."

"Daisy—" Warrick interrupted. "Is there anything you need to take with you? Can I help you collect your things?

"Oh, all right. I'm going. I wasn't asking for details." She took her reticule and her hat and started for the door. "But just out of curiosity, my lady, what do you charge? You know, from a purely business perspective?"

"Daisy!" Warrick put his arm about her waist and hustled her toward the door. "We can discuss it later."

When she was gone, he turned back to the room and surveyed the rose-infested chamber. He knew Daisy had a peephole into the public room, and that would be perfect for Fallon to use to observe her father. But she also needed somewhere to hide if something went wrong or Bayley demanded a more private place to talk. "This armoire might be the thing," he said, crossing the room and opening the door. It was full of—what else?—roses, but he liberated them, making space for Fallon.

She watched him quietly, and he wasn't certain he liked the thoughtful expression on her face. "What are you thinking about?" It was a dangerous question to ask a woman. He should know as he had two sisters and two sisters by marriage.

She shook her head. "Nothing, really."

He didn't believe that, but he was smart enough to let it go. Finally, a woman who didn't need to share her every thought and feeling.

"I'm not offended by Daisy's remarks, if that's what you think."

Or perhaps she did want to share.

"She means well," he said, checking the time on his pocket watch. He still had several hours in which to survey the layout of the brothel and make last-minute adjustments to his plan.

"I know, and I do play the role of a courtesan. It's not as if I'm a lady."

Warrick set down a vase of flowers and took Fallon by the shoulders. "You're more of a lady than most of the so-called ladies of the *ton*. You're kind, intelligent, fearless."

She shook her head. "Oh, I'm not fearless. Kind and intelligent and—don't forget—fascinating, I will give you, but not fearless."

"And what are you afraid of?"

"My father," she said softly. "I don't know how I'll feel seeing him after all of these years. I thought he was dead. I thought I was alone in the world." She shrugged. "But now I don't know what to think."

"There's nothing to think, Fallon. You don't owe him anything, and you're better off without him."

"I know."

"And?"

She glanced up at him, those dark eyes full of unshed tears. He knew she'd never let him see her weep, and somehow that made the knife in his gut dig even deeper. "He's my *father*," she whispered. "No matter what he's done or who he is, he will always be my father."

Warrick let out a slow sigh. He felt the same way about his father. The man was an ass who'd disowned him because he hadn't followed Society's dictates for what the third son of an earl should do with his life, but that didn't mean he didn't love his father and miss him.

That didn't mean he wasn't thinking about what he could do to mend their relationship. Even if Lady Edith was out of the question, there must be something. There must be some way his father could forgive him for Edward.

"And this is not what we should be thinking about right now," Fallon said. "You have plans to make, I'm sure. And after tonight, you'll have your answers and we won't have to hide in your town house or creep about in dusty tunnels."

He wanted to believe this meant there was some future for them, but he knew Fallon too well. What she meant was that after tonight their relationship was over.

"And so I won't see you again." Warrick made it a statement.

"Why would you? We live in different worlds. You have your mother and Lady Edith." She waved a hand and moved away from him. "And I have... I have to find some way to repair the damage you did to my reputation at Alvanley's ball."

"Is that all you care about?" he asked, his voice harsher than he wanted, but he was angry now.

"My reputation is my life. I keep my standing only by being highly sought after. If anyone can have me, I might as well be out on the streets like Daisy was."

"And you've never wanted anything else?"

She blinked at him. "As in marriage or children? Those things aren't for me."

"Goddamn it, Fallon. It doesn't even matter, does it?" He was stalking toward her now, backing her up against a wall.

"What doesn't matter?"

"That I love you."

"You say that now." She put a hand out to stop him from coming nearer. "But what does it really mean? You want me for your mistress? How do you think Lady Edith would feel about that?"

"I don't care. I'm not going to marry Lady Edith." He grabbed her hand and yanked her to him.

"Your mother seems to think otherwise."

"In case you haven't noticed, I'm not a child. I'm a man. I make my own decisions, and I'm going to marry you."

She stared at him. "No, you're not."

He pushed her back against the wall. "The hell I'm not. You're mine, Fallon, and I'm going to have you, one way or another."

She sputtered a protest, but he took her mouth with his, cutting her words off. He didn't really care what she had to say at the moment. What did he have to do to prove he was in love with her? To prove he didn't care what his mother thought? To prove nothing but the two of them mattered?

Her mouth moved against his and her arms went around his neck. Someday he would have her forever, but that day was not today. Presently, he would have to content himself with this moment. Right now, it would have to be enough.

Fourteen

FALLON EXPECTED HIM TO BE ROUGH. SHE LIKED rough. She wanted rough. But Warrick wasn't going to give her what she wanted. She was learning he was contrary in that way.

His mouth met hers in the slowest, most mesmerizing kiss she had ever experienced. Like a glass of spirits, the kiss fired a hot trail of tingling heat from her lips to her belly. His mouth moved slowly over hers, taking, then pulling away. She had to reach for him, capture his mouth with hers, until the teasing left her so frustrated, she wrapped her hands in his hair and held him firm against her.

Finally, he obliged her by kissing her deeply and passionately. She couldn't think when he kissed her this way. Couldn't remember her own name, much less what she wanted. She only knew she wanted more, more of this and more of him.

"Warrick," she murmured against his mouth and heard him growl softly in the back of his throat. He liked it when she used his name. "Warrick," she said again.

His hands, which had been planted on the wall just

above her shoulders, reached for her. Through the silk of her gown, she felt the warmth of his touch on her waist. He gripped her hard, his fingers splayed and moving slowly upward.

Yes. This was what she wanted. Her breasts were heavy and aching with need, her nipples hard and erect, waiting for his touch. But his hands seemed to inch at a maddeningly slow pace, while his tongue teased and twined with hers.

"Touch me," she demanded.

His hands stopped their trek, and she could feel his light, careful touch against the bandages on her cracked rib. How could he remember to be so careful at a time like this? She didn't care. She wanted him, and if she suffered for it later, then that was a small price to pay.

His fingers gradually splayed, his thumbs reaching up to stroke the underside of her breasts. She shivered as pleasure zinged through her. She arched her back and sighed. "More."

His fingers brushed her nipples through the fabric of her dress once then twice, and she shivered in anticipation. But he continued to tease her with light caresses until her head was spinning with need. "Please," she all but cried when his fingers circled her hard nubs oh-so-lightly. "Please."

And then she felt his hands on her skin, the rough calluses of his thumbs on the bodice of her gown as he yanked it down and freed her breasts. She broke their kiss and allowed her head to loll back as he touched her with his hands and his mouth. This was what she wanted. This was what she'd been longing for.

And when he took one of her nipples in his mouth, twirling his tongue around it then giving it a hard suck, she cried out in pain and pleasure. She was panting now, her whole body alive with sensation and need, a gnawing need that begged to be satisfied.

"Take me," she ordered, moving her hand between them. He was hard for her, and she opened the fall of his trousers so that he sprung warm and solid into her hand. She stroked him and was rewarded with a low growl. "Hike my skirts up and take me."

"Not yet." His breath feathered against her cool skin, heating it and making her shiver. He suckled her again, and she bucked against him. She had never wanted a man so much. She had never needed one.

And she had never known pleasure like this.

One of his knees parted her legs and pushed against her, making her cry out. She was all but ready to explode from his slightest touch, and she pressed against him in frustration. "Now," she all but sobbed. "Now. Please."

"Say the words, Fallon. Tell me what I want to hear."

She had to struggle to understand him, much less think what he could possibly want from her. And then she knew, and she stiffened. Yes, she wanted him, was ready to say anything to have him inside her, but she wasn't in the habit of playing games. If she told him she was his, she would have to mean it. He wanted to marry her. The very thought was ridiculous. Absurd.

And wildly romantic.

A small firework of hope burst inside her. Perhaps he really did love her. Perhaps he really did want to marry her. It seemed impossible, and she would do nothing to fan the flame of that hope, but she couldn't quite bear to extinguish it either.

She wanted to hold on to that dream, treasure it, for just a little while. And perhaps if she kept the dream small, when Warrick extinguished it, the pain wouldn't be so great.

"Warrick ——"

"Say it, Fallon. Mean it."

"I'm yours," she whispered. "I'm yours."

His mouth covered hers, and he pulled her hard against him. "Always."

"Always," she echoed.

He held her tightly, kissing her until she was dizzy and drugged from the pleasure. And then his fingers were on the flesh of her thigh, tracing a slow, burning path upward. When he finally reached the juncture of her thighs, she gripped his shoulders so hard, she feared she would hurt him. His arms slid around her, cupped her bottom, and lifted her. She felt his hard erection against her and welcomed it. When he thrust inside her, she cried out at the blinding pleasure. She had never known she could feel this way. Nothing before it could compare.

He moved inside her, slowly, increasing his speed until she was pistoning with him, reaching for that elusive climax that seemed impossibly sweet. And when she found it, she cried his name and clutched him tightly, afraid if she let go, she would dissolve into a puddle of burgundy silk on the floor. She felt him swell and thrust, and then he too cried out. Lowering his forehead so that it rested on her shoulder, he fought to catch his breath. She knew the feeling. For some reason, she had the urge to comfort him, and she patted him on the back and kissed his cheek.

He lifted his head and looked at her. "What just happened?"

"You tell me. I'm not nearly the expert I pretend to be."

He smiled at her, a lopsided, satisfied smile.

"Then it's not like that for you all the time?" she asked.

He shook his head. "It's never been like this with anyone else. And you?"

"I can't even remember anyone else before you."

"Good." He lowered her gently to the floor, and she allowed her legs to fold beneath her so she sank to the ground. She rested her head against the wall and closed her eyes.

"Are you well?" he asked, squatting beside her.

"Fine. I just need a moment to…" Breathe? Recuperate? Stop falling in love? "Rest."

"I'll help you to the couch. You'll be more comfortable."

She shook her head. "I'm fine here." Waving him away, she said, "Go and do what you must. I know you want to be ready."

He kissed her nose. "I'll check on you in a moment."

When he was gone, she adjusted her gown and tried to repair the damage to her hair. The upsweep had actually fared well. She pulled her knees to her chest and rested her chin on them. Closing her eyes, she allowed her thoughts to drift back to Warrick's mouth on her mouth, his hands on her body, his gaze on her face when he'd told her she was his.

You're mine, Fallon.

Men had tried to possess her before. Men had tried to own her and control her, and she'd easily turned them away. But Warrick didn't want to own her. He wanted to love her. He wanted to marry her. She shook her head. How could a seasoned soldier be such a romantic? They could never marry. He deserved someone like this Lady Edith, who would make him proud and please his parents. Fallon was better off alone. It was safer that way.

Fallon laughed bitterly. Perhaps Warrick wasn't as romantic as she thought. Perhaps he was just brave, while she was afraid of losing her heart.

It had happened once before, and she still winced from the pain the memory brought her. Frankie had been one of her father's boys. That's what her father had called them—*his boys*. He'd never so much as called her *daughter*, but then he didn't have much use for her, even though she was as good a pickpocket as any of her father's gang.

Mostly Bayley's Boys, that's how they referred to themselves, ignored her or kicked her when she walked by. That was how her father and brother treated her, and they were used to following Arthur and Joseph's lead, lest they get a smack or a punch. But Frankie was different. Frankie never kicked her, never spoke harshly to her, and often smiled at her when the others weren't looking. Fallon had had precious little kindness in her life, and she would anticipate a smile from Frankie for days. When she received one, she felt as though she could run as fast as one of those fancy horses everyone bet on. Her heart and soul simply soared.

And then one night she stumbled across Frankie in an alley near home. She was coming back from Bond Street, where she'd been picking pockets, and she was hurrying because she knew her father would be waiting to see her take. Frankie had stepped out and called, "Maggie."

She'd jumped at least a foot then put her hand to her heart when she saw who it was. "You're like to scare me half to death," she'd said.

"I'm sorry." He stepped out of the shadows, and there was that smile. It melted her inside, and she forgot where she'd been going, forgot she'd been in any hurry whatsoever.

They'd talked for a few minutes. Fallon couldn't remember what they'd discussed now. It had probably been something about her father's latest scheme or the trouble one of the gang had gotten himself into, but Fallon remembered the feeling she'd had when she walked away.

She felt happy. It wasn't something she was used to, and she could hardly wipe the smile off her face when she finally reached home.

Her father had done that for her, smacking her around for being late and chiding her for her small take, though she suspected it was more than any of the other boys had delivered. She'd gone to bed without dinner, but she hadn't cared. The gnawing in her belly was replaced by the fullness of happiness. She'd dreamed of Frankie's smile.

She dreamed of Frankie. He had always been the most handsome of all her father's boys. He had wavy brown hair that fell over his forehead in a curl, big brown eyes, and dimples in each cheek. He was tall and strong and always dressed well. When Bayley's Boys walked the streets, the girls' heads turned to watch Frankie go by.

After that first meeting, Fallon and Frankie met every few days, furtive meetings and quick exchanges because both of them feared the consequences should her father ever see them together. But they hadn't been afraid enough, at least she hadn't. The first time Frankie kissed her had been the best day of her life. She'd just turned fifteen, and she couldn't imagine anything more wonderful than the feel of Frankie's lips on hers.

Except his promises. He promised they'd run away together. He promised he'd marry her. And one evening, after a series of long, breathless kisses, he'd told her he'd always love her.

She'd lost her heart to him that day, and her virginity not long after.

And then everything changed. Frankie no longer sought her out. He ignored her when they did see one another, and his smiles all but disappeared. She'd tried to talk to him when she saw him out on the street, but he'd told her to go home. And then one evening she saw him disappear down an alley with a two-bit whore, and she knew she'd been used.

She knew she'd meant nothing more to him than that whore.

Fallon had spent the better part of each night for a week sobbing silently into her dirty pillow. And then her father had taken her to meet Lucifer, and she knew she was doomed. She was going to be sold as a virgin, and she was no longer a virgin. It hadn't seemed to matter so much before, when Frankie had been promising to run away with her, but by the time she met Lucifer, Fallon knew she would never get away.

And she knew her father would kill her.

But Warrick wasn't Frankie. He wasn't a seventeen-year-old boy with one thing on his mind. Warrick wasn't a handsome boy taking advantage of an inexperienced girl. Fallon was no girl, nor was she inexperienced. No one had ever made her feel like Warrick did. Many men had told her they loved her, of course, but she'd never been tempted to believe it. She'd always only played the part of the courtesan, never lived it. She preferred the role because it allowed her to keep a measure of independence most women didn't have.

Could she give up that independence to marry Warrick?

Fallon clenched her hands, rose, and stalked the room. Why was she even thinking such ridiculous thoughts? Why was she even allowing such notions into her head? This was how one got hurt. She couldn't allow herself to love Warrick, and she couldn't believe they had any future.

And she would make sure that, after tonight, they never saw one another alone again.

※

Warrick forced himself to put thoughts of Fallon aside and concentrate on his work. Usually he was very good at this sort of single-mindedness. It had probably kept him alive on more than one occasion. But today little flashes of Fallon kept intruding. When he was moving the furniture in the public room to ensure his exits weren't blocked, he thought of the way her lips parted when she moaned. When he was hiding his pistol and knife where he could reach them if need be, he thought of the heaviness of her breast in his hand and the hard nub of her nipple against his tongue. And when he was warning Daisy's girls to stay upstairs and out of the way, he thought of the curve of Fallon's thigh when he lifted her skirt and the slick, tight feel of her when he'd entered.

Finally, all was ready, and with a half hour left before the rendezvous, he went to speak to Fallon. He found her pacing Daisy's chamber, her expression not one he'd seen before. "What's wrong?" he asked from the doorway.

She looked up, just taking notice of him, and pasted on a smile. If he hadn't known her as well as he did now, he would have believed it. She was that good at pretending. But he did know her now, and he knew that was not her real smile.

He went to her and took her hands. "Why are you nervous?"

"I'm not—"

"Fallon, don't pretend with me. I can see it on your face." He opened his hands to show her her clenched hands. "And in your body."

She swallowed. "I haven't seen my father for years. Thinking of him now has brought up so many bad memories."

"He'll never know you're here." Warrick led her to a small panel in the wall. He pushed it in and slid it aside, revealing a peephole that afforded a view of the common room.

"Clever," Fallon said, peering into it.

"I imagine Daisy likes to know who or what is waiting for her on the other side of this door. You can see your father and still be safe if you stay here."

"You don't need me?"

He took her hands. "I need you to be safe."

She smiled. "And that's why you've dragged me halfway around London and pushed me out of moving carriages."

"I admit," he said, "I originally had other ideas, but my feelings toward you have changed. If I had my way, you wouldn't even be here tonight."

"And what were your ideas for this meeting?"

"Fallon…" He turned away. He didn't like to think of how he'd originally planned to use Fallon.

She grabbed his elbow. "Tell me."

He searched her dark eyes and sighed. He wasn't going to be able to refuse her anything. "I planned to use you only as a last resort, only if things weren't going well."

"That's a comfort." She frowned. "I think."

"I could threaten your father with a source, you, who could testify to all his crimes and lock him up for good. And then when I brought you out, I knew he'd be so shocked, it would give me the advantage I needed."

"And what's your plan now?"

"To keep you as far from that bastard as possible." He kissed her cheek. "It's late. I have to go." He started for the door, but she came after him.

"Warrick, if you need me, I'm here."

He grinned. "I won't need you. Stay here. Don't reveal your presence, no matter what happens." He squeezed her hand and opened the door to the public room. He only hoped Fallon was good at taking orders and kept her head about her.

He wasn't at all certain his plan was going to work.

He seated himself on one of the sagging couches and was just peering at his pocket watch when he heard the clip clop of horses and the squeak of carriage wheels.

Midnight.

Bayley was right on time.

Warrick gave one last glance at the couch cushion where he'd hidden his pistol and rose. The first man to enter was Gabriel. He had a large cane, and his foot was bandaged. He hobbled into the public room. "You," Gabriel said with a sneer. "You're going to pay for what you did. You're going to pay dearly."

Warrick took a breath. Gabriel's appearance was an unexpected and unpleasant development. Warrick had thought he would only be dealing with Bayley and his men.

"Let me talk to him first," another man said, moving into the doorway. Warrick had never met him, but from the descriptions he'd heard, he knew it was Joseph Bayley. Bayley was short and wiry. He had small eyes and a thin mouth. His busy mustache and beard were attempts to hide the scars on his face, but they weren't entirely successful.

Knife scars, Warrick thought. *From Fallon.*

Bayley was dressed in black and used a black walking stick. It didn't appear ornamental, but Warrick would keep his eye on it anyway. Walking sticks were good hiding places for knives.

As Bayley stepped into the light, Warrick struggled to see any trace of Fallon in this man who was her father. Except for the petite stature and the dark hair and eyes, she didn't resemble him.

Several men moved in behind Bayley. They were young and inexperienced. Warrick didn't dismiss them. Sometimes the young, inexperienced thugs were the ones who were just rash enough to do something stupid.

And deadly.

"So," Bayley said, "you've finally come out of hiding."

"I wasn't in hiding," Warrick answered. "But neither was I making myself an open target."

"And now you are?" Bayley asked. "That makes my task easy." His small eyes roamed the room, looking for Warrick's men, looking for traps.

"And what is your task, precisely?"

"To kill you."

"Why?"

"How the hell do I know why?" Bayley asked. "I don't care. I kill you and I get paid. Blunt. That's all I care about."

"Who's paying?"

"That's not your concern."

"I beg to differ, considering I'm the one he wants dead."

"You'll be dead in a moment, and it won't matter." Bayley signaled to one of his men.

"Why don't we sit down and discuss this like civilized men?" Warrick said, moving toward the couch where his pistol was hidden. He'd counted on Bayley talking before he had to begin defensive maneuvers.

"I don't have time to waste talking to you."

Bayley's man moved forward, and Warrick abandoned the pistol and angled his foot toward the thin, all-but-invisible string attached to the leg of a chair. He was just about to trigger the trap when Gabriel lurched forward. "Wait a moment. I thought I was going to be the one to kill him."

Bayley's man paused and glanced at his leader. Bayley frowned. "Get out of the way, or I'll have you shot as well."

Gabriel pulled a pistol from his coat. "Not if I shoot you first." But instead of pointing the pistol at Bayley or his man, Gabriel turned it on Warrick. Warrick had a second in which to gauge the direction of the ball, and he dove for cover as the ball screeched past him. He landed near a side table, fumbled for the knife he'd hidden there, and rose with the knife in hand.

"Fool! You missed!" Bayley said. "Get out of the way."

One of Bayley's men pushed Gabriel aside, and the one with the pistol stepped forward. Warrick stuck his foot out and tripped the wire. Scalding water crashed down on the men's heads from a pot suspended above.

Bayley jumped aside just in time, but the other men were hit and began screaming. Warrick lunged for Bayley, but the man moved with surprising agility for a man with a cane. He was on his feet again, and the cane came down on top of Warrick's head.

Devil take it, he thought as his head exploded in pain. This was not going well. He rolled to the side to protect his head and got a blow in the ribs. Warrick kicked out and got another blow. He'd dropped his knife and curled into a ball on top of it. Bayley would think he was wounded, and when he bent closer, Warrick would stab him through. For good measure, Warrick groaned. It was not difficult to sound like a man in pain. His ribs were definitely bruised, and he was going to have a knot on his head.

But he wasn't dead. Yet.

Bayley moved closer, and Warrick tensed to spring, just when Daisy's door opened.

"No, wait! Don't touch him!" Fallon cried.

Warrick closed his eyes. Now he was as good as dead.

Fifteen

FALLON STARED AT HER FATHER. IT WAS REALLY HIM. She couldn't believe he was standing before her in the flesh. It was like seeing a ghost, but he was flesh and blood.

He blinked at her, narrowed his eyes, and said, "So it's true. I didn't believe Gabriel when he said you were alive."

She swallowed, tried to find her voice, and couldn't.

He stepped closer, and she caught his scent. He still smelled of boiled potatoes and stale gin. She shivered, the memories rushing back at her like a windstorm.

"I looked for you," he said. "When I could move again. I was going to kill you. Slowly. I thought someone else had gotten to you first. I hoped."

Warrick was rising, and she had the urge to move closer to him. Funny how a moment before she had thought to protect him, and now she was the one feeling the need for protection.

Her father looked from Warrick to her, and she saw the flicker in his eyes. She knew that flicker. He had an idea. "You've done well for yourself." He looked her up and down. "I knew you were going to grow up to be a beauty, Maggie."

"It's Fallon now," she said, her voice raspy.

Her father grinned. "You always did think you were too good for the rest of us. Gabriel says you're a well-paid courtesan now. I suppose you weren't so different from us after all. You became a whore just like your mother."

Fallon shook her head. "You don't know anything about me." She saw Warrick was standing and stepped toward him. "We're leaving now, and if you know what's good for you, you'll forget you ever saw us."

Everything happened so quickly, she didn't have a moment to think or react. One moment she was backing toward Warrick, and the next moment her father had his arm around her neck and something cold and hard was pressed to her temple. Fallon could tell by the look on Warrick's face that the situation was less than ideal. He'd moved toward the couch, and somehow he had a pistol in his hand as well.

"Let her go, Bayley," Warrick said, aiming the pistol at her father—and consequently also at her.

"What's she to you, Fitzhugh?" her father asked. "Are you her protector?"

"Let her go, or I'll shoot you."

"Oh, I don't think you will," her father sneered. He backed up, pulling her along with him. "But I *will* shoot *her*. I owe her a slow, painful death, but I'll take my chances when I can."

"What do you want?" Warrick asked.

"No!" Fallon said. "Don't bargain with him. He'll never keep his word."

"Shut up," her father said, digging the pistol into her temple. "You want her back?"

"Let her go now, and we'll talk," Warrick said.

"I don't think you're in a position to bargain, Fitzhugh."

Fallon closed her eyes. She'd made everything worse. Somehow, in her attempts to save Warrick, she'd doomed him.

"Here's what I want, Fitzhugh. Meet me tomorrow at half past midnight at the Serpentine Bridge in Hyde Park. Come alone and unarmed, and bring the names of the other Diamonds in the Rough with you."

"Why?"

Fallon had already deduced why, and she supposed Warrick had as well. But he was trying to stall for time, and for that she loved him. Unfortunately, it was too late. Her father was in the doorway, and he was going to pull her into the street and then into a waiting carriage.

She was never going to see Warrick again. She was never going to see anyone or anything again.

"Be there, or I kill her." He yanked her out the door, but Fallon latched onto the doorway and levered herself back inside.

"Don't go, Warrick. He'll kill me anyway. Don't—"

Her father yanked her backward, and she stumbled to her knees. Her survival instincts resurfaced, and she rolled away then jumped to her feet. If she hadn't been wearing the heavy gown, she might have gotten away. But she snagged her toe on the hem and went down again. It was just enough time for one of her father's men to grab her and pull her back. She screamed, and her father backhanded her hard enough to cut off the sound. Fallon tasted the familiar tang of blood.

"Get her in the coach," he said. The man threw her in the vehicle, and she landed on the floor. She immediately grabbed the door handle opposite, but it was locked. And then her father kicked her arm away. His next blow landed on the side of her head, and she closed her eyes and sank into darkness.

She prayed she never woke up.

❧

Warrick stood in the doorway of The Merry Widow and watched the carriage drive away.

She was gone. Fallon was really gone, and he had no illusions she would survive the night, much less until his rendezvous with Bayley. A wave of dizziness swept over him, and he gripped the back of a chair. For a moment, the room swam and he was back on the battlefield. He could smell the tang of fresh-spilled blood and hear the wheeze of a man drawing his last breaths. But the wheeze was nothing compared to the wails of the dying men. Cries of "Help me, please" and "Mother! Mother!" rent his ears.

He couldn't help them. He couldn't help any of them. But he couldn't leave. He had to search. He had to try.

A shot rang out, and he jumped, whirled, and reached for his pistol. He had it in his hands and spun around, looking for the gunman.

"Warrick."

He aimed and cocked the hammer.

"Warrick, no!"

He blinked, tried to still his shaking hands, and focused on the man in front of him.

No, it wasn't a man, not a French soldier, but a woman.

Daisy.

"There you are. That's all right now. Come back to us." She turned to the clerk coming in behind her. "Get him a glass of wine. Hurry."

"Daisy." His hands were still shaking, and he couldn't seem to lower the pistol.

"Put it down now, luv." Slowly, she put her hand on his wrist and lowered the weapon. "I tripped over a chair, and the sound took you unawares. That's all."

The clerk returned and handed Daisy the wine. Warrick took it and sipped. Daisy watched him, and after he'd drunk about half the glass, she said, "What happened? Where's the marchioness?"

Warrick closed his eyes. "Gone. Bayley got her."

"Who is this Bayley?"

Warrick shook his head. How did he describe Bayley?

"What does he want with her?" Daisy asked.

"To leverage her against me. But he'll kill her before he lets me have her back."

"Then you just have to get her back before he hurts her." She put her hand on his shoulder. "You can do it, Warrick. I know you can."

Warrick put his head in his hands. He wanted, desperately, to be the man Daisy thought he was, the man Fallon needed. But he wasn't a hero. He'd saved Daisy's brother, and that was the extent of his good deeds. He hadn't been able to save the others.

He hadn't been able to save even one man drowning in his own blood on the field that day. Instead, he'd climbed over their ravished bodies, adding one last insult to their final moments.

He'd lived another day, and the faces and voices of those men lived with him.

"I don't even know where to begin, Daisy. I could find him. I know I could, but there's not time for that."

"Well, maybe he can help you." She pointed to a heap in the corner, and Warrick rose. In Bayley's haste to get away, he'd left Lucifer's man behind, and Warrick had hit him over the head with his pistol. He hadn't thought anymore about Gabriel, but now Warrick narrowed his eyes. Daisy might just be right.

Warrick felt a renewed sense of purpose, of hope. He shook off the ghosts clinging to his boots and marched to Gabriel's crumpled form. He nudged the man with his toe, and Gabriel groaned. "Leave me alone, bastard."

"Get up, or I'll shoot your other foot."

Gabriel opened his eyes. "What do you want from me?"

"Get up, and you'll find out."

If Warrick was going to save Fallon, he had to get to her before tomorrow night.

And Gabriel was going to help, whether he wanted to or not.

❧

When Fallon woke, she was cold and aching. The floor beneath her was hard and damp, and when she opened her eyes, she saw nothing but blackness. Her hands were bound behind her, and her arms had long ago lost all feeling, but she managed to struggle to her knees. Besides the pain in her head from the kicks she'd sustained and the numbness in her arms, she was otherwise unharmed.

But she knew that wouldn't last.

She twisted her hands behind her, testing the strength of the bindings. They were tight, but if she worked at them, she might free herself. The floor above her creaked, and she paused and held her breath. Footsteps sounded and then moved away, and she began to twist her wrists again. Pins and needles of pain sliced through her arms as the nerves woke, but she ignored the sharp pricks and continued to pull at the bindings.

She felt them give enough that she chanced a smile. If she could just get free, she knew she could find her way out. Escape was her only hope, her only chance.

The rope burned into her skin as she twisted her hands and attempted to pull them free. Sweat or blood dripped onto her fingers, but she ignored it. She knew the moisture would make her task easier. She flexed one of her wrists, and despite the excruciating pain, tried easing it through the bindings. "Not yet," she muttered and worked her hands again.

She heard the footsteps again, but this time she didn't pause. She was close, and every second counted now. But the footsteps didn't fade this time. They grew louder and then she heard the rattle of a key.

No.

A slice of light appeared above her, and she squinted and averted her face. The light grew brighter and the footsteps louder as her father descended the steps, carrying a lantern. "I thought you might be awake."

Fallon scuttled backward, looking for some protection. She felt vulnerable and exposed with her hands immobilized. The light illuminated her surroundings, and she saw she was in a dark cellar. Broken chairs and tables had been piled high in one cramped corner, and in another was what looked to be the remains of a pianoforte. All around were dead mice and rat droppings. She swallowed and gauged her escape options.

If there were any windows, they'd been boarded up and concealed. She didn't spot any doors, either. The only escape route looked to be the entrance her father had just used.

She took a deep breath and fought the overwhelming sense of doom threatening to crush her. She couldn't give up now. She had to stay strong.

Her father paused on the last step and hung the lantern on a nail hammered into one of the wooden beams. "So, my darling daughter, it seems we have much to discuss."

"I was never your darling, and there's nothing to discuss. You can go back to whatever hole you crawled out of."

Her father didn't give her the satisfaction of a response. She hadn't expected him to. He had always been a master at concealing his emotions. She had been an eager student and learned to do the same. But now she wished he would show irritation or amusement or something! He moved toward one of the chairs and righted it. The back was torn apart, but it had four legs and appeared steady enough. Her father sat on the chair, crossed his legs, and blinked at her.

"I have nothing to say to you."

"You will."

She shook her head. "You should be dead."

"If you'd had your way, I would be. As it is, I'm very much alive. But soon, my little Maggie, *you* won't be."

❧

Warrick shoved Gabriel back against the wall of Daisy's chamber. "You'd better tell me something before I become angry."

Gabriel's nose was bleeding, and the blood had run down his chin and splattered on his white shirt. "I don't know where he hides. He keeps it a secret."

"You can find out."

Gabriel winced as Warrick shoved an arm under his chin and pressed on his throat. "No." He wheezed. "He'll kill me."

"I'll kill you."

Gabriel sucked in a breath and shook his head. "You won't."

Warrick stood still for a moment, then swore. Gabriel was right. He wasn't going to kill the man. He'd seen too much death and destruction in his life to ever be the cause of more. He wasn't afraid to kill, but it was a last resort. Besides, killing Gabriel wouldn't get Fallon back. She'd been in Bayley's hands for two hours now, and with each passing moment, she was in more and more danger.

Warrick hung his head. "You're right," he said,

sounding dejected. Then he brought his right fist up with lightning speed and sliced Gabriel across the face with a powerful uppercut. The man's head snapped back and hit the wall with a resounding thud. "But that doesn't mean I won't make your life painful." Warrick eased his arm back, and Gabriel sank to the floor.

"Bastard," he muttered.

Warrick bent and put his face close to Gabriel's. "Start talking."

Gabriel narrowed his eyes. "I hope he kills her. I hope he passes her around to all his men and then kills her slowly and painfully."

Rage welled up in Warrick. Somehow Gabriel had seen right into his deepest fears. He knew what the man was doing. Warrick had done the same thing himself on many occasions—make the tormentor angry so that he forgets his true purpose. It bought Gabriel more time.

But even though Warrick knew Gabriel's tactic, it didn't stop the panic bursting inside him. He could hear the clock ticking, and he felt powerless to help Fallon. He was running out of time. He shook Gabriel, knowing that would get him nowhere, but unable to stop himself. "Tell me where she is, you piece of filth. Talk!"

Behind him, Daisy's door opened with a loud creak.

"Go away, Daisy. You don't want to be part of this," Warrick said, never taking his eyes from Gabriel's pain-filled gaze.

"It's not Daisy," a quiet, feminine voice said. "But you're close."

❧

Fallon stared at her father and willed him to stand, move around, do anything but stare at her with that piercing gaze. He had the same small eyes, eyes like a rat, but eyes that had the range of a hawk. He never missed anything. She couldn't work her bindings while he was looking at her, no matter how small her movements. He'd just secure them again, and she'd lose all the ground she'd won.

"You almost did it, you know," he said, tapping a hand on one knee. Fallon noted his fingernails were clean and his hands much whiter than they used to be. Once his hands had been covered with grime and lacerations. Despite the filth, he'd always managed to have dainty hands, small fingers that tripped lightly and stealthily into a pocket. Now his hands looked like those of a gentleman. She could only imagine how her own appeared at the moment. She'd never be able to show them for the rest of her life.

Not that her life was looking to be very long at the moment.

"You almost killed me." He was staring at her, his face contorted into a look of hate and malice. "If not for your friend, what was his name? Oh, yes, Frankie."

Fallon felt her insides tense, but she worked to keep her expression neutral.

"Frankie came in just as I was taking my last breath. He saved me, that boy. I always knew he was going to be useful one day. That was the only reason I didn't kill him when he started tossing your skirts."

Now Fallon couldn't stop the jerk of surprise. Her father smiled, knowing he'd won.

"That's right. I knew about you two. I knew all

along. Do you think anything happened on my streets I didn't know about?"

"But…" Fallon closed her eyes. She didn't want to go back. She didn't want to remember that time, the girl she'd been, but the longer she was in her father's presence, the more she became Maggie again. She could all but feel her silk gown turning scratchy and cheap against her skin. She could feel the dirt under her fingernails; she could smell the stench of rotting rubbish.

"If I knew, why didn't I kill you?" her father said, finishing her thoughts. "Because I wanted to make some money off you first. You were a whore, just like your mother, only you were easier on the eyes than she ever was. I could have made a fortune off you."

Fallon curled her lip. "You make me sick. I was your daughter."

"And I knew you well." Bayley rose. "After all, what did you become if not a well-paid whore?"

Fallon closed her eyes, willed Maggie back into the past where she belonged. "You don't know anything about me, and you never will."

"And I don't care. I'm only keeping you alive long enough to get Fitzhugh." He stepped toward her, and Fallon couldn't help but shrink back.

"Who's paying you for him? I hope it's a great deal for the risk you're taking. You'll be the one dead before all of this is done."

"Not likely, but I'd kill ten Fitzhughs for the price I'll be paid." He lunged for her, and before she could jerk away, he snatched the ruby necklace at her throat. He held it up to study it in the dim light. "Pretty but nothing." Dropping the necklace to the floor, he ground it under his boot. "These are nothing compared to what I'll receive." He held up a fist and shoved it under her nose. "Rubies as big as my fist. Three of them."

She must have made some doubtful expression, because he pushed his knuckles into her lip.

"Don't believe me? I've seen them. I've touched them. Those rubies are going to buy me a new life far from here."

"Too bad Fitzhugh will kill you before you ever see those rubies again."

He kicked her back, and without her hands to catch her, she fell hard on her shoulder. His boot slammed into her middle again, and she let out a gasp of air. She could feel the rough dirt from the floor biting into her cheek, and she concentrated on that rather than the pain tearing through her.

She knew there would be more pain. So much more before this was over. Fallon closed her eyes against the next blow, but it didn't come. She slit her eyelids and blinked at the boots approaching her. They gleamed and shone even in this dim light. She closed her eyes, opened them again, and followed the boots to a knee clad in tight, buckskin breeches. As her gaze traveled higher, over the brushed wool coat and the fine linen shirt and cravat, she stared into a face she knew well.

Frankie smiled, showing his dimples. "Hello, Maggie."

❧

Warrick watched Lily, dressed in a dark blue ball gown and sparkling sapphires, step into Daisy's rose-strewn chamber. She made the roses look cheap. She made everything pale beside her delicate porcelain skin.

"What the devil are you doing here?"

She smiled. "Nice to see you, too."

"I didn't send for you."

"And you weren't going to." She glanced over her shoulder, and Warrick saw Daisy standing in the doorway, her mouth ajar.

"Daisy, might you give us a moment?" Warrick asked.

"But she's... she's—"

"Yes, I know. The Countess of Charm."

Daisy's eyes were wide. "First a marchioness, now a countess."

Warrick wanted to tell her they weren't real titles, but he supposed to an abbess like Daisy, a notorious courtesan's sobriquet carried as much weight as a real title of nobility.

"I promise we shall have a few moments to chat when I've spoken with Fitzhugh," Lily said, going to the door where Daisy stared at her. "We shall sit and sip tea, I think."

Daisy nodded. "Tea. I'll fetch some. Only the best for you, my lady."

"Thank you." And she closed the door on Daisy's eager face.

"They don't call you charming for nothing," Warrick remarked.

"I'm glad to hear you say so. Now, might I inquire what you have done with my friend Fallon?"

Warrick scowled. "I don't need your help with this, and if the Secretary knew you were here, he'd have both our heads."

"Well then we'd better not tell him." She peered around Warrick to catch a glimpse of Gabriel. "I won't tattle if you won't."

He sighed. "Lily…"

"I'm assuming this man might have some knowledge of Fallon's whereabouts. From what Daisy said, she's been taken by her father." Lily shook his head. "I knew when I spoke to her this afternoon she was in danger."

"I will get her back."

"Yes, you will." Lily moved past him, bent, and studied Gabriel. She placed a gloved hand under his chin, heedless of the blood that would ruin the expensive kidskin. "Now, good sir," she said, "start talking, because I promise you that though Fitzhugh here won't kill you, I have no such qualms."

Warrick blinked and a glint of steel winked from her gloved fingers. She pushed the knifepoint into Gabriel's flesh until he gasped in pain and surprise.

"I only know rumors," Gabriel hissed, obviously attempting to move his chin as little as possible.

"Oh, good. I do adore hearing the latest gossip."

Warrick rolled his eyes, but he didn't interfere. He watched and listened as Lily charmed Gabriel into revealing all.

Sixteen

FALLON STARED AT THE MAN BEFORE HER IN COMPLETE bewilderment. She knew that face so well. And she hated it, too. She would have been happy to imagine Frankie with a knife in his back, rotting on the bottom of the Thames.

He put his hands on his hips and grinned at her. "Well now. You grew up, didn't you?"

She wanted to say something pithy and sarcastic, like *Well, that's usually the way of things*, but instead she blinked at him owlishly. How could he look so much like the boy she remembered? She felt fifteen again—awkward and unsure.

He crouched in front of her. "I hear you're a fancy man's whore now. Got a title and a new name. Is that true?"

She blinked at him. He was still undeniably handsome. His eyes were a deep, dark brown with gold flecks. His hair was thick and lustrous. His teeth were perfect. And when he had smiled, it had always made her stomach flip.

In her experience, his smiles melted every woman he came across.

But then her gaze narrowed on a patch of dark stubble on his cheek. He must have missed it when shaving. So he wasn't perfect after all. He had flaws.

She straightened. And for all his manly beauty, she'd been wooed and pursued by men just as handsome. Men with titles and intelligence and wealth. What was Frankie but a criminal? He was still working for her father and living in this hole, while she had a town house in Mayfair and more ruby necklaces than she could count.

Well, that wasn't true. She had counted them, and she had three. But they were hers. She hadn't stolen them. She had made something of her life, even if that something was mostly a lie and not very respectable.

If nothing else, she had escaped Joseph Bayley.

"Why are you here?" she asked, using her best *ton* ballroom intonation. "Don't you have unsuspecting girls to seduce?"

Frankie's brows shot up. He'd expected her to cow before him as she always had. But not this time. She was going to be dead shortly, and she wasn't going to go without settling old scores.

"You weren't hard to seduce. You all but begged me to toss your skirts up."

She shrugged. "I cared about you. Obviously, I was a fool, but at least what I felt was real."

He snorted. "And is that what you tell all those dukes and lords when they're climbing in and out of your bed?"

She smiled. "Let me tell you about my bed, Frankie, seeing as you'll never be in it. It's covered in silk sheets, draped with a canopy encrusted in rare jewels, and I have a bottle of French wine on the bedside table." This was a bit of an exaggeration, but she did have the silk sheets.

Frankie stood. "I was the first to have you." He shrugged his coat off. "And I'll be the last. You'll die with the feel of my body still on your skin."

"You always were a romantic." She darted a glance at her father, but he only looked annoyed. He probably didn't like that he had to wait for Frankie to rape her before he could kill her. But Fallon was not going to be raped or killed without a fight. Not caring if they saw her struggles now, she twisted her wrists again, sending renewed pain into her numb arms and burning her already chafed skin. Was she clinging to false hope or did the bindings feel looser?

Frankie reached for her, and she kicked her feet out, catching him hard in the jaw. He swore and fell back, landing unceremoniously on his bottom. From across the room, her father cackled. "This is more entertaining than I expected."

Just wait, she thought, and pulled one hand free of the ropes. *Just wait.*

❧

"I have to admit," Warrick said as he and Lily raced along the dark, wet streets of Seven Dials, "Gabriel knew more than he let on."

"Men like that become powerful by knowing everything about everyone. It was only a matter of convincing him to tell us what he knew."

A steady drizzle was falling, and drops of rain rolled off Warrick's hat and onto his neck, chilling him. He was already deathly cold inside. If he and Lily were too late...

She took his hand. Even wet and pale with cold, she looked strong and vibrant. "We'll find her, Fitzhugh. Don't worry. Look, there's the bakery now." She pointed to a shop with a worn sign showing a piece of bread. The windows were dark and grimy, and the display in the front did not boast any of the shop's wares.

"That must be it," he said, pausing and ducking back into the door of a hat shop. If Bayley's men were watching, he didn't want to be spotted. "Any suggestions for how we handle this?" he asked Lily, who had ducked out of the rain beside him.

"You're asking me?" She raised a thin brow. "This is your area of expertise, not mine."

"You handled the interrogation well."

"All right. You should look for a back door and go in that way. Despite my boasts to Gabriel, I'm no good at hand-to-hand combat. I'd be more of a liability to you than anything else. But I can knock on the front of the shop and pretend to be lost. That might distract whoever Bayley has patrolling long enough for you to sneak in and find Fallon."

"Good idea. But as soon as Bayley's men tell you you've got the wrong shop, get out of there." He cut a glance at the door to the shop and imagined Lily standing in its shadows. This was why he had retired from the Foreign Office. He hated having to risk the lives of others. He hated the gut-wrenching fear encompassing him now, the fear something would go wrong and he'd be responsible for not one but two deaths tonight.

He was already responsible for so many deaths—maybe not directly, but hadn't his missives and documents led to the deaths of hundreds of men? True, they saved the lives of his own countrymen, helped the British win the war against Napoleon, but he couldn't forget the cries of those French soldiers. When a man was dying, nationality ceased to matter.

"Fitzhugh." Lily put a hand on his arm. "Are you ill?"

He clenched a fist and forced his thoughts away from that faraway battlefield and back to the one before him. Fallon needed him. If he could save her, perhaps it would atone for some of the wrongs he'd done.

"I'm fine." He took a breath and willed it to be so. "But remember what I said. I want you safely away as quickly as possible. We can meet back here or at The Merry Widow."

"Of course."

"Lily." He took her hand. "They're men and they're bored and they're going to try to detain you. You have to—"

She shook her head. "You worry about Fallon. I can handle Bayley's men."

He didn't doubt it. With a last check of his pistol and dagger, he started across the slick streets toward the dark alley behind the shop.

❧

"Oh, you're going to pay for that," Frankie said, rising to his feet. "You're going to be very sorry."

She notched her chin up and stealthily shook the bindings off her wrist. She was free now, but her arms were still prickling with numbness and pain. "Then make me sorry," she said. "I don't think you can."

"She's not afraid of you, boy," her father said. "Maybe I should have kept her and gotten rid of you."

Frankie whipped around. "She's the one who tried to kill you, old man. And I'm the one who's going to get you those rubies. Don't you forget it."

He'd turned his back to her, a fatal error she would have never made were she still a thief on the streets. Fallon wasn't going to allow the opportunity to pass her by. She jumped to her feet, wobbled unsteadily, and flew at Frankie with all she had. He wasn't expecting the attack, and her swift kick to his lower back had him falling to his knees. Her arms were still pulsing with pain, so she gave him another kick and wished she had worn her half boots instead of these useless slippers.

Her father was screaming something at her now and coming toward her, and she knew she had no choice but to use her arms. She glanced about for something to grab and spotted a broken piece of crate. A nail scraped her hand, and she turned the wood just as her father came within striking distance. She swung out awkwardly but effectively, the wood slicing him across the cheek and drawing blood.

Her arms burned and throbbed in protest, but she gritted her teeth and swung the piece of wood again—this time at Frankie. Frankie ducked, and she missed. Her aim was off because her arms were shaking. He lunged at her again and managed to knock her to the ground. The shard of wood went flying, and helplessly, she watched it land across the room with a clatter.

"I've got you now," Frankie said with a grin. He

was on her in a moment, his body like a sack of flour. She could barely breathe much less move. His hands were all over her, his hot breath in her face. She tried pushing him away, but her arms were useless.

Even if she'd had her full strength, she did not think she could have managed to push him off. She could still do some damage, though. She struck at him with her hands, tearing at his hair and then at his face. He stopped his assault long enough to grasp her wrists and hold her still.

Fallon closed her eyes as he pushed her hands to the floor. His legs clamped around her waist, and she knew she was trapped now. He was going to rape her and then kill her. There was no escape this time. She couldn't wriggle out of his grip like she had the bindings.

She felt his moist, sweaty hand on her breast and clenched her jaw. She tried, one last time, to free her hands by moving them from side to side, but he held them tightly with his unoccupied hand. Still, her movement had revealed something of interest. Cautiously, she flexed her fingers and felt the warm metal of something lying on the dirty ground beside her. A blade? A knife? A shard that had long since come free of whatever it belonged to? Whatever it was, she had it within her reach. She fumbled with her fingers and managed to close her hand on it. It pricked her, and she sucked in a breath.

Now, how to free her hands...

Fighting Frankie would only make him clutch her that much tighter. But if she gave in—no, he wouldn't believe that. If she were immobilized...

"Frankie," she said breathlessly, gasping for air. It

wasn't much of an act. She couldn't catch her breath with all of his weight on her abdomen. "I can't breathe. Please."

"You don't need to breathe. Very shortly, you won't be breathing at all." She heard fabric rip and felt his fingers on the bare skin of her chest.

"Frankie, I'm going to faint." She'd never fainted in her life. "I can't…" As hard as it was to make herself go limp, especially with him pawing her, she let all the tension and strength flow out of her arms and legs until she was completely at his mercy. He didn't seem to notice. She could tell by his movements, he was busy getting himself ready to enter her. Everything in her wanted to fight back, to scream, to struggle, to buck and claw and tear.

She fought the urge and made herself lifeless.

His hand thrust between her legs, and she felt bile rise in her throat. He wasn't going to release her. He was going to rape her, and she was going to sit here and allow it to happen.

Don't move. This is your last chance…

He kicked her legs open and raised her skirts.

Please, please, please.

And then she felt it. His hand loosened on her wrists, tightened again, and then when she didn't fight, loosened. She would have one chance. One.

She held her breath and swung her arms up in an arc.

✎

Warrick stepped inside the shop. The lock had been easy to pick, which told him Bayley and his men weren't worried about intruders. They felt safe.

He could hear voices toward the front of the shop, a high one that must be Lily's and a lower one that was one of Bayley's men. Warrick doubted Bayley only had one guard, so he'd have to watch for the second one. He slunk along the wall, keeping to the shadows, and caught a glimpse of Lily standing in the doorway. She was talking earnestly, and he could have kissed her. If she could just keep the guard occupied for ten more seconds, Warrick would be out of sight.

He reached a staircase, put his hand on the banister, and was halfway to the top when he heard a distant crash. It wasn't coming from upstairs. The sound of voices from the doorway below ceased, and Warrick knew the guard was listening.

It must be Fallon. Warrick's heart soared. If she was fighting, she was alive. But she wasn't upstairs. Where, then?

There must be a cellar. He flew back down the stairs and searched for a cellar door. He found it under the stairs and pulled it open. The screams grew louder, and heedless of the danger, he ran down the stairs with his pistol in his hand. The cellar was dark, and it took a moment for his eyes to adjust. When they did, he blinked, uncertain whether or not to believe what he was seeing. Fallon stood over the body of a man who lay face down on the floor, writhing in pain. She held something in her hand, and from the dark smears on her fingers, Warrick supposed whatever it was was covered in blood.

"Warrick." Her voice was full of relief, and he realized she must have feared he was another of Bayley's men coming for her. He took a quick inventory of her, noting her torn bodice and the disarray of her hair. If anyone had dared touch her, he would gut him and serve the man his own entrails. His gaze knifed to the man on the floor.

"Are you hurt?" he asked, his voice deadly calm.

"No—" Something in the shadows caught her attention, and she turned her head. Too late, Warrick saw who claimed her attention. Joseph Bayley lunged from the darkness and grabbed Fallon around the waist. His arm locked hers in place, immobilizing the hand holding the weapon.

"Fitzhugh," Bayley croaked. He had a streak of blood running down his cheek and a nasty gash above it. Warrick had no doubt who was responsible.

Fallon struggled against her father's hold then stilled. In the gloom, Warrick sensed the knife more than saw it.

"I knew she'd bring you to me one way or another."

A deadly calm settled over Warrick. "You have me now. You can let her go." He dropped his pistol and kicked it out of reach. In the back of his mind, he could hear the screams of those dying men on the battlefield, and he willed them away. They faded but would not cease.

"I don't think so," Bayley said. "She and I have matters to settle, but I will make you a bargain. I won't kill her until after I've killed you."

"Get out of h—!" Fallon hissed before her father jerked her and cut off her words. Warrick's gaze met hers, and he saw the anger and fire in her eyes. He saw the pain too. Bayley was hurting her. He glanced at her neck and saw the rivulet of blood making a slow, crimson path to her collarbone.

Her mouth moved. *I'm not worth it.*

Warrick shook his head. There, she was wrong. "This and more," he said quietly.

"What?" Bayley barked.

"Let her go." Warrick held out his hands. "I'm unarmed. You can have me, collect your prize, live out the rest of your life in"——he glanced about in disgust——"comfort."

"Do you think me that much a fool, boy? Pull the knife out of your boot. Do it slowly now, and toss it this way."

Warrick gritted his teeth and unsheathed the knife. With a flick of his wrist, he sent it flying into the gloom behind Bayley.

"Now, we're going to make a trade, nice and easy like," Bayley said. "You take her place."

"No!" Fallon cried before Bayley shook her, silencing her.

Warrick didn't like it, but it would give Fallon a chance at escape. That was, if she would run. Lily was probably still out there, hiding, watching the shop. She would catch Fallon, take her home, get her to safety. Fallon would be safe.

And he would be dead.

"All right," Warrick agreed. He looked at Fallon, eyes hard. "When I take your place, you run. Get out of this shop."

"No!"

"Do it, Fallon! Don't make me die for nothing."

"Oh, isn't that romantic," Bayley cooed. "I feel all warm inside."

"Stubble it, Bayley, and let's get this done." Warrick's gaze never left Fallon's eyes. He gave her a hard glare, and she glared right back. He wasn't certain if that meant she'd follow his orders or countermand them. In any case, he was out of time.

Bayley shifted Fallon so that the knife was still at her neck but she was off to one side. Warrick indicated the empty space before him with a flick of his eyes. "As soon as I have you, I let her go."

"Very well." Warrick swallowed and took a step forward. He'd always thought, at the end, that everything in the world around him would slow. He'd remember sweet moments from his childhood—a lullaby his mother sang him or a horse ride on his father's back. The memory of the first girl he'd kissed would flash before him or the first time he and his friends at Oxford had gotten drunk. He was certain he'd always remember the splendor of the palace when he'd been first called before the King and Queen or the anguish he'd felt when he'd had to take a life for the first time, even though it was the life of an enemy.

But he thought of none of these things. His mind was filled with images of Fallon—her smile, her frown, the feel of her hand in his, the sound of her voice. For a moment he longed for what might have been. They could have had a life together. He could have been happy with her. He could have made her happy.

But he was a fool for ever thinking it so. He'd always known marriage and family weren't within his reach. His gaze was still locked on Fallon's face as he took his last step into Bayley's reach. The screams that haunted Warrick for years rose in pitch and crescendoed as he took his last breath and stepped forward.

～～

Frankie was screaming. The sound startled Fallon, and she had to control the impulse to jump lest she cut her own neck on her father's knife. She felt the tremor run through her father and knew this was it. This was her only chance. Frankie came to his knees, and Fallon squirmed away from her father.

"Now!" she yelled at Warrick.

Her father reached for her, but it was too late. The moment's distraction had cost him, and Warrick was right there to take advantage. She paused a second to admire Warrick's quick reflexes. His hand shot out, grabbed her father's wrist, and shoved him back until he was pinned to the wall. She heard some sort of scuffle from that corner, but her attention was still on Frankie. His hand had been on his cheek and now it came away, covered in sticky blood.

"What the devil have you done to me, you bitch?" he screamed, rising unsteadily to his feet.

"You're not so pretty anymore, Frankie," she said. "In fact, I should think the ladies will be more eager to run from you than to you in the future."

"I'm going to kill you." He lunged for her, but she ducked and sidestepped behind him. He rounded on her, quickly, and she was forced back. In her peripheral vision, she saw Warrick and her father struggling. She couldn't see who was winning, but she prayed it was Warrick. She took another step back as Frankie advanced, and her foot kicked something solid. She glanced down, saw it was Warrick's pistol, and dove for it.

Unfortunately, Frankie saw it too. He reached for it at the same time she did, and their hands locked on the weapon together. "Let go!" she ordered, but she knew it was futile. His strength would win this one. They both tugged at the weapon, and when he yanked, she let go. Frankie stumbled back, and she turned to Warrick. She could see his back and the slumped form of her father in front of him.

Good. He'd won that battle. She'd bought him that time, and she could only pray it was enough. At least now he had a chance. She looked at Frankie, and took a deep breath as he raised the pistol.

"No!" Warrick rammed into Frankie, sending the ball wide and clear of her. He knocked Frankie down and the two men melded into a tangle of arms and legs. Fallon ran first to her father, ensuring he wouldn't interfere in the fight. But his eyes were wide and unseeing. Her gaze traveled from his waxy face to the knife protruding from his belly.

She could feel no joy in his death, only relief. "Good-bye, Da," she whispered and closed his eyes.

She rose slowly and turned back to the men who were now rolling about on the floor. She moved closer, trying to see how she might aid Warrick. Frankie rolled over, and Warrick looked up at her. Blood and dirt were smeared across his face. "Get out of here!" he ordered.

"Not without you."

The men rolled again, and Warrick was on top. He punched Frankie hard enough to cause real damage, but Frankie didn't flag. Instead, he reached for Warrick's neck, took hold, and shook Warrick. Fallon swallowed in sympathy and glanced around for some sort of aid. She spotted the pistol lying in a corner and rushed to pick it up. "Frankie, let him go," she said, pointing the pistol at the men.

Good thing she had no intention of firing it. She'd never get a clear shot.

"I'll kill him and then you," Frankie hissed.

"Shoot him!" Warrick told her. Fallon didn't have the heart to tell him she didn't know how to prime the thing much less fire it. The men rolled again, and Warrick was on the bottom with Frankie's hands about his throat. Even in the murky light, Fallon could see Warrick's face was turning an unhealthy shade of purple.

Frankie lifted Warrick's head and slammed it into the floor. Fallon winced.

"Shoot him!" Warrick croaked.

She couldn't shoot him, but she could do something. While Frankie choked the life from Warrick, she rushed up behind him, raised the pistol, and brought it down hard on the back of his head. He turned to her, angrily, and she hit him across the face. Her hand exploded with dull pain, and she stepped back to cradle it. She was glad she had. Warrick threw Frankie off and struck the other man hard in the nose.

Fallon heard the crack and blinked. And then Warrick's arms were around her, and she was hauled against his chest. He smelled of dirt and sweat and blood, and she had never been so glad to bury her head into a man's chest before.

"Why didn't you run?" he asked her, holding her so tightly she didn't think she could have answered even if she'd wanted to. He pulled back. "We have to get out of here. Can you run?"

She nodded. She was bone-weary, but seeing him

gave her renewed strength. She felt at that moment she could do anything with him beside her. Hand-in-hand, they started up the stairs and, breathless, pushed the cellar door open together.

A giant stood before them, arms crossed, frown permanently etched into his features. Warrick sighed, and Fallon almost turned back. The man reminded her of Titus, her butler. But Titus would never hurt her. This man was obviously of a different mind-set.

"Now wait a moment, chap," Warrick said, holding his arms up as the man stepped forward. "There's nothing to fight for any longer. Your employer is dead."

The giant was still coming, so Fallon added, "It's true. He has a knife sticking out of his belly. Go see for yourself."

The giant reached for Warrick, grabbed him by the shirt, and shook him. Fallon screamed and stepped aside to avoid being slammed by one of Warrick's doll-like limbs. She grabbed one of the giant's arms and tried to pry it down so he would release Warrick, but she was lifted off her feet. The giant shook her off and slammed Warrick to the ground. Warrick landed in a heap in the corner. Fallon blinked and stepped out of the giant's reach, but he wasn't looking at her.

He lumbered forward, intent upon Warrick. When he bent to grab him again, Fallon did the only thing she could think of. She jumped on the giant's back. It was like riding a small, untamed horse. The giant whirled around, reaching for her, trying to grab her. She held on, wrapping her arms around his neck and squeezing. Her efforts left her breathless but seemed to have no effect on her father's man.

"Warrick!" she screamed when the giant swiped her with one great paw.

"Coming," he mumbled. She could see him attempting to rise, using the wall to pull himself slowly to his feet. And then something tapped her shoulder and when she looked that way, something hard and heavy was thrust before her.

"Here, try this," someone said.

Fallon didn't question it. She raised the crowbar and slammed it over the giant's head. He stumbled but didn't fall. Fallon shook her head. Was the thing even human? He was still grabbing for her, careening wildly to and fro, and she was losing her one-armed grip. She took a last try at him, her aim ineffective, and slid off his back and onto the hard floor.

Lily—*Lily?*—took the crowbar, stepped neatly forward, and lowered it with a loud *thunk* on the giant's head.

The man went down like a large tree, narrowly avoiding flattening Warrick, who managed to lurch to the side.

Fallon blinked and stared open-mouthed at Lily. "What are you doing here?"

Lily offered her bare hand and Fallon almost hesitated to take it. Her own hands were filthy, and Lily's skin was still pristine white. Lily grabbed her hand and pulled her to her feet. "Pretend you don't see me."

"Pretend I… what is going on?"

Warrick wrapped his coat around her, and Fallon nodded her appreciation. Her dress was in tatters.

"If that is all then?" Lily said, looking at Warrick.

"Thank you," he said. "You should go."

Lily squeezed Fallon's arm, then turned in a whirl of black cape and was gone.

Fallon shook her head. "I don't understand. What is going on?"

Warrick took her arm and led her from the shop. "You and I are going home. This is over."

Fallon began to nod, to agree, and then she stopped. "What is it?"

"It's not over yet. I know who hired my father to kill you and the other spies."

Seventeen

WARRICK KNEW HE SHOULD INTERROGATE FALLON immediately. After all, this was the information he'd been seeking for weeks. If she knew who the traitor was, then he owed it to King—or at least Queen—and country to find said traitor and bring him to justice before another of the Diamonds in the Rough turned up with his throat slit.

But Warrick couldn't seem to care about all of that at the moment. Fallon was standing before him, and she was alive. Right there, in the middle of Seven Dials, he pulled her into his arms and held her. She was dwarfed by his voluminous greatcoat, but he rested his cheek on the top of her hair, which still miraculously smelled of jasmine. "I thought I'd lost you," he whispered into her chestnut tresses.

She pushed him back with both hands, and he stumbled with incredulity.

"You *should* have lost me," she said. "You were a fool in there." Fallon nodded her head toward the dark shop in the distance.

Warrick stiffened. "Pardon me?"

"No, I won't. How could you risk yourself and the lives of the other spies by coming in after me? That was exactly what my father wanted, and he almost succeeded in killing you."

Warrick raised a brow. "I beg to differ—"

"You may beg all you want, but your actions were foolish and idiotic. I'm no one and nothing. You have a duty to your country to save the other spies and ferret out the traitor."

"And you say I'm the fool."

She put her hands on her hips. "Think whatever you like, but you know if another man in your position had acted as you did, you would chastise him severely." She shook her head. "And all because you fancy yourself in love with me."

"Fancy?" He clenched his fists. "*Fancy?*" he roared, unable to contain his fury any longer. A window above a nearby shop opened, spilling light onto the damp, muddy street, and somewhere a baby started crying. "I have never *fancied* a thing in my life. I'm no squealing woman or smooth-faced schoolboy." He grabbed her by the arms and hauled her forward until their noses were all but touching. "If I say I am in love with you, you can damn sure believe I am."

"Then take 'er to bed already!" a voice called out from a nearby doorway. "So the rest of us can get a wink or two."

Warrick glanced about and saw half a dozen faces peering out at them from doors and windows. He took Fallon's arm and led her away from their audience. It had started raining again, and he felt the sting of the drops as they hit his face. He pushed her into the doorway of a shop and out of the rain. "If anyone is a fool," he hissed, "it's you, Fallon. You don't realize your own worth."

She shook her head. "No, Warrick. *You* don't realize it. I'm worth nothing. I'm not even Fallon. I'm Maggie, and I'm nothing but the daughter of a thief and a whore. And that man you were fighting in there? That horrible man? I gave him my maidenhead when I was only fifteen."

Warrick's hands tightened on her arms.

"That's right. You have no idea where I've been or what I've done. You don't love me. You don't even *know* me."

He stared at her for a long time. "Yes, I do," he said quietly. "I do know you, Fallon."

"I told you, I'm—"

"No, you're not. You're not Maggie anymore and you haven't been for a long time. I don't care about your past, and I don't condemn you for it either. It made you the woman you are today."

"And what is that but a high-priced whore?"

"We both know that's not true. I don't see a courtesan when I look at you." He reached out and smoothed a wet tendril of hair from her cheek. "When I look at you, I see a woman who is beautiful, brave, and resourceful. I see a woman who's not afraid to fight. I see a woman who has more strength and resilience than ten of her so-called betters."

She shook her head, disbelieving. "You're daft."

"Maybe." He grinned. "But I don't care. I'm going to marry you, Fallon."

"What?" She took a step back. Was he back to

marriage again? "No, you're not. Your mother will never consent to that."

"Good thing I don't need my mother's consent to marry."

"But your father…" She gestured with her hand as though that simple expression could illustrate the utter ridiculousness of his proposal.

Warrick nodded. "Honestly, I will be sorry to widen the distance between my father and me. But if he doesn't choose to accept you, that's his loss."

"No." She shook her head and moved back another step. "I'm not going to marry you. I don't want to marry you or anyone, and I don't love you."

Warrick's heart twisted, but he forced a smile on his face. Reaching for her, he pulled her against him. Her hands were ice, and he could feel her shivering. "I don't think you quite understand," he said, rubbing her arms to warm her. "I'm not asking you."

She stiffened. "Oh, well, if you think you're going to *order* me to—"

"Fallon." He put a finger over her lips. "Stubble it." He lowered his mouth to hers and claimed her cold lips with his own warm ones. She was stiff and unyielding, but gently he coaxed and persuaded her to soften to him. When her hot little tongue met his, he had to remind himself where they were, lest he push her up against the doorway and take her right there. A crack of thunder boomed above them, and the rain began in earnest. Warrick broke the kiss, smoothed his hair back, and squinted. "I'd better get you home and into something warm and dry." Like his bed. "Let's start back for The Merry Widow and pray my coach and driver haven't been carried away by Daisy's… neighbors."

He pulled her along behind him, and before they'd reached the brothel, his coach steered toward them. "I've been driving around looking for you, sir!" his coachman said, jumping down and opening the door for them. "Get in, and I'll have you home warm and dry in no time."

"Thank you, James," Warrick said, helping Fallon in and then climbing in after her. The rain beat on the roof of the carriage, making conversation all but impossible. Warrick didn't mind. At this point he had nothing more to say. And Fallon looked as though she were half in a daze. He supposed he should have done things properly, taken her hand, told her how ardently he admired her, asked her to be his esteemed wife. But neither of them had ever been much concerned with propriety, and he was tired of waiting for her to realize that she loved him as much as he loved her. Perhaps after a few years of marriage she would come to see they were perfect for each other.

His gut clenched, but he refused to acknowledge that nagging voice that warned him that she didn't love him and never would.

When they reached his town house, a bevy of servants greeted them with every comfort imaginable. They were both bundled off to warm baths, given hot tea and hearty soup, and tucked into beds cozy from bed warmers. And when all the hubbub died down, and the house was silent but for the rain pinging against the windows, he rose, pulled on a pair of trousers, and padded to Fallon's room.

He opened the door, and she turned her head to look at him. "Go away. I'm tired."

Warrick closed the door and locked it. "How are you feeling?" he asked as he approached the bed. Her dark hair gleamed in the firelight; several droplets of water from her bath still clung to it, shimmering like stars in a river of night.

"Tired." She rolled over, presenting him her back. The covers slipped, and he saw she was wearing a white linen shift. Pretty and proper—and he couldn't wait to strip it off her.

"I was lying in bed, thinking about you."

"You'd be better served by going to sleep."

He reached out and touched her hair, and she shivered. "I was imagining what I'd like to do to you."

"I was imagining sleeping." But her voice faltered, sounded unconvincing.

"Were you? What if I gave you something else to imagine?" His fingers pushed the hair off her neck, and he bent and kissed the delicate skin. She took a quick, sharp breath.

"I don't want—"

"You don't want me to kiss you here." He slid the sleeve of her nightshift off her shoulder and kissed the golden skin there. He reached around and pulled the ties on the bodice, then pushed the garment down, baring her back. "Or here." He kissed the smooth skin in the center of her back, and she whimpered. His hand slid around to cup her full breast. "Or here." Her nipple hardened against his palm, and she rolled on her back. He knelt beside her and drew the linen down over her round breasts. "But perhaps your imaginings tend in a different direction all together. Perhaps you'd like to imagine me between your legs, my tongue teasing you, opening you…"

She closed her eyes and arched into his fingers as they stroked her nipples.

"Would you like to imagine that, Fallon?"

"No, damn you." Her voice was husky.

"Then tell me what you want." His hands slid down, over the curve of her hips. He pushed the counterpane aside and grasped the hem of her nightshift. "Do you want to go to sleep?" He pulled the linen over her calves, her thighs, higher.

"You know what I want." She took his hand, put it between her thighs. She was already wet for him, and he had a moment where he had to reach for control. "Kiss me."

"Where?"

"Everywhere."

He began with her mouth, that lush, ripe mouth that had been made for kissing. He imagined men dreamed about that mouth, about the pleasures it could bring them, and he took possession of it. He kissed her deeply, cupping her cheeks, trailing his fingers over her soft skin. When she was arching against him, he traced her jaw then dipped to her graceful neck. "I want to kiss you everywhere," he murmured against her ear.

"You could skip some places." Her fingers dug into his back. "And spend more time in others."

He chuckled. "Are you that eager for me?"

"No." She was like a petulant child who refused to say yes even when the thing she wanted was right in front of her.

"Good. Then I shall take my time." His lips brushed over her collarbone, his tongue teased her shoulder blade, and she sighed with mounting desire and impatience. Her legs were wrapped around him, the heat of her cupping his erection, making resisting her increasingly difficult. But he was going to take time to minister to her breasts. He stroked them until the nipples peaked and then took first one and then the other in his mouth. He rolled them over his tongue, nipped at them, sucked until she was panting and crying out.

"Warrick, please."

Without warning, he dipped between her legs, spread them, and touched his tongue to the pink folds. She jumped and her hands dug into the sheets around him. Her thighs were quivering and stiff, and he caressed them with his fingers. "Open for me." He kissed the inside of each thigh, rubbing his lips against their silkiness. "Give yourself to me."

He could all but feel the war within her—desire fighting independence, willfulness fighting need. And finally her muscles relaxed, and she opened for him. He kissed her, teased her, tasted her. Her skin was warm and smelled of scented soap, but underneath it was her own exotic scent, and it all but drove him mad. She gripped his hair and arched her hips against him, and he plunged one finger into her, feeling her tighten against him as she cried out. He didn't take his tongue from her, instead he wrung every last ounce of pleasure from her, and when she melted, he paused then stroked her with his finger.

"No." She tried to push him away. "Enough. Let me give you pleasure."

"In time," he said, parting her folds and stroking her. She jumped.

"Warrick, I can't." But her breath was already coming in short gasps, her body straining eagerly.

"You can. Give yourself to me. Surrender."

"I can't," she all but wept, but her hips were moving in tandem with him as she clawed at the sheets in frustration. He rolled his thumb over that most sensitive spot then dipped his tongue and flicked it against her. She screamed, and he tapped his tongue to her mercilessly. "Please," she begged him. Her hands were on her breasts, her neck arched back. "Please."

He stroked her hard and this time when she came, she was crying. Her climax was long and hard, and he could feel her body devouring every last morsel of pleasure. When it was over, she collapsed and closed her eyes. "No more."

He sat and opened his trousers, pushed them over his hips. Her heavy-lidded eyes watched him as she lay limply on the bed.

"We're not through yet," he said, and to his surprise, she wrapped her legs about his waist and guided him into her.

❧

He was hard and heavy and exactly what her body was craving. She didn't think she could climax again, but she needed him inside her, needed him to fill her. She buried her face in·his shoulder, closed her eyes, and allowed herself to savor his smell, the feel of his skin, and the knowledge that she was safe in his arms. She'd been more afraid than she wanted to admit, even to herself, that she would never see him again.

She was falling in love with him. What woman wouldn't when he could do things to her with his mouth and his hands and his body most women only dreamed about? Even now as he thrust and rocked inside her, she could feel the pleasure building and spiraling upward. But this wasn't only physical. There was more to him—the way he put her first, the way he insisted he loved her, the way he promised to flaunt all custom to marry her.

Ridiculous.

But then so was the way she was feeling at the moment. She could not possibly climax again, and yet her body arched and strained.

He groaned. "Come with me, Fallon."

She shook her head. It was too much.

"Let go."

She couldn't have said why the challenge terrified her so. Perhaps because letting her guard down also meant letting him in. What would she do if she fell in love with him?

He reared back so that he was looking down at her. His face was bronze and covered with a fine sheen of perspiration. His brown hair was mussed and tousled about his face. She could see from his clenched jaw that he was straining with the effort of holding back his own pleasure. For her.

He reached between them, stroked her. Fallon couldn't help herself. She arched against him.

"Oh, yes." He gripped her hips hard with one hand. "I can't hold on."

She felt him swell and pump inside her, and it sent her over the edge. But this time the climax was slow and warm and delicious. It seemed to infuse her entire body with a heat as thick and sweet as honey. She closed her eyes and saw only Warrick's face, Warrick's intense gold-flecked eyes.

Afterward, he held her, stroked her hair and her back. She wanted to sleep, but her thoughts were restless. The events of the night played over and over in her mind. Her father was finally dead. He'd been just as horrid as she remembered him, and yet, somehow she'd hoped all this time she'd been mistaken, that seeing him as an adult would change her perspective.

And Frankie... how had the man she had thought she once loved turned into something out of a nightmare?

He'd never cared for her. She knew that now. Somehow the certainty of that fact made it easier to let go of all her childhood fancies. Warrick was correct. She was no longer Maggie Bayley. She'd been Fallon for some time now, and she should stop looking over her shoulder and fearing Maggie would return.

But who was Fallon? She wasn't a courtesan and never had been. Oh, she'd enjoyed the lavish lifestyle and the admiration of Society's most eligible men, but she could not imagine giving her body to a man she did not care for. At the moment, she could not imagine giving it anyone other than Warrick.

She was certainly not a marchioness of mystery, and she was no longer certain she wanted to perpetuate the myths about her. But what else was there for her? She wasn't like Juliette, who had grown up on a farm and would be perfectly happy returning to the countryside.

Fallon had never even been near a cow, and truth be told, she was a little afraid of them and not so fond of horses either.

And Lily. Well, Fallon didn't even know what to think of Lily at the moment. Fallon had thought *she* had secrets. Obviously, Lily had secrets of her own.

It was almost dawn before she finally fell asleep, and when she woke, she was alone. She wanted to roll over and sleep the rest of the day away, but she had to talk to Warrick about the rubies her father had mentioned.

She sat, thought about ringing for Kitty to help her dress, and then decided perhaps she would have tea and scones first. Her stomach growled, and she decided she needed fortification before seeing Warrick again. She reached for the bell just as a commotion erupted outside. A familiar voice demanded, "I will see my lady!"

She knew that voice, and she hastily pulled the counterpane over her breasts and up to her chin. A sharp rap sounded on the door, and it opened. But Titus did not stick his head in. "My lady, may I enter?"

She sighed. Why not? Everyone else had been to see her. "Yes, Titus."

He ducked and entered, glanced at her, and then fixed his eyes on the ceiling. "I am sorry to disturb you like this, my lady." With Titus in the room, it suddenly seemed very small. It was easy to forget how large and imposing he was if one hadn't seen him for a few days. The top of his head was only a few feet from the ceiling, and his broad chest was puffed out in what might have been indignation.

"It's my fault, Titus. I'm certain you were concerned for my safety and welfare. I should have sent a note."

"Mr. Fitzhugh sent one, my lady, but I wanted to see for myself that you were here of your own volition."

"I am, yes." Fitzhugh had sent a note? "Ah, Mr. Fitzhugh thought his home would be safer."

Titus's huge fists clenched at his side. Fallon had always wondered how he managed to complete delicate tasks when one of his hands was as large as her head. And she realized now she had offended him. "Oh, but Titus, I didn't mean to imply I would not be safe at home."

He swallowed. "That is quite all right, my lady. You must go where you think best."

"Oh, Titus." She sighed. How was she possibly going to mend his hurt feelings now? "You know I would rather be home."

"Is it possible you could share the source of your distress, my lady? So that we at the town house might be prepared?"

"Ah…" She really wanted to tell him. Any concession at this point would have smoothed over his roughened feelings. "I cannot, but I assure you I will be home soon. If you could—"

"What is the meaning of this?" Warrick stormed into the room, his gaze sweeping it and taking in first Fallon and then Titus. "Who is this?"

"Titus. He's my butler."

Warrick blinked. "Oh, of course. I remember now."

Titus did not look at him. The servant kept his gaze on the ceiling.

"Is everything all right?" Warrick asked.

"Yes. Titus was merely concerned for my welfare. I've assured him I am well."

"Good."

"If that is all, my lady," Titus said, "I will take my leave."

"Thank you, Titus. And I do promise to be home very soon."

He nodded, padded silently out of the room, and closed the door behind him. Warrick's gaze flicked back to her, and she saw the flicker of heat in his eyes. It amazed him that after last night he could still want her. Even more, it amazed her that warmth was flooding into her own belly and her nipples were hardening. "I need to talk to you," she said. "It's about what my father said."

He nodded. "I had planned to ask you about it but wanted to wait until you were awake."

"I'm awake."

"I see that." His gaze dipped to the counterpane. "Is it possible you might dress before we discuss the matter? I might be able to concentrate more if I didn't know you were one flick of my wrist from being naked again."

Fallon smiled. "I have faith in your powers of restraint."

He raised a brow. "Do you? That faith seems a bit misplaced."

"In any case, I have some information I believe will be useful."

"You said you knew who the traitor was."

"And I do—only I don't have his name."

Warrick sighed. "No, that would be too easy."

"But my father mentioned something about a man with rubies. He said the man would pay him with three rubies as large as his fist."

"Did you believe him?"

"I can see no reason for him to lie."

Warrick paced away from her, and she could see his mind was no longer on seduction. He was reasoning something out, if the furrow in his brow was any indication, and why that furrow made her want to throw off these sheets and lure him back to bed was beyond her. There was something enticing about intensity in a man.

"So whoever it is has wealth," he said, going to the window and opening the drapes. "I thought as much. But rubies as large as one's hand..." He made a fist and looked down at it. "Rubies of that nature imply great wealth, and rubies like that aren't common." He looked at her. "Have you heard mention of anyone possessing such jewels?"

She shook her head. "No, but it might not be someone who moves in London Society. At least, not in my circle."

Warrick turned back to the window and parted the curtains again. She admired the way his back tapered into a slim waist and how his tight breeches molded to shapely thighs. "I think I must make a visit to Threadneedle Street."

"What's there?"

He faced her. "The Bank of England. I might have it wrong, but it's a start."

"I don't understand. Do you need money?"

"No, but I'm betting that whoever owns those rubies also insured them."

"There are hundreds of places he could insure them."

"True, but not all of them could support an insurance policy that large."

"All right. I'm coming with you."

He closed his eyes. "I bloody well knew you were going to say that."

"I'm involved now," she told him. "I was almost killed over those rubies last night, and I want to see who is behind this."

"I suppose you'd better get dressed then."

"You aren't even going to argue?"

He sighed. "Madam, I no longer see the point."

Two hours later, they stepped out of the shadow of the bank and into the bright afternoon sunshine. "Well, that didn't go well," Fallon said.

"It went as I expected."

She frowned. "If you expected them to tell us they wouldn't give us access to the insurance records, then why did we make a trip here?"

"Because I wanted to refresh my memory."

Fallon's hand froze in the act of opening her parasol. "Oh, no."

Warrick raised his brows.

"You are not going to do what I think you're going to do."

"That depends." He took her arm and led her away from the bank. "What do you think I'm going to do?"

"Break into the Bank of England," she said in a whisper.

He nodded. "Oh. Yes, I am going to do that. That manager knew about the rubies. A hundred to one says there are insurance documents stored in the bank. Do you want to come with me?"

She wanted to say yes. She wanted her time with him to go on forever, but if she didn't end it now, then when? The sooner she made a fresh start, the better.

"I'm not coming back with you." She paused at the curb and looked to and fro for Fitzhugh's carriage.

"It's just there," Warrick said, pointing. "My coachman is already headed this way."

"Good." She swallowed. "Have him take me home."

Warrick frowned at her. "My home?"

"No. My home." Her stomach clenched, but she did not retract the words.

"I see." He was looking at her with those direct eyes, and she made herself look away. If she continued looking into his eyes, she was going to give in and do whatever he wanted. Again. "So that's it then?" he asked.

She took a breath, ignoring the hitch in it. "Yes. I think it must be."

"I disagree."

"Then we will have to agree to disagree. You have your life, Warrick, and I have mine." She kept her gaze on the gray stone facade of the building before them.

"I believe I proposed we unite the two."

The carriage stopped in front of them, and she blinked at the sun's brightness reflecting off the gleaming black conveyance. She angled her parasol to block the reflection. Now her eyes were watering because of the damn sun.

"And I considered your proposal," she said, now looking at his cravat. Best to avoid his eyes at all costs.

"Did you?"

"Yes, and it will never work. I'm sorry. You and I are from two very different backgrounds. Your family will never accept me, and I..."

He took her arm and forced her to look into his eyes. "And you? What about you, Fallon?"

"And I don't want to marry." She straightened her back. "I like my independence." This much was true. Marriage was for prim little misses and those who miraculously found love. It was not for her kind.

"You are such a good little liar, but you can't lie to me. I know you, and you're afraid."

She bristled and snapped the parasol shut. "Afraid of what?"

"You tell me."

"Nothing."

"Liar."

She stepped back. "Mr. Fitzhugh, I had thought we might remain friends, but I see now that is quite impossible."

"Don't talk to me like I'm one of the men vying to be your protector."

"Then stop acting like one," she snapped.

She regretted the words instantly, and regretted them even more when he stepped back and away from her. His face was granite, his expression stony, but in his eyes she saw a flash of pain. "Warrick—" She reached out to him, but he stepped out of reach and flagged a hackney coach.

"Marchioness, I think you might be more comfortable in this hack." He paid the jarvey and handed her up before she could even protest. For the first time since they'd met, his hand did not linger on her body. "I will have your things sent posthaste."

"Thank you."

"Good day." And he walked away without a backward glance.

Eighteen

THE BANK OF ENGLAND KNEW WHAT IT WAS ABOUT, Warrick mused as he picked the last lock on the back entrance. But he had been trained by the best, and his training hadn't failed him yet. He felt the lock click into place and pushed the door open. "Not bad for a man who's out of practice," he murmured to himself, stowing his lock-picking tools in the small leather case in which he carried them and dropping it in his great coat.

He slipped into the bank and closed the door silently behind him, then locked it from the inside. He wished he had a lamp, but he hadn't wanted to risk alerting the Watch if he happened to pass by and see a light in the window. Warrick's eyes were already adjusted to the dark, but he took a moment to survey his surroundings. He was in a back room, most likely where the employees entered and exited. What he needed was the records room.

He knew from experience that the vault was under the bank on the first floor. He'd been there with his father years ago. He'd noted a staircase leading to another level this afternoon and watched bank clerks winding their ways up and down its marble steps. What was on the second level? Offices? Perhaps stored records? It was worth investigating.

He made his way silently through the bank and up the staircase. The second floor was darker and also better insulated from the exterior windows. Warrick pulled a tinderbox from his coat and lit a spunk. He unearthed an old candle from his pocket and lit the wick. Slowly, he perused the plaques outside doors until he found one that read *Records*.

He smiled. If he was a pirate, X would have marked the spot. He turned the knob and swore. Who the devil locked a records room? And how was he supposed to hold a candle with one hand and pick a lock with the other? He looked about for a table or chair to drag over, but the corridor was annoyingly sparse. He tapped the door. It wasn't very thick. Perhaps he could kick it down...

He heard a scrape and a thump and instantly blew out the candle and ducked. Silently, he crawled to the staircase and peered through the rails. Below, nothing and no one moved. Had he imagined that noise?

He slowed his breathing and closed his eyes, listening. He heard the clop of horses on the street and the distant cry of a flower girl, but nothing—wait! There it was. The shush of the carpet as someone stepped lightly on it. Tiptoeing.

So it wasn't the Watch or a night guard. He wouldn't tiptoe, and he'd be carrying a lamp. The ground floor was still shrouded in darkness. A thief? He'd locked the door behind him, but as he'd proved, it could be picked.

Whoever it was appeared to be searching the ground floor. Warrick couldn't risk discovery, which meant he was going to have to deal with the intruder. Silently.

He pulled the dagger from his boot and made his way stealthily down the stairs. Hugging the banister and keeping to the shadows, he took one step at a time, glad they were marble and unable to creak. From this vantage point, he couldn't see the interloper, which was a good thing as Warrick didn't relish being spotted on the staircase. He reached the ground floor and heard a rustling to his left. Keeping his back to the staircase, he used the shadows to stay hidden.

A shadow across the room shifted, and Warrick discerned a caped figure crouching before the door to the lower level. Whoever the man was, he was trying to access the vault. Shifting his dagger in his hand, Warrick eased forward. He could move almost silently, but the thief appeared to sense him because he turned. Warrick ducked behind a desk, waited, and when he heard the scrape of a lock being picked, he moved in. Closing the distance between them, he stepped behind the man and put a knife to his throat. "Don't move. I don't want to kill you."

"I'm not so certain of that."

Warrick dropped the knife and grabbed Fallon by the shoulders, hauling her up so that she was facing him. "What the devil are you doing here? I almost killed you." The hood of her cape fell back, revealing that sweep of thick dark hair and the honey curve of her cheek. But he wasn't going to look at her, to fall in love with her again. She'd made her feelings clear.

"Not a very nice greeting, considering you invited me."

"Madam, I believe our conversation following the invitation served to rescind it. I ask again: What are you doing here?"

She looked down, and her lashes were dark smudges on her smooth cheeks. "I don't know. I suppose I wanted to know who the man with the rubies is."

"Why?" Warrick released her and crossed his arms over his chest. "He doesn't want you dead."

"I care about you."

"Do you? That's heartening. I thought you had a heart of stone."

"Listen, I—"

A beam of light pierced the darkness of the bank, and Warrick grabbed Fallon and hauled her down to the floor. "Shh! It's the Watch."

"I know who it is."

The beam made a slow path over the desks and chairs in the bank, and Fallon pointed to a desk nearby. Warrick nodded, and they scurried underneath it. The space was tight, even with his knees pulled up to his chin. It would not have accommodated them both if Fallon had not been so petite. Pressed against her, he could not help but be reminded of the warmth of her skin and the feel of her lips against his own. Her light exotic perfume tantalized his senses, and he turned his head away.

He could hear the thump, thump of the Watch's boots outside the building, but he knew the light would not find them under the desk. "Were you seen breaking in?" he whispered.

"Of course not. Were you?"

"Do you mean to insult me?"

"No more than you insult me."

The beam flashed near them, and Fallon put her hand on his arm. They both sat immobile and silent. Then the beam faded and the Watch's footfalls receded.

Fallon did not remove her hand. "I didn't like how we parted this afternoon."

He glanced at her, the dark shape of her beside him.

"That's why I came tonight. I didn't want that to be the end."

"You might have sent me a note."

"I'm no writer. I wouldn't have known what to say."

"Why don't you simply admit you're in love with me?"

Her hand tightened on his arm and then she released him. "I do care about you."

"Care? Do you break into the Bank of England for everyone you care about?"

"I care a *great deal*."

"What are you so afraid of, Fallon?"

"I'm not afraid!" she all but yelled.

"No, of course not." And he was no fool. He was not going to *persuade* her she loved him. He was not going to beg for her affections. Either she loved him enough to risk herself or she did not. He was going to regret walking away for the rest of his life. He was going to die a little inside every time he read about her in the papers or saw her across a ballroom. He was going to die wanting her, but if he continued to chase her, he would die loathing himself. She would have to come to him. He was already standing on the edge of the precipice. If she wanted him, she'd have to cross the divide.

He pushed out from under the desk and brushed his coat off. "Go home, Fallon. I don't need your help." He started back up the staircase, leaving her crouching under the desk. He wanted to look back at her. He wanted to will her to come after him. Instead, he concentrated on walking away from her and tried to ignore the stabbing sensation somewhere midchest.

∽

Fallon watched him go, watched him deliberately take one step at a time away from her. How she hated him. She was humiliated. She had come here and risked everything, and he had told her he did not want her.

Why *had* she come?

He wasn't worth this. No man was worth it. She knew that to be true. Why did she keep breaking her rules for this man? She was never going to marry. She was never going to fall in love.

Except she had fallen in love, and it was perfectly inconvenient. He was all wrong for her. He was an aristocrat. He was a spy. He knew all her secrets.

And he was walking away from her.

Good. She should let him go. She should go home, sleep for three days, then make a grand appearance back into Society. She should meet with Lily, and the two of them could plan a triumphant return.

Except, when she thought of Lily now, she thought of Warrick. Lily had more secrets than Fallon could have guessed, and she didn't think she could go back to sitting in Lily's drawing room, sipping tea, and pretending everything was as it had been. Pretending they were both celebrated courtesans, when privately neither of them resembled that in the least.

And the truth was, Fallon did not want that life anymore. She did not want a life where she didn't see Warrick every day. She did not want a life without him in it.

And that was why she had come here tonight. That was why she had left her safe, warm home in the middle of the night, traveled halfway across London to Threadneedle Street, and knelt in a dirty alley to pick the lock of the Bank of London.

If she were caught, she would most certainly be hanged. And yet, here she was—and she'd do it all again, too. She was that much of an addlepate.

Her heart thumped hard, and she could hardly manage a breath. But she had to go after him. She couldn't lose him. It was never going to work. She was going to end up alone and miserable when, in the end, he threw her over for a woman of his own station. But she would have him until then. Until that last moment, she would sleep in his arms, hear his voice whisper her name, feel his lips on her skin.

She shot up, bumped her head loudly on the underside of the desk, and winced. "Warrick!" she shouted then grimaced. She was going to get them both caught, and that was hardly the romantic scene she wanted.

She rubbed her head and crawled out from under the desk. He was no longer on the staircase, and she rushed up the stairs after him. Her cloak swirled behind her, and she lifted her skirts almost to her knees as she raced up the steps. It seemed to take days to reach him. Who would have thought a bank would have so many stairs? Finally she reached the top and was greeted with dark silence. "Warrick," she hissed.

Nothing.

"Warrick!"

She stared down the corridor. Had he gone right or left? Why had she not thought to bring some sort of light? Very well, she would go right and see where that led her. Hands out in front of her, she started down the dark corridor. "Warrick? Where are you?"

How could he not hear her? Was he still here? What if he had left? What if she was alone in the empty bank? She shivered. Of course he hadn't left her. How would he have exited from the second floor?

"Warrick?"

"Are you trying to alert the whole of London?"

She jumped and, hand on heart, flattened herself against the wall. She still couldn't see him. "Warrick?" she whispered.

"I told you to go home."

"I can't. I... Where are you?"

She didn't hear him move, but suddenly he was before her. How did he manage feats like that? She could just make out his dark eyes in the gloom. She reached out to touch him, and he stepped back. "Do you need an escort home? Wait downstairs, and—"

"No, that's not it. I—it's you. I need you."

He sighed. "Fallon, we've been through this."

Oh, dear God. She had waited too long to tell him. He really didn't want her anymore. She had driven him away. Her heart clenched, and she fought a wave of dizziness. "No. I came to say…" Her throat constricted. Why was this so difficult? "I mean, what I want to say is that…" She took a deep breath. "I love you."

He didn't speak, didn't respond. She waited. Wasn't he supposed to take her in his arms and tell her he loved her too? Wasn't he supposed to kiss her or embrace her or… well, something other than simply stand there?

"Did you hear me?" she asked.

"Yes."

She could feel her cheeks flame with heat. That was it? That was his response? She was such a fool. The last time she had said those words, she'd been fifteen and the man she'd said them to had betrayed her days later. Now she'd said them again, and the man to whom she was giving her heart didn't want her either.

She almost laughed. Perhaps she was cursed. Perhaps this was God's way of punishing her for all her sins. And she deserved punishment. There had been many sins and few for which she was sincerely contrite.

"I'm sorry," she finally whispered more to herself than to him. She was sorry she had not been braver sooner. She was sorry she had allowed that tiny flicker of hope he'd sparked to flame into something more. "I'll not waste another moment of your time." Fallon moved past him and started for the staircase. It appeared quite blurry for some odd reason. She reached the banister, placed her hand on it, and took a shaky step.

"Wait."

She almost toppled down the steps at the sound of his voice.

"Why? Why do you tell me this now?"

She clenched the banister, feeling the ridge of the smooth wood under her fingertips. "I don't know."

"Not good enough." His hand gripped her waist, and he turned her to face him. "Why did you come here tonight?"

"Because I missed you," she whispered. "Because I..." Her throat constricted again, and she tried to swallow the enormous lump.

"You missed me. Go on."

"Because I didn't want to be without you." She looked down, and he notched her chin back up with a finger. "I couldn't stand the thought of not being with you." She put her hands on his chest, felt the warmth of him through the wool greatcoat. Suddenly the words she'd fought for rushed forward like a river whose dam has broken. "I know this will never work. I know you can't possibly marry me, but I don't care. I want you anyway."

He shook his head. "And you think that's love?"

She took a shaky breath. "Yes."

"Fallon, you don't know anything." But instead of releasing her, he pulled her into his arms and kissed her. She was too shocked to react at first, but then his warm mouth coaxed hers open, and she was kissing him back with everything she had. She didn't understand what had happened or what he had meant when he'd said she knew nothing. And she didn't care. Warrick was kissing her. Warrick was holding her.

His hands fisted in her hair, tugging her head back gently so he could kiss her neck, her earlobe, her collarbone. She shivered, a languid, liquid heat poured through her, warming her and making her tingle.

"You're wearing too many clothes," he murmured when he reached the prim neckline of her gown.

"So are you." She wanted to divest him of his coat and shirt. She wanted to run her hands over his firm chest and that flat abdomen. She wanted to nip his broad shoulders and wrap her legs around the dent of his waist.

With a growl, Warrick pulled away from her. "This isn't the time or the place," he said. Fallon stared at him. His breath came in rapid huffs, and his eyes were dark with passion.

"You *do* want me," she whispered.

He laughed. "Of course I want you. I told you, I'm in love with you."

"But I thought—I mean, when you told me to go—"

He cupped her face with his hands. "I am going to tell you this one more time, Fallon. I have no expectation you will comprehend this time, but I'm ever hopeful. *I love you.* I will always love you. I know you don't believe me. I know you don't trust me, but it's true."

She smiled. She did believe him, and she wanted to think his *always* meant forever. "I love you too."

He kissed her again, gently and almost sweetly. "You've no idea how much I've wanted to hear you say so. And now, if we're to have any future together, we had better discover the identity of the man who wants me and the other Diamonds in the Rough dead."

"The man with the rubies?"

"Exactly. I found the records room, and if you will

hold the candle for me, I'll pick the lock and we can search the insurance policies."

Fallon raised her brows. "That sounds tedious."

He took her hand and led her down the corridor. "One can't be abducted or involved in a carriage chase every night." He retrieved his tinderbox, lit the candle, and handed it to her. Then she watched as he opened a small leather case and took out what appeared to be professional lock-picking tools. This was why she loved him. How could she love a man who didn't have some useful skills?

"Those are very nice," she said, peering over his shoulder.

"Thank you." He glanced up at her. "Could you hold the candle so I might see the lock?"

"Oh, of course." She watched as he selected an instrument with a long, thin, metal protrusion and inserted it into the lock. He twisted and turned the instrument, and she leaned closer to get a better look.

"Fallon." He sounded as though his teeth were clenched. "This is hard enough without you leaning over my shoulder."

He went back to work, and she glanced at the other tools in the case. There was one with a bent end she thought might work better on a lock of this sort.

He swore, removed the pick, and then inserted it again. "Lift the candle, please."

The candle was lifted, but she recognized frustration when she heard it.

"Why don't you try—"

His hands stilled, and she closed her mouth, realizing her mistake. If she'd learned anything masquerading as a courtesan, it was never to give a man advice. They did not appreciate it and rarely took it, even when it was perfectly logical and obviously the best possible solution to their problem.

He swore again and ran a hand though his hair. Fallon pressed her lips together.

"What?" he said, without looking at her.

"I didn't say a word."

"You were going to say something earlier."

She shook her head. "No."

He rose. "I'm going to have to kick it down."

She winced. "That's rather loud, and tomorrow the bank manager will know a thief was here."

"Do you have another suggestion?"

A suggestion was similar to advice, in her experience. Fallon hesitated. "Perhaps I could try picking the lock."

Warrick moved aside. "By all means." He gestured to the door. "Have a go."

She was wary of his solicitousness, but she didn't relish waiting all night for him to pick the lock or having the Watch discover them when he made a racket by kicking the door down. She handed him the candle, and he held the pick out to her. She took it, knelt, and replaced it in his case.

"You're not going to use the pick?" he asked.

"Not that one, no." She extracted the curved pick, studied the lock, and inserted the instrument.

"That one is not going to work," he said from behind her.

She jiggled the pick gently then turned it to the left.

"The lock is such that you need a straight pick."

She turned the pick to the right.

"That kind will damage the mechanism if—"

Snick. Fallon pulled the handle and opened the door. Without a word, she replaced the curved pick in the case and handed it to him. "Lovely tools," she said. He stared at the tools, then at her. She thought, for a moment, he might say something, but he merely pocketed the tools and gestured for her to enter the records room.

The room was spartan and consisted of a long table, several chairs, and rows and rows and rows of files. It did not have a window, so Warrick lit a lamp and directed her to search the row of files on the far wall. He began with those on the wall near the door. Fallon took one look at the boxes of files and sighed. This, she supposed, was why she would not make a good spy. There was far too much drudgery involved. But she began sorting through files, glancing at page after page of dull documents, looking for any mention of rubies. Several times she thought she found something interesting, but the rubies were part of a set of jewelry, and she knew the rubies she wanted were not in a setting.

"That was impressive," Warrick said.

Fallon started. She'd become so accustomed to the silence that his voice startled her. "Pardon?" She glanced at him. He was standing by a stack of files, thumbing through them. The warm glow from the lamp made his skin look burnished and glinted off what appeared to be auburn pieces in his chestnut hair.

"The way you picked the lock," he said, without looking at her. "It was impressive."

"Oh." She went back to her files. "I have plenty

of experience picking locks. It's not something I'm proud of."

"There are some who would envy your skills."

She gave a bitter laugh. "Thieves and cutthroats."

"And spies."

She glanced up at him. "You would have succeeded with the lock. Eventually. You simply selected the wrong tool."

"In my business, every second matters. Selecting the wrong tool can mean death."

"Then I'm happy you are retired." She didn't like to think of him risking his life. She didn't like to think of him injured or dead. With renewed vigor, she began sorting through files. But she looked up when his shadow fell over the parchment before her.

"I'm trying, in my clumsy way, to say thank you."

She looked back down. "There's no need."

He kissed her cheek. "There's every need. You're an extraordinary woman, Fallon. One day you're going to believe that."

They studied files until Fallon's back ached, her shoulders felt taut as the wire of a pianoforte, and the words swam before her eyes. Finally, Warrick said, "It's not here. Or, if it is, we've not time to find it. I've seen dozens of large insurance policies. The rubies might not be insured, or they could be insured elsewhere."

Fallon stretched her back. "Where?"

"Perhaps Child's Bank on Fleet Street."

Fallon frowned. She had no desire to stray that close to the Temple Bar.

"Perhaps Hoare's."

Another Fleet Street bank. "Surely we can't break into every bank in London."

"No. I'll have to take a different direction." He shoved a box of files back on the shelf. "Right now I want to go to bed." His gaze met hers. "But not alone."

She smiled. It seemed she'd been waiting for years to be in his arms again.

Once they were in the alley again with the Bank of England locked securely behind them, he asked, "How did you come here?"

"Hack. I had him leave me a few streets away." She could see the sky lightening to a pewter gray. Dawn was coming.

"I did the same. We'll not find one at this wee hour."

Fallon sighed. "I suppose that means we walk."

He offered her his arm. She took it and they headed for Threadneedle Street. They had not gone far when a voice called from the darkness, "I've been waiting for you."

Nineteen

WARRICK REACHED FOR HIS PISTOL BUT FROZE WHEN he heard the sound of a pistol being cocked.

"Put yer hands where I can see them."

Warrick lifted his hands and glanced at Fallon. Whatever happened, he couldn't allow any harm to come to her. Most likely this was nothing more than a simple robbery. He would toss the thief a few coins and they would all walk away. Fallon looked back at him, drops of water in her hair. The night air was damp and heavy. A slate-gray fog curled about his ankles like a hungry cat. He could hear the distant sounds of farmers' wagons hauling their goods into town. London was opening a groggy eye. In a few more moments, someone would happen by.

"You were in the bank for quite a spell," the thief said.

Fallon's eyes widened, and Warrick knew what she was thinking. How had the man known they'd been in the bank?

"What's it to you?" Warrick asked. He itched to turn his head, to see the man properly.

"Just you keep facing as you are," the man said.

"My face ain't nothing to see. You almost got me caught, ye did. The Watch are suspicious in these parts. Can't be bribed either."

"If all you want is the few coins I have on me, take them and be gone," Warrick said. "It's late, and I want my bed."

The man laughed. "Pretty girl like that at yer side, I bet you do. But that's not all I want."

A shiver of unease skittered up Warrick's spine. "What else could you want?" He moved closer to Fallon, shielding her with his body.

The man laughed. "Not yer ladybird. I want you, Mr. Fitzhugh. You have a price on yer head, and I intend to claim it."

Bloody hell. Exactly how many men did the traitor with the rubies have after him?

Warrick turned, and the man stepped hastily into the shadows. Warrick couldn't see him at any rate. He had the collar of his coat up and his tricorn hat pulled low over his forehead. "Turn back around." The man's voice shook slightly.

Good. He wasn't a professional. "What exactly do you intend? Will you shoot me dead on the street? I imagine that will attract some attention." Warrick took a step forward.

"Don't come no closer."

"Or else you will shoot me? You've already told me that is your intention. What do I have to lose now?" He stepped closer again, and the man stepped back.

"Warrick, be careful," Fallon said.

"Listen to the chit. You'd better be careful."

"Or you will shoot me?" Warrick took another step

forward. "You'll do that anyway." He was facing the pistol now and could see the man's hand shaking on the hammer. At this rate, he'd be shot accidentally. But Warrick could also see a little of the man's face. He was young, no seasoned killer. He wasn't much older than the boys Warrick had seen dying on the battlefields of the Continent.

The boy raised the pistol higher. "Keep yer hands up."

There was fear in his voice, fear and desperation. The combination made Warrick's ears roar as though a spring gale buffeted his face. Warrick closed his eyes, willed the memories of the battle away. But the boy's voice and his face had triggered something. Suddenly, the sky was stained crimson from the distant fires. Smoke scorched his nostrils and snaked along the muddy ground. Warrick could hear the battle cries again. He could hear the screams of the horses and the distant booms of cannon fire. The ground beneath him shook, and he braced his legs to keep his balance on the slippery ground.

From far away, he heard someone say, "What's he doing?"

Fallon was calling out to him. "Warrick, are you ill?"

He looked for her, but the smoke from the battle was too thick. He couldn't see her. He had to reach her. She shouldn't be here. She should be safe, home in London. He was reaching out for Fallon, straining to touch her, crawling over the bodies of the dead men again, slipping on their slick blood, falling in a pool of excrement and severed limbs.

No! He would not go back. He would *not* go back. With a roar, he rushed forward, heedless of the dead men he trampled. He knocked the enemy down and fought with a rage he hadn't felt since the war. "I'm not going back!" he shouted. "I won't do it."

Thud. Thud. Thud.

"Warrick!"

Fallon was screaming. He could hear her. Where was she?

"Warrick! Stop. You'll kill him."

Someone grabbed his arm and he struck out, pulling the punch at the last moment when he saw it was Fallon. She gasped, stumbled, and fell backward.

The battlefield faded away, and he was back in London. A gray fog—not smoke—rolled by him, and the pewter sky—not crimson—hung with the promise of rain. The sounds of the city, of horses' hooves clopping, vendors crying, and wagons lumbering through the streets surrounded him. Slowly, the battlefield faded into the corners of his mind, where he knew it would wait and watch for another chance at freedom.

"Fallon!" Warrick was beside her in an instant, lifting her into his arms. "I'm so bloody sorry. Are you all right? Did I hurt you?"

"No." She gripped his face. "I tripped on my cape, but I'm fine. What happened? I screamed your name, but you didn't seem to hear me. You almost killed him." She looked past Warrick. "Perhaps you did kill him."

Warrick turned and saw the young man lying on the ground. His tricorn hat had tumbled off, revealing a head of long, dark blond hair. His face was streaked with blood. Warrick moved closer to the boy, and the lad raised a weak arm. "No more."

Thank God. The boy wasn't dead. Warrick's gaze flicked to the pistol that had fallen from the boy's hand. He leaned over and scooped it up, tucking it into his pocket and out of the boy's reach.

The boy moaned again, and Warrick hauled him up. "Who sent you?"

"No more," the boy moaned.

"I'm not going to hurt you, if you answer my questions."

"No more." The boy's head lolled back, and Warrick sighed. He knew he hadn't beaten the lad so badly the boy couldn't talk.

Fallon put her hand on Warrick's shoulder. "Let me try."

Warrick started to protest, then realized she probably had the right of it. The boy was too terrified of him at the moment to speak.

Fallon knelt beside the boy, and Warrick frowned. He didn't like to see her kneeling on the dirty street. "What is your name?" she asked softly.

The boy's eyelids fluttered. "Wha?"

"Your name?" She bent over him, so he could see her face.

"John."

"John, I'm Fallon. Are you well enough to sit?"

The boy struggled to his elbows, and Warrick stepped forward to assist. But Fallon shook her head, and Warrick stepped back into the fog. When the boy was sitting, Fallon said, "Now, tell me who sent you here to kill Mr. Fitzhugh. I assume this isn't a personal matter but that someone is paying you."

"I ain't going to get paid now." He tossed a

contemptuous look in Warrick's direction and spit out a tooth.

"Your reward is your life," she said. "And if you want to keep it, tell me who sent you."

The boy looked at her then looked over at Warrick. Warrick crossed his arms over his chest.

"I don't know his name, and I never seen his face. But he's a gentleman, I know that. I could hear it in his voice. He sounds like that one there." He hooked a thumb at Warrick. "I couldn't see his face, it were too dark, but I saw his boots. They were expensive, like. I believed him when he said those gems were real."

"The rubies?"

He blinked at her. "You seen 'em?"

"No, but I've heard of them. He showed them to you?"

"He did. They was huge. I'd like to have done just about anything to get my hands on one of those."

Warrick rolled his eyes. As though the boy would know what to do with a ruby once he had it.

"When and where did you see these rubies?" Fallon asked.

Warrick had to give her credit. She was getting the boy to talk and asking all of the right questions. A few drops of rain plinked on Warrick's face, and he peered up at the foreboding sky.

"He had them right here in London. Met him over on the East End in a pub. Thought he was just one of those gents slumming it, then he pulls me aside, buys me some gin, and shows me them rubies."

"When was this?" Warrick couldn't resist interrupting. His pulse had started to race. The traitor was in London—or had been recently. It was drizzling in earnest now, the water beginning to dilute the splatters of blood on the street.

The boy glared at Warrick. "I ain't talking to him," he said to Fallon. "I'm talking to you."

"Of course." Her gaze never left the boy's. "When did you meet this man?"

The boy shrugged. "Couple of days ago."

"Then he's in Town now?" she asked.

"I should think so. Said I had until"—the boy lifted his fingers and counted—"day after tomorrow, which I suppose is today already, to do the deed. I was to meet him at a fancy ball in two days' time." Another dagger-like glance in Warrick's direction. "I'd get paid then."

Fallon frowned. "A fancy ball? Whose ball, and how would you gain entrance?"

The boy shook his head as though speaking to a child. "I'd hide in the gardens."

"Whose ball?"

"I don't know the name. Some lord or other with deep pockets."

"How were you to find it? Did the gentleman with the rubies give you the address?"

The boy scowled. "I don't read, Miss Fallon. He told me, and I remembered." He tapped his head.

"What was the number?"

The boy cut another glance at Warrick. He leaned closer to Fallon. "Thirty-six Berkeley Square."

Warrick's world tilted, and he reached out to clutch a lamppost for support.

"You know it?" the boy was asking Fallon. She shook her head. "No."

Warrick took a deep breath and tossed a few coins at the boy's feet. The boy scrambled to grab them, and Fallon stood.

"This ought to cover a visit from your doctor. After that, I'd advise you to stay in bed, because if I see you again, I'll kill you."

The boy glared at him. Warrick held out an arm, and Fallon took it. "Let's go before the skies open up and soak us."

They found a hack just as the rain began in earnest. Warrick started to give the jarvey his address, but Fallon interrupted with her own.

"Why did you do that?" Warrick asked when they were inside.

"Who knows how many other hired men this gentleman has after you? For right now it might be best for us to sojourn at my town house."

"What about Titus?" Warrick asked darkly.

Fallon raised a brow. "He is a little scary, isn't he?" They sat in silence for a moment, then Fallon said, "Who lives at thirty-six Berkeley Square?"

Warrick would have sworn she had her gaze fixed on the boy when that information had been revealed. But somehow she'd seen his reaction.

"My mother and father."

"You don't think—"

"No. My father isn't trying to have me killed." At least Warrick didn't think the earl hated him that much. "But my mother is hosting a ball."

"Ah." Fallon nodded. "The ball with the famous Lady Edith."

"Precisely. Obviously our man has an invitation."

"I suppose this means you will be attending."

He looked at her. Was that jealousy in her voice? "*We'll* be attending. It's time you met my father."

✥

Fallon did not think it time she met the Earl of Winthorpe. In fact, she could have done quite nicely never meeting the man. But she wasn't going to argue the point with the sun rising, her head pounding, and Titus glaring at Warrick from the vestibule of her town house.

"Titus," she said, smoothing her hair back into place, though she couldn't have said why, as it was a lost cause. "Would you tell Cook to delay breakfast? I think we shall sleep first."

She glanced at Warrick, and he nodded agreement. He looked exhausted. His eyes were rimmed with red. Insomnia or not, it was time he slept.

"My lady," Titus said, his severe tone making her jerk her attention toward him. "Might we have a word?"

"What is it?" Fallon handed her cape to her lady's maid with an apologetic smile for the dirt.

Titus hesitated and shifted.

"Go ahead, Titus. You may speak freely."

Her butler gave Warrick a dark look, but before Titus could speak, Warrick said, "I know what this is about. You want me to go. Do I have the right of it, Titus?"

"Yes, sir." Titus's tone on the *sir* was far from respectful. "It's not proper, you staying here."

Fallon sighed. "Titus, I am a courtesan. Men are supposed to visit me here."

Titus frowned but didn't argue.

"Titus," Warrick began. "Let me put your mind at ease."

"Warrick, you go on. I'll speak to Titus."

"Actually, I think it might be better if Titus and I spoke in private."

Fallon raised her brows. "You want to speak to my butler in private?"

Warrick nodded. "If you don't mind." He indicated the door to a small parlor. "Might we speak in here for a few moments?"

Titus nodded and, to Fallon's shock, lumbered into the parlor. What exactly was going on here? She watched, stupefied, as Warrick followed and then closed the parlor door.

Anne came forward. "May I help you to your room, madam?"

Fallon shook her head. "No. Go on ahead and prepare my chamber. Make sure there are two glasses of wine on the nightstand." It was not a usual request, but Anne only nodded and disappeared into the servant's domain.

Fallon edged closer to the parlor door, leaning her ear against it. Her footman was coming toward her, but she waved him back impatiently.

"—think I understand what is going on here," Warrick was saying.

Well, she was certainly glad someone understood.

"You see yourself as a sort of guardian for Fallon."

"I *am* her guardian," Titus answered.

It was news to Fallon—who had been on her own since fifteen, and who was past the age of majority—that she had a guardian. Especially one on her own payroll.

"And naturally you have concerns about me and my intentions."

Fallon rolled her eyes. This was like some sort of grand farce. She employed Titus. *She* had saved *him*. She remembered meeting the giant. She had been new to the world of the demimonde and still learning her way. The Earl of Sin had set her up in her town house with Anne and a footman. Sinclair had even loaned her his own butler, Abernathy, to help put the house in order. And what she had learned from Abernathy was that she needed a good butler of her own. Of course, she had no idea where to search for one.

And then she had been on her way home one evening—or rather one early morning—and passed by a group of men beating what appeared to be a giant. It was five against one, and she had never liked to see odds like that—even if the one did appear to be, on first inspection, the equivalent of three ordinary men.

She'd ordered her coachman to stop, and he hadn't argued, though they had not been in the best part of Town and he had no real means to protect her if things did not go well. She'd taken a small, dainty pistol she carried for show from beneath her seat, climbed out of the carriage, and faced the thugs down. She didn't know quite how she'd done it, but she managed to convince the thugs that they should load Titus into her carriage, and she was driving away before the men could question her.

She'd taken Titus home and nursed him back to

health. He had stayed on, gradually taking on more and more of the household responsibility until he was virtually running the place. She'd never asked where he'd come from, why the men were assaulting him, or who he'd been. In return, he didn't question her.

And they'd gotten on well for years. But now, apparently, she'd crossed some invisible line, and Titus intended to challenge Warrick.

"I do, sir," Titus answered, sounding very much like an actual butler. She supposed he was an actual butler, though she couldn't have said exactly when the transformation occurred.

"My intentions are honorable," Warrick was saying. Fallon put her hand on the door, intending to go in and stop the nonsense at once. Warrick didn't have to explain himself to Titus. But Fallon didn't push the door open. Something made her hesitate.

"So you say, sir," Titus answered, "but I have reason to doubt."

"Understandable. But I assure you, Titus, I intend to marry your mistress."

Fallon had known Warrick was going to say that. He had fastened onto the idea of marrying her, and no matter how much she tried to convince him they would not suit, he hadn't let it go. Truth be told, she didn't want him to let it go. And perhaps that was why she was eavesdropping. She needed to know if Warrick still wanted to marry her.

"And if she does not want to marry you?" Titus asked. Fallon smiled. Only Titus would think to ask such a question. Of course, he'd helped throw out many a determined suitor who would not be persuaded she was not interested in playing the role of wife for the night.

There was a long silence, and Fallon could picture Warrick frowning and clasping his hands behind his back. "That is her decision, of course. But I think it would be a foolish choice, considering she is in love with me."

Fallon opened her mouth to respond that it wasn't a foolish choice at all, but she remembered she wasn't supposed to be listening. And since Warrick had probably guessed she was listening, she stepped away from the door and started up the stairs to her bedchamber.

She tried to ignore the way her heart thudded, tried to tell herself it was the exertion of climbing the stairs so quickly. She tried to tamp down the bubble of excitement that arose when Warrick's words echoed in her mind.

I intend to marry your mistress.

But bubbles were notoriously difficult to control. As a child, she'd tried to catch them on her finger, but more often than not, the bubbles escaped her. And when she did catch one, it inevitably popped immediately. The bubble of excitement escaped her, rising and rising until she could not help but skip, giddy with exhilaration. Warrick loved her. Warrick wanted to marry her. She had never thought she would marry, but now images of Juliette's recent wedding flickered in her mind. Fallon wanted what Juliette had had—the lovely dress, the fresh flowers, Warrick in his morning coat, looking at her with that expression of love that melted her heart. She realized she wanted what Juliette had with her duke. She wanted someone who would

love her more than was right, more than was proper,
and more than convention deemed appropriate. She
wanted someone who would tell Society and all of its
social dictates to go to the devil. The Duke of Pelham
had done just that for Juliette, but he was the exception. She had no hope Warrick would do the same
for her.

Fallon closed her eyes and pictured the sunlight
streaming through the church on Juliette's wedding
morning. The stained glass windows had reflected a
shower of sapphire, topaz, ruby, and amethyst on the
marble floor. Those same colors had danced across the
back of Juliette's silver-embroidered wedding dress.
Fallon remembered thinking it the most beautiful sight
she had ever seen. How she longed to be the one with
the spray of color frolicking over a pale silk gown.

Oh, please, Fallon prayed. *Don't allow this bubble to pop.
Not yet.* She wanted to enjoy it, just for a little while.

When she entered her bedchamber, she was pleased
to note Anne had drawn a bath for her and scented
it with a few drops of the jasmine oil from India for
which she had paid far too much.

Anne helped her undress, and Fallon dismissed her,
luxuriating in the warm bath water until all the tension
oozed out of her shoulders and her head ceased to
ache. She was beginning to doze when she heard
Warrick's deep voice. "That's a lovely scene. I should
have come up sooner."

She didn't open her eyes, but she smiled. "If you'd
waited too much longer, I would have been asleep."

"You should sleep. You must be exhausted."

She opened her eyes. "We'll both sleep. After."

He shook his head. "You know I never sleep."

She straightened, clasping her arms around her knees. "Why is that? Are you afraid of your dreams?" The fire in the fireplace flickered, making his face appear all shadows and hard planes. His black clothing was severe and unrelieved against the backdrop of the bright jewel tones in her bedchamber. Behind him, beads on amethyst-, emerald-, and opal-colored pillows glittered like cat's eyes.

"They are not pleasant. How are your ribs? Do they still pain you?"

She touched her side and realized she could hardly feel the injury any more. "My ribs are much better, but you are changing the subject. We're speaking of you. What happened tonight outside the bank? You seemed to go away for a few moments, and when you returned, even I was frightened."

Warrick ceased pacing. "I apologize. My behavior was unforgivable."

"Hardly." She reached for her towel, stepped out of the tub, and began to dry off. "I can forgive quite a lot. And, really, there's nothing to forgive. I only wanted to understand."

When he didn't speak, she glanced at him. His eyes were so dark with desire, she almost dropped the towel. "Could you hand me my dressing gown?" she asked. Anne had left the ruby silk gown draped on the end of her bed.

"I could, but it would obstruct my view."

"I promise to take it off again, slowly, when we're done talking. But, for the moment, I want your complete attention on our conversation."

"I make it a policy never to argue with a naked woman." He handed her the gown, and she slipped it on, cinching the sash in the front.

She took his hands, pulled him to the bed, and sat while he stood before her. "Tell me," she said quietly. "Whatever it is, it won't change my opinion of you. You already know my secrets. If you do want to marry me, you have to share some of yours."

He raised a brow. "So you *were* listening at the door."

"You will have to do better than that to divert this conversation."

With a sigh, he sat beside her. His thigh was solid and warm against hers, and she leaned her head on his shoulder.

"My doctor has called my condition soldier's neurosis. I feel like some sort of hysterical woman when I speak of it in those terms, but I don't have any others."

"And what is soldier's neurosis?"

"Basically I cannot seem to escape the war. At times my mind goes back to it, and the images are so real, I feel as though I am there again. I can hear the cannons, I feel the ground tremble beneath my feet, I smell the blood and the overturned earth, I see the mangled bodies of the men I knew. I search. I crawl over bodies because I'm searching for something or someone." His voice caught, and she reached over and took his hand again. "Don't ask me to describe it any further. It is not something I want you to imagine. It's too horrific."

"And this is why you cannot sleep? Your dreams bring you back to those horrors?"

"At times they do, but almost anything can trigger an episode. That boy tonight—something about him reminded me of... another boy. Before I knew it, I was back on the field, reliving it all."

"And when I spoke to you, you thought I was one of the soldiers?"

"No." He turned to her, took her by the shoulders. "You brought me out of it. Your voice helped me to return to reality."

"Is there anything to be done for this neurosis? Any treatment?"

Warrick gave a bitter laugh. "*Time heals all wounds* is the advice I received."

"I'm certain that's true, but I think we can do better than that." She reached for her sash and unfastened the knot.

"What are you doing?" he asked.

"Taking your mind off war and battles and death. When I'm done, you won't be able to think at all." She released the sash and allowed the gown to sliver open.

"Fallon, you should rest. You're tired."

"We're both going to rest." She bared one shoulder. "Later."

"I…"

She bared the other.

"If you're going to argue, you should do so quickly. I'll be naked soon, and you know your policy concerning nude women." The gown slipped farther until it rested precariously just above her nipples. They were hard, and the silky material chafed and rubbed.

"I find," Warrick said, drawing the garment down slowly so that her breasts were bared to him, "the policy also applies to half-nude women." He brushed the back of his hand over one breast, and before Fallon could forget her intention to seduce him, she stood and allowed the gown to pool at her feet. Warrick let out a low groan. "I could not resist you, even if I wanted to." His warm hand stroked the curve of her waist. "You are exquisite."

She smiled. She had been complimented thousands of times in her role as a courtesan, but she had never believed a single statement. But she could see Warrick meant every word. She was far from exquisite. She looked like every other woman, and she had her flaws. She was short, and her legs were not at all long and slender. But Warrick didn't see any of that. He looked at her as though she were perfection personified.

She could have loved him for that alone. And perhaps his insistence that she was somehow special, even though he knew she was as common as any other person they should pass on the street, was the reason she had fallen in love with him. But it was not the reason she loved him. In Warrick she saw the contrasting qualities of strength and vulnerability. He could support her, buoy her, protect her. But he needed her too. He needed her to help him forget all he had seen and done. No one had ever needed her before, and after years of being told she was worthless and then more years of being an ornament for a ballroom, Fallon yearned to be needed.

With a light push, she toppled Warrick so he fell back onto her large bed. She loved the look of him—those broad shoulders, the beginnings of a beard darkening his face and making him look somewhat dangerous, the intensity in his gold-flecked eyes. She wanted to take him then and there. But this was about helping him to forget. She wanted his mind filled with images other than those of war and battle. She turned, bent, and pulled his boots off, first one foot and then the other.

"Oh, good God." His voice sounded tight and barely leashed. When the second boot dropped to the floor, he sat, spun her around, and kissed her. "Bend over like that again, my love," he whispered.

"Not yet." She separated them using two fingers and then pulled off his coat and his shirt and opened the fall of his trousers. "You *are* ready." She pulled him up and slid his trousers off, running her hands along his muscular thighs and cupping his bottom. He jerked, and she leaned forward and kissed his flat abdomen.

"You are killing me. I do not have this much restraint."

"Oh, I think you do." She pushed him back to a sitting position, admiring the way the firelight burnished his skin. "Later, when you fall asleep, this is what I want you to see." She lifted her hands and caressed her shoulders, imagining her own hands were his. She slid down her body until she reached her breasts then cupped and stroked them. She watched his eyes grow impossibly dark and his breathing grow labored as she circled her nipples with her fingers. She was aching for him now.

Her hands slid down over the curve of her stomach, tracing the swell of her hips, then brushing her thighs. Slowly she inched toward the juncture of her thighs until one hand rested there, parting her folds.

Warrick seemed to sway as she dipped one finger

inside. She was wet for him, growing more aroused when she saw his hands grip the bed, his knuckles white. She moaned, imagining her finger was him, imagining herself pinned beneath him as he took her unmercifully. She closed her eyes, allowed her head to fall back, and moved her hand faster. Just as she neared climax, Warrick grabbed her wrist.

She opened heavy lids and smiled at him.

"You're not going over without me."

"I want you inside me," she whispered, kissing him. His mouth was eager against hers, and his hands slid up and down her body, making her shiver. He strayed closer and closer to her core as his tongue played with hers, and she knew if he touched her there, she would come apart in seconds. She broke the kiss and moved to his neck, kissing him tenderly and working her way down his chest. She took time to explore that part of him, tracing the hard muscles with her tongue, running her fingers over the smattering of hair. He had scars here and there, and she lovingly kissed each one, imagining some day she would know the story behind each.

She moved her body down his, rubbing her breasts against him as she neared his abdomen. There she took her time exploring. His hands were gripping her shoulders, and she knew he was barely holding on. With a smile, she flicked her tongue out, tasting the head of his erection.

"Fallon!" He tried to sit, but she took him in her mouth before he could pull her away. She looked up at him, her eyes teasing him, and saw he was watching her raptly. She moved up and down the length of him, loving the feel of him, the taste of him. She could have brought this to an end right then, but she wanted him inside her. If she was selfish, then so be it.

"Lie back on the pillows," she instructed, and they both moved fully onto the bed. Slowly, she straddled him, taking him inside her inch by inch. His hands clenched her hips almost painfully, but when he finally filled her to the hilt, she could think of nothing but the way he felt. She rocked, pleasure swirling and building within her as she moved. She arched her back and took him hard and fast. Her hips pistoned, and she cried out as she shattered. She was sinking against his chest when he flipped her over.

Her eyes snapped open as he pinned her wrists to the bed with one hand. "We're not done."

She looked down. "*You* are not done." She licked her lips. "Come here."

"No. It's my turn."

She shook her head. Her body was boneless and limp. He couldn't possibly… and then his mouth was on her breasts, sucking and licking, and she found her hips arching and the tension once again building.

"You like that."

"I like everything you do to me." She tried to touch him, but he held her wrists to the bed.

"I'm in charge now," he said, swirling his tongue around her erect nipple. She would have fought any other man who dared to restrain her, who had the audacity to tell her he was taking control. But she found herself surrendering to Warrick, strangely thrilled that she was his captive, in his power. His hand traced her ribs and her belly delicately and then one knee nudged her legs apart. His hand parted her, and he gazed at her for a long time. She tried to close her legs, but his hand wedged them open. She was completely revealed, and the way he was looking at her made her breath come fast and hard.

"Take me," she pleaded, arching toward him.

"Not yet." His finger slid over her, and she caught her breath. She all but cried when he slid two fingers into her.

"You are so wet."

"For you." Her hips bucked as his thumb circled her, sending bolts of pleasure through her. She rocked her hips against him, her body straining for release, just as he withdrew his hand. "No!"

Now she fought him, her arms straining against his hold. But he was merciless, pinning her to the bed. "Shall I tease you with my tongue or thrust into you, hard and fast?"

"Hard and fast," she begged. "Make me come."

"Oh, I will." He released her hands, and she rejoiced that she could finally wrest control back, but then his head dipped between her legs, and she found all she could do was to fist her hands in his hair as his tongue teased her unmercifully. She was screaming for release when he finally entered her, filling her so completely that she all but wept.

"Hard. Fast," she begged, and for once he abandoned his tenderness and complied. He drove into her, and with each thrust she screamed his name. Waves of pleasure crashed over her again and again and again, each one slamming into her and rendering her weak and wanting more. Finally, *finally*, he lifted her legs onto his shoulders and drove into her. She watched his face as he came.

"Fallon," he groaned, and the sound of her name on his lips sent her over. The pleasure seemed to crash through her for hours. Her body took and took until at last they both lay still, legs and arms wrapped around one another, both wet with perspiration, and too sated to even think of moving.

His arm tightened around her, and she turned her head to kiss his temple. His eyes were closed and his breathing heavy.

"You're safe with me," she whispered. "I won't let you go. Now, sleep."

And he did.

Twenty

WARRICK WOKE SLOWLY, LISTENING TO THE UNFAMILIAR sounds around him. There was the distant chime of church bells, the raised voice of a nanny calling to a small child, and the hushed murmurs of servants somewhere nearby. Even closer was the sound of someone breathing deeply. He opened his eyes and his gaze fell on Fallon. Her hair was spread on the pillow beside him, and she had one arm flung carelessly above her head. Her dark lashes brushed against a cheek still red from his beard, and her swollen mouth was slightly parted.

She looked completely at peace, and Warrick realized, with a shock, that until a moment ago, he had also been at peace. He could not remember the last time he had slept so soundly or so dreamlessly.

He looked at Fallon again. This was her doing. She was good for him. She brought him back from that raging whirlpool of memory that continually reached out greedy hands to suck him in. He'd seen men go mad because they could not put the horrors of war behind them. At times he feared he was destined for that path himself, but Fallon gave him new hope. She was an anchor he could reach for when the whirlpool threatened.

She didn't trust him, of course. She didn't believe him when he said he would marry her. And why should she? He supposed men lied to her all the time, and he had been trained in the art of lying. But he had been nothing if not honest with her.

There was no doubt marrying her would be a sacrifice. His family would never again receive him. He would never mend the split with his father. They would be ostracized from good Society—not that Warrick gave a damn. He couldn't even remember the last time he had stepped foot in his parents' town house, not to mention the country house. They had cut him off long ago when he refused to leave the Foreign Office to take some ridiculous position as a vicar. Warrick couldn't think of any service he was less suited for than the clergy, and when he'd been promoted and become one of the Diamonds in the Rough, he knew he had found his true calling. He and the other three diamonds had been instrumental in stopping Napoleon's relentless siege of the Continent. They, along with others, had been able to provide Wellington the information he needed to win at Waterloo.

Warrick couldn't regret his decision to become a spy, even if it meant his father was ashamed of him. Some things were more important than the Earl of Winthorpe's approval, though his father doubtlessly disagreed. Warrick looked at Fallon again. His family would not welcome her with open arms. Fortunately, he and Fallon had a day to prepare before the ball, and he would prepare by paying his mother a visit and convincing her to allow him a look at the guest list. Perhaps a name or two might stand out.

He glanced at the window and judged it still early. His mother would not even be receiving callers yet. Hell, he didn't even know if it was her day to receive calls, and he didn't really care. He did care that he would have to leave Fallon behind. If he wanted to see that list, it wouldn't serve to annoy his mother. But sooner or later she would have to accept he was in love with Fallon.

As though hearing his thoughts, she stirred beside him. He rolled onto his side and stroked her cheek, trailing down to her shoulder then her arm. Her mouth turned up in a lazy smile, and her eyes fluttered open.

"Did you sleep?" she asked, her voice husky with sleep and perhaps something more.

"I did, thanks in no small part to you."

"I was happy to oblige."

His hand moved to her hip, caressing the silky skin there. She stretched and threw one leg over his hip. "I could sleep for another twelve hours."

His hand trailed to her bottom. "Don't let me stop you."

"I'm afraid you're rather distracting."

"I shall take that as a compliment, and beg your forgiveness because I cannot seem to resist you."

He kissed her lips, pulling her bottom closer so she cupped his hard erection.

"Mmm, I don't want you to resist me." She kissed him back, a lazy lingering kiss that fired his blood. Her hands wandered over his back, down his sides, and came to rest on his hips. Her teasing fingers left him breathless as she inched closer and closer to his erection. Finally, when he was about to groan, she took him in her warm hand and stroked.

"Fallon." He buried his face in her neck, letting the sweet scent of jasmine wrap around him. He nibbled her neck, felt her shiver, then she guided him to her core. She was warm and wet, impossibly inviting. He wanted to wake up like this every morning. He rocked inside her gently, allowing their passions to build. There was no hurry, no frenzy. He wanted to savor every second with her—her every sigh, her every response.

Finally, he rolled on top of her, and she smiled up at him, her eyes still cloudy with sleep and also with passion. She wrapped her legs around him, and he moved inside her, so slowly he thought he would go mad. The climax built and built until he could not stop it from crashing over him. He felt her tighten around him, and she sighed a soft, "Yes," before she crashed too.

He pulled her into his arms, held her until her breathing grew deep, and she slept. And then he left her.

❧

The park in the center of Berkeley Square was flooded with sunshine and the twitter of birds. Daffodils swayed in the light breeze that whipped his great coat, and that same breeze brought to his ears the tinkle of voices from the nearby patrons enjoying Gunther's ices.

It was a splendid day. The last remnants of rain

sparkled and dried in the warm, spring sunshine, and everywhere around him budding flowers opened one eye and considered showing their colors.

The town house of the Earl of Winthorpe looked every bit as peaceful as its surroundings. Its gray, stately exterior was flanked by large flower boxes, whose blooms dared not wait until the other blossoms of London decided to flower. Color spilled from the boxes just as dignity emanated from the large edifice.

Warrick had many memories here. He could remember standing outside, as he was now, as a boy, eating his ices with nothing more important on his mind than whether he should play with his toy soldiers or his ball that afternoon. He could also remember standing here as a man about to leave for the Peninsular Wars, stealing a last glimpse of home over his shoulder, feeling the bleak coldness of the house and his dismissal as much as he felt it in the chill, damp air around him.

This town house had been home, as much as Embrey Abbey in Cardiff, the ancestral homes of the earls of Winthorpe. He and his brothers and sisters had grown up here, and as he stood outside now, he could not help but feel the tug of nostalgia.

But he was here with a duty in mind, and he must not be swayed from his purpose. It was almost two o'clock, which was perfect, as his mother would be all but done receiving calls for the day. He climbed the steps to the door and knocked on the brass knocker three times. Dalton, the butler who had been in residence for as long as Warrick could remember, opened the door. If he was surprised to see the Winthorpe's prodigal son returned, he did not indicate such. He merely nodded and said, "Mr. Fitzhugh." He opened the door wide, and Warrick stepped inside. He handed his walking stick, greatcoat, and hat to a waiting footman then said, "I'm here to see my mother, Dalton."

"Of course, sir." The butler must have been ancient, but he hadn't aged so much as a day in Warrick's estimation. He still had the same unsmiling countenance, the same drooping jowls, the same steely gray hair and steely gray eyes. "Your calling card, please." He held out a hand.

Warrick refrained from rolling his eyes. "I haven't one with me." He couldn't have said if he had one at all. He was not in the habit of making calls. He supposed his own butler could have unearthed them for him, but he hadn't thought to ask when he'd stopped home for a quick change. His valet had fussed when he said he didn't have time for a shave, and Dalton's gaze on him now made Warrick wish he had listened to his valet. His day's growth of beard made his cheeks burn under Dalton's critical eye.

"I see. If you will wait here a moment." Dalton and the footman disappeared, the footman in one direction and Dalton toward the drawing room. Warrick shoved his hands into his pockets and studied the house. Little had changed since he had last been here. The ceilings were still soaring, the art still classical, the potted plants still green and perfectly tended. The silence of the house was familiar, as well. He had remembered being chastised more than once as a child for stomping up and down the stairs when he should walk like a young gentleman. Suddenly, there was a shriek followed by a laugh. Warrick started then turned as a young boy scampered by, chasing a battered ball. Another boy followed, and in their haste to retrieve the ball, they tangled legs and fell in a heap at Warrick's feet. Giggles erupted as the boys rose to their knees and then abruptly ceased as they glanced up at Warrick.

"Good day," he said.

Both boys gave him grins so reminiscent of his older brothers, Warrick could not fail to know their identities. One of these boys was Henry and the other must have been Charles. These were his nephews, but how could they be so big? He had last seen them as babies.

"Good day," the boys said, as they rose.

"And who are you?" the taller one with a mop of thick black hair asked. This one must be his eldest brother Richard's boy. No one but a future heir would presume to speak so to a stranger.

"I'm your uncle, and you must be Charles." He pointed to the boy with the black hair. "And you," he nodded at the shorter boy, "must be Henry."

Henry grinned, but Charles's brow furrowed. Good God, the boy was the spitting image of his father. "Uncle? But Uncle Anthony is here already."

"I'm your Uncle Warrick." He leaned down and whispered, "The one they don't talk about."

Henry giggled, and Charles shot him a warning look.

"It's all right," Warrick said. "I'm here to see your grandmother."

"Charles!" Warrick recognized the voice immediately. It was his brother Richard. A moment later Richard strode into the vestibule, stopping short when he spotted Warrick. He recovered himself quickly. "Warrick, this is a surprise."

"I'm sure," Warrick said. "I didn't realize I was interrupting a family gathering."

"You're not." With a wave, Richard sent Charles and Henry back into the parlor from whence they'd emerged. Charles went readily, but Henry dragged his feet and glanced over his shoulder. The boy reminded Warrick of himself at that age.

"The ladies are going shopping with Mama, and Anthony and I thought the boys could play together in the park." He gestured to the square.

"I'm certain they will enjoy that. The weather is splendid today."

"Yes, it is."

Anthony, in his vicar's garb, emerged from the parlor, a young boy following him closely. "Charles said Uncle Warrick was here, but I didn't believe it until I saw it." He swept the boy into his arms in one motion then gave Warrick a hard hug in the next. Anthony and Warrick were the closest in age and had always been boon companions. Now, as Anthony hugged him, Warrick caught the scent of the child he held, something sticky and sweet and perfectly innocent. His heart wrenched.

Anthony stood back. "Have you met George?"

"I don't think I have." Warrick smiled at the child. "I thought you had a daughter."

Anthony nodded. "Mary couldn't leave her lessons. She has a very strict governess." He grinned, and Warrick grinned as well.

"It's a surprise seeing you here," Richard said.

"I came to see Mother."

"Didn't think you were welcome," Anthony said. "That's how we treat war heroes, you know."

Warrick smiled. "I don't have an invitation, but I wanted to speak to Mother about the ball tomorrow night."

"Are you attending?" Anthony asked. "Mama will be thrilled."

Richard put his hands on his hips. "She'll be thrilled you are here now. Lady Edith is with Anne and Frances in the drawing room."

It took Warrick a moment to place Anne and Frances. They were his sisters–in–law, but he could not immediately remember which was married to Anthony and which to Richard.

"Mr. Fitzhugh," Dalton said, appearing again. "Shall I take you to the countess?"

"By all means." He nodded to his brothers and started up the steps. How many times had he climbed these steps as a child? How many times had he and Anthony charged down them, playing Henry V and the Battle of Agincourt? Would his own children ever know this place? Would they ever play with their cousins or face the withering glances of Dalton?

Dalton opened the drawing room doors and announced Warrick. He entered, and three ladies turned to study him. One was his mother, and the others must be Anne and Frances. He remembered them now, the blond was Anne, and she was married to Anthony. The brunette was Frances, Richard's wife. She looked as though she wore a rod in her gown.

"Ladies." He bowed. Warrick heard a commotion behind him and Anthony and Richard, along with the boys entered. The boys immediately ran to their mothers, who smiled at them indulgently. Anne took George upon her lap.

"Warrick," his mother said, "this is a surprise. You remember Lady Edith, do you not?" She gestured, and he turned to see a woman standing behind him. She was more beautiful than he remembered, and Fallon's opposite in almost every way. She was tall and thin, stately in her demeanor. Her wheat-colored hair fell in charming curls about her face and neck. Her eyes were light, a green or blue, and sparkled with laughter. She looked young and fresh and innocent.

She came forward, holding her hand out to him. "Mr. Fitzhugh, so good to see you again."

He took her hand and bowed. "Lady Edith, it's been far too long."

"Indeed, it has." She gave him a mischievous smile and then retreated to the couch beside Frances. Henry climbed onto her lap, unbidden, and she accepted him happily, apparently unconcerned that he might wrinkle her pale pink gown.

"To what do we owe the pleasure of your company?" his mother asked. "I do hope it is to confirm your attendance at the ball tomorrow. As I'm certain you noticed, the frenzy of preparations has begun."

Warrick had noticed no such thing. If the servants were in a frenzy to prepare, they were masking it well. "I will be at the ball."

"Oh, good!" Frances said. "Lady Edith has been saving a waltz for you."

Well, that was nicely done, Warrick thought. Frances was going to make one hell of a countess one day.

With little choice but to oblige, Warrick said, "I look forward to it, Lady Edith." She smiled, exchanging a look with Frances. Warrick was struck by how comfortable she seemed surrounded by his family. She fit in, whereas he had always felt like an outsider.

"Your father will be pleased to see you," his mother said.

"Will he?" Warrick asked, looking away from Lady Edith.

"I daresay he will," Richard answered. "He's become nostalgic of late."

Anthony laughed. "Which is Richard's way of saying he regrets banishing you." Anthony was standing next to his pretty wife, and he put a hand on her shoulder. She covered it and gave him a warm look. "You should come to the ball," Anthony said, "and the two of you can make amends."

Warrick studied the small, happy group. The scene was so heartachingly domestic he could barely make himself stay rooted in place. This was what he wanted. This was what he had dreamed of through all those months of war. Only the thought of returning to London, marrying, and having his own children had kept him going through the worst of it. He looked at his brothers, with their wives and their sons, and he envied them. He had never envied them before, but now they had something he wanted.

His gaze strayed to Lady Edith, who would be the perfect addition to his family. She gave him a knowing smile. He looked at his mother, who nodded at him. She would not be so pleased when he arrived with Fallon on his arm tomorrow night.

He tried to imagine Fallon sitting with this group and found it difficult. She was at ease with the men of the *ton* but had little experience with the ladies. And in Warrick's experience, it was generally the ladies who determined whether or not one was accepted into Society. When he did marry Fallon, would he be dooming her to a lonely life of rejection? She knew her place now. She would have no defined place as his wife and a former courtesan.

"I will attend the ball," Warrick said, looking at his mother. "And I was hoping I might take a look at the guest list."

His mother frowned. "Whatever for?"

"It's state business, so I'm not at liberty to say."

His mother straightened. "I am sure you can have no reason to investigate any of *my* guests."

"Nevertheless, I was hoping to peruse the list."

His mother sighed. "I suppose that would be all right." She rose, excused herself, and led him to a small parlor on the first floor, where she completed all of her correspondence. She took several sheets of vellum from the drawer of a dainty rosewood desk and handed them to him. "Is this the real reason for your visit today?"

"I'm pleased I was able to see Richard and Anthony."

She held her hand up. "Say no more. You've answered my question." She started for the door, then paused. "You are coming to the ball alone, are you not?"

Warrick kept his gaze on the vellum.

"I see." His mother shook her head. "Warrick, do think what you are doing." She gestured toward the stairs. "Think what you are throwing away."

"I've thought of little else, Mama."

With a huff, she left him alone to peruse the long lists of lords and sirs. None of the names stood out, though. All of the guests were exactly the men and women he would expect to appear on a guest list for a ball given by an earl. He replaced the vellum and turned toward the door to see his father standing within its frame. Warrick had not seen the man, except from across his club, for several years now, and he was surprised at how much the earl had aged. Hair that had once been dark brown was now peppered with gray. His strong face and bold features appeared slightly shrunken and lined. He'd put on a stone or more as well, and Warrick noticed his father leaned heavily on a walking stick. Realizing he had been staring, Warrick recovered himself quickly and bowed. "My lord."

"I did not expect to see you here, sir."

"I needed to speak to Mother."

"You will be attending the ball tomorrow night?" his father asked.

"Yes, my lord."

"Capital. We can speak more then."

Warrick nodded. He supposed this was as close as his father got to welcoming him back. "Yes, my lord."

His father moved aside, and Warrick took the gesture to indicate a dismissal. He exited the parlor, nodding at Dalton, who stood guard at the door. But before the butler could open it, the earl spoke again. "Your mother tells me you have taken up with a courtesan."

Warrick halted and glanced at Dalton. Dalton kept his gaze focused on the nothing in front of him. Warrick attempted to imagine how his mother might have broached the subject of their youngest son and a notorious courtesan and decided he did not want to think too hard about the more intimate aspects of his parents' relationship.

"Her name is Fallon," Warrick said, turning,

"That matters not. I was a young man once," the earl said. "I understand the lure of pretty women, but there is a time in a man's life when he must put all of the frivolities of youth aside. You are one and thirty, sir. Your mother and I would like to see you settled."

Warrick clenched his fists. He remembered his father calling his work for the Foreign Office a *frivolity* years ago. It appeared now he was to be forgiven for that folly and chastised for another. "Fallon is not a passing fancy, my lord," Warrick said. "When you meet her—"

His father shook his head. "Do not be so bold, sir, as to think you will introduce me to a common trollop. What you do with her on your own time is your affair, but you will not sully this house by bringing a whore into it."

Warrick contained the rage that exploded within him but just barely. "You mean a whore who is not titled, I think. I saw the guest list, my lord, and I do not believe most of the women on it can claim they have not strayed at one time or another from their marriage bed."

"I will not dignify that comment by acknowledging it."

Warrick nodded and started for the door again. So many years had passed, and yet so little had changed. He and his father would never make amends, it appeared. Dalton moved slightly, then stilled when the earl spoke again. "Warrick, one question."

If the earl hadn't used his Christian name, Warrick

would not have stopped. But there was something about hearing his father refer to him so familiarly that tugged at a part inside him—a place dangerously close to the center of his chest.

"You can't think to marry this woman, can you? You must know that would be disastrous for both of you."

"The Duke of Pelham—"

"Yes, yes, I know all about that fiasco, but you are not a duke, nor are you one of the wealthiest men in the country. Money and status often buy forgiveness, not to mention that the duke had a somewhat eccentric father and an impeccable reputation before his fall. Society will overlook one transgression from a man of Pelham's character. You will not be afforded the same courtesy."

"That is a price I am willing to pay." He started for the door again, but his father caught his arm. Warrick all but jumped at the earl's action. He could not remember the last time his father had touched him.

"I am only going to say this once," the earl hissed in Warrick's ear, his voice so low even Dalton, who stood a few feet away, could not have made out the words. "Do not throw your life away. If you marry this woman, you will be dead to me and to your mother. I am trying to make amends for our past, but you must meet me part of the way."

Their gazes met, and Warrick stared at the tears in his father's eyes. The urge to embrace his father all but overcame him. It had been so long since he'd felt he had a father at all.

"Give me another chance, son," his father whispered. "Let's begin again tomorrow." The earl squeezed Warrick's arm and released him. Slowly, he withdrew until Warrick was standing in the vestibule alone with Dalton. Warrick looked at Dalton, but the servant stared straight ahead. Warrick shook his head. Had he imagined what had just happened?

He moved toward the door and Dalton opened it. With a nod, Warrick passed through it and walked back toward the park. He had intended to return to Fallon's town house after his visit with his mother, but now something held him back. He told himself he would not be good company at the moment, and he started for home. Well aware his residence was probably being watched, he took a back way and entered the gardens through a locked, hidden door only he knew about. He locked it again behind him, entered the town house cautiously, and made a cursory search. He startled several of his servants, but otherwise everything appeared to be in order. A quick discussion with his butler told him no one had come to call and nothing suspicious had occurred in his absence.

He went to his room and left strict instructions that he was not at home—to anyone.

Once in his room, he jotted down as many of the names of his mother's guest list as he considered noteworthy. Only a dozen or so of the men in attendance had amassed the kind of wealth necessary to obtain three large rubies. He went to the window, leaned on the casement, and scanned the names. One of these men had to be the traitor. He knew all of them, though he only knew one or two well. Still, none of them gave him even a moment's pause. But one of them wanted him dead, and Warrick wished his instincts had not chosen this day to fail him.

Twenty-one

By ten the next morning, Fallon had to admit the painful truth to herself—Warrick was avoiding her. He'd left the morning before without so much as a good-bye. He had not sent any sort of word all day, and when she sent a note to his town house, her messenger had returned with her missive, saying Mr. Fitzhugh was not at home and no correspondence was being accepted.

Fallon's belly had felt sick and tight, but she tried not to think the worst. Lily had stopped by the night before to invite Fallon to attend the theater, but Fallon said she didn't feel well and stayed home. That had probably been a mistake. Fallon was not the sort to sit at home waiting for a man to call on her, but that was exactly what she had done.

Her only consolation was if she had gone to the theater with Lily, she would have done nothing but talk about Warrick the entire time. Obviously Lily knew him better than she had pretended, and Fallon was eager to know the connection between her friend and her lover. But something told her she'd get little information from Lily and then she'd end up pushing the matter and embarrassing herself.

So she'd stayed home, hating herself for her weakness and hating Warrick for making her think he'd loved her. Though, there again, she had no one to blame but herself.

Finally, after pacing her chambers most of the day and avoiding her lady's maid, who wanted answers as to Fallon's plans for the night, she retreated to Lady Sinclair's town house. There she found Lily and the countess sipping tea in the spacious drawing room. With its cream-colored furnishings, high ceilings, and white moldings, the room was serene and peaceful. The countess embraced her warmly, and Fallon felt a little of the blackness hovering about her like a fog lift.

Until she saw Lily's face.

"What is it?" Fallon asked, pulling out of the countess's embrace. "What is wrong?"

"It's nothing." Lily tucked a newspaper beside her on the chair.

"There's something in that paper," Fallon said. "Is it about me?"

"Why do you always assume everything in the papers is about you?" Lady Sinclair asked, taking her seat and gesturing to the empty chaise longue across from Lily.

Fallon shook her head. "You are correct, of course. I hope it isn't about you or Juliette." She took the cup of tea the countess offered her and sipped. She might have wished it were brandy, but oolong would do for the moment.

"How are you, my dear?" the countess asked.

Fallon was about to respond, when Lily said, "How are things with Mr. Fitzhugh?"

Fallon jumped to her feet, spilling tea on her gown in the process. She set the cup on the floor and lunged for the paper. Lily let out a small scream but surrendered the paper readily enough. It only took a moment for Fallon to find the Society column and the item about Fitzhugh and Lady Edith. Apparently they had both been spotted at the Earl of Winthorpe's residence yesterday afternoon, and sources close to the earl said his youngest son had been quite taken with the young lady.

Fallon felt the room grow dark, and she dropped the paper on the floor. Lily was beside her in a moment. "The papers exaggerate everything, Fallon. You know that." She took Fallon's arm and led her back to the longue. Fallon sat on it, feeling like some sort of lead marionette.

"You are as white as a sheet," the countess said from far away. A few moments later much-needed brandy was pressed to Fallon's lips. Fallon drank it and closed her eyes, and when she opened them again, the world had stopped spinning.

"I knew it," she whispered. "I knew something was wrong."

"I am certain nothing is wrong," Lily said. "The papers—"

"He hasn't seen me or written to me since he went to his father's house. He told me he wanted me to go to the Winthorpe ball with him tonight, but he hasn't sent any word at all and the ball is only hours away!"

Lily knelt beside her, her green eyes filled with

concern. "If Fitzhugh said he was taking you to the ball, he will take you. He is a man of his word."

Fallon's eyes narrowed. "And how do you know so much about him? What, exactly, is your connection?"

Lily glanced at the countess.

"Now isn't the time to discuss that," Lady Sinclair said smoothly.

Fallon shook her head. What exactly was Lily hiding? Apparently the countess knew—and was keeping Lily's secret. Fallon took a breath. "If Fitzhugh hasn't thrown me over, then why haven't I heard from him?"

"Oh my!" The countess pressed her hands together. "You're in love with him!"

Fallon frowned. "And why does that make you look so pleased? You told me a few days ago not to fall in love with him."

"Only because I knew that *would* make you fall in love with him."

Fallon glanced at Lily, but Lily only shook her head, looking as confused as Fallon felt.

"Oh, you were already in love with him," the countess explained, sipping her tea. "But I knew telling you not to fall in love with him would only make you more so."

"That's ridiculous," Fallon protested. "I'm not that contrary."

The countess raised her brows and sipped her tea. Fallon looked at Lily, but Lily was suddenly intensely interested in her white gauze sleeves.

"Fine." Fallon sighed. "I am contrary. Perhaps *that's* why he prefers Lady Edith."

"Fallon!" Lily grasped Fallon's arm gently.

"He doesn't prefer Lady Edith," Lady Sinclair said, "but I meant what I said when I came to see you. His mother is a woman who achieves her purposes. She wants Fitzhugh married to Lady Edith. If he goes against her wishes, and I imagine, those of his father, he will lose much."

Fallon pressed her hands to her eyes. "Exactly. He's thrown me over."

Lady Sinclair rose and joined Fallon on the longue. "Do you have so little faith in his love for you? I daresay if he has thrown you over, then he doesn't deserve you."

Fallon's belly tightened, and she fought the urge to be sick. *This* was why she never fell in love—this wretched nauseating feeling she knew would only grow worse. It would be eclipsed, though, of that she was certain. The stabbing pain in her heart would render the roiling in her belly insignificant. And there was nothing she could do to conquer these feelings, nothing she could do to stop the pain. She would have to push through it. She would have to continue on, no matter how much she felt like dying.

"He has not thrown her over," Lily said. Fallon was barely listening. She wanted to go home, crawl in bed, and pull the covers over her head.

"But he is thinking the matter over," the countess said. "He will choose Fallon, but by then she will have given up on him. She will refuse to see him and ruin everything."

"I am sitting right here," Fallon said. "And I know where this is going, and I am not going to be a part of it." She rose. "I'm going home."

"Oh, no you are not," the countess argued, pulling

her back down. For a small woman who used a walking stick, the countess was remarkably strong. "You are going to allow Fitzhugh to prove his love."

Fallon stared at her. "Fitzhugh isn't the Duke of Pelham, my lady, and I'm not Juliette. Fitzhugh is not going to make some grand gesture."

"We shall see."

"No, we shall not." Fallon rose again. "I am going home." She was halfway across the drawing room, when Lady Sinclair's words stopped her.

"I suppose if you prefer to run and hide, rather than fight for what you want, there is little I can do."

Fallon clenched her fists, staring blindly at the pale blue and white striped silk chair by the door. If only she could keep moving and reach the chair, the handle for the door would be at her fingertips.

"I had no idea you were such a coward."

Fallon whirled around.

"Countess!" Lily gasped.

Lady Sinclair waved a hand. "It's true."

"No, it's not," Fallon said through clenched teeth, "but I'm not going to prove it by marching into the Winthorpe ball uninvited."

A small, devious smile spread over Lady Sinclair's face. "Excellent plan, my dear. Abernathy!"

Fallon gave Lily a pleading look. "Now what is she doing?"

Lily shook her head, bewilderment on her face. Abernathy, the Sinclair's butler, opened the drawing room door. "Yes, my lady?"

"Inform his lordship we are attending the Winthorpe ball tonight."

"Of course, my lady." He nodded. "Is that all?"

"I do not think I responded to the invitation," Lady Sinclair said, leaning on her walking stick and rising. "Repair that oversight."

"Of course, my lady."

"Thank you, Abernathy."

Fallon shook her head. "Are you going to go to the ball to bash Fitzhugh about the head? If the man must be convinced he loves me—"

"Oh, hush!" The countess waved her stick at Fallon, forcing Lily to duck. "I'm merely giving the man an opportunity to prove his love to you once and for all. Lord knows it will take considerable effort to make it through your thick skull."

"I do not have to listen to this."

"Oh, yes, you do. Not only will you listen, young lady, but you will do exactly as I say." The countess glanced at Lily. "You too."

Lily nodded quickly. Fallon had the ridiculous urge to inform the countess that she was not her mother, but she kept her mouth closed. The countess had done more for her than anyone Fallon had ever known. She was not going to refuse a request by Lady Sinclair.

And her capitulation had absolutely nothing to do with the fact that Lady Sinclair scared her to death.

"Now"—Lady Sinclair rubbed her hands together—"we have work to do."

Four hours later Fallon and Lily stood in front of a looking glass and admired the results of the assault. Lady Sinclair had summoned a veritable army of modistes, hair stylists, and maids to turn Fallon and Lily from courtesans into princesses.

At least that was how Fallon felt.

She stared at the woman in the mirror and tried to find herself somewhere. She had been dressed and styled and primped many, many times before but always the effect was exotic and sultry. The woman looking back at her looked young and innocent. Her dark hair had been pulled back from her face and secured in a sophisticated chignon, which was held in place by a small diamond tiara. That was the only adornment she wore, if one did not consider the gown. It was a rich red and hopelessly out of style. The skirt was too full, the waist too low, and the neckline all wrong—and yet, Fallon loved it. She looked like a princess, and she actually twirled from side to side to watch the ruby-red skirts swish. In the lamplight, the beads flashed and sparkled. The gown might not have been the current style, but it was classic.

Beside Fallon, Lily, who was dressed similarly in a sapphire gown, smiled. "I feel like I should look about for my throne," she said as one of the modistes fussed with her hem. "I cannot fathom where Lady Sinclair has been hiding these gowns and for what purpose she had them made in the first place."

"I shudder to think what else she has hidden. If Fitzhugh had run off to Arabia, would she produce some sort of harem attire?"

"I assure you I have no harem attire," Lady Sinclair said, moving into the room.

Fallon pressed her lips together. She should have known Lady Sinclair never missed anything. The countess studied her long and hard, made several suggestions to the modiste and the hair stylist, and finally nodded her approval. "You will do."

Fallon laughed. "High praise indeed. Tell me, are we going to a masquerade? You can't possibly think to have us dress so for the Winthorpe's ball."

"Not to mention," Lily added, "Fallon and I have not been invited."

The countess shook her head. "I have never understood that expression—*not to mention.* If one is not going to mention something, why follow the phrase by mentioning it?"

Lily opened her mouth to explain then closed it again, looking perplexed.

"In any case," the countess said, "you will attend as my guests."

Fallon took a deep breath. "I really do not think this is a wise idea."

The countess raised her brows. "I assure you, my dear, if the idea is mine, it is wise. And stop clutching your belly. You look as though you will cast up your accounts at any moment."

Fallon felt as though she might. The situation worsened by the moment. Just the thought of seeing Warrick made her heart gallop. She felt like such a fool. How was she going to hold her head high when he cut her, ignored her, and danced with Lady Edith? She took a step back.

"Oh, no!" The countess was before her immediately. Again, for a woman who needed a cane, she moved remarkably quickly when she wanted. "Whatever you were thinking of just now, cease."

"I am not attending the ball. I have better things to

do with my time." She shook her head, undeterred even by the cutting glare the countess leveled on her. "And I do not wish to be humiliated."

"Fallon, you *can* do it. You're strong—" Lily began. Lady Sinclair held up a hand, and the gesture was enough to silence Lily.

"Leave us for a moment," she said to Lily. "Wait in the vestibule, if you do not mind."

"Not at all." Lily all but ran for the door. Fallon wished she could escape too.

"All of you," Lady Sinclair said to the remaining modistes, maids, and hairdressers. "Please, leave us."

The room emptied as quickly as it had filled earlier in the day, and Fallon felt the weight of dread in the heavy silence.

"You can't scare me into going," Fallon said. But, truth be told, she wasn't so certain.

"I had not intended to scare you," the countess answered. "I am merely going to ask you to go."

Fallon swallowed. This was indeed worse.

"Have I ever asked anything of you, Fallon?" Lady Sinclair questioned. "Have I ever asked so much as a single favor?"

Fallon shook her head. "No."

"I am asking you now. Please go to this ball."

It was the *please* that did her in. That and the fact that she owed the countess everything, and it was true, Lady Sinclair had never asked for anything in return. Fallon bowed her head. Who was she to use humiliation as an excuse? The countess knew humiliation better than anyone. For years she'd been pitied by almost every one of her friends and acquaintances because Lord Sinclair kept three mistresses. Had Lady Sinclair ever denied the accusations, even though they were patently false? No, she had allowed everyone to believe the rumors, even fostered them, because those rumors helped Fallon and the other members of The Three Diamonds.

And now Lady Sinclair was asking for a favor in return. How could Fallon deny her? She owed the countess everything.

Fallon offered her arm. "I am happy to accompany you, my lady."

Lady Sinclair smiled. "Fallon, you will thank me for this; you do realize that, do you not?"

Oh, how Fallon wished that were true.

◈

Warrick was late to the ball. Even by Society's standards of fashionable tardiness, he was late. It was his own fault, really. He'd had second thoughts about bringing Fallon. He didn't like to admit it, but it was true. His father's words had affected him, and even more than his father, the domestic scene he'd witnessed yesterday in his parents' drawing room had affected him.

How he wanted that domesticity for himself.

But he did not want it with any woman but Fallon. He wanted her more than anything else. If his father was prepared to deny his son because of Warrick's choice in wives, then his father be damned. Lord Winthorpe was making the mistake, not Warrick.

But he'd mulled the issue over too long. He knew that now. He should have gone to Fallon immediately or at least sent some word. Instead, when he finally arrived at her town house in order to escort her to the ball, Titus informed him she was not at home. Warrick had been prepared to search her residence, even if it meant fighting Titus to do so—a terrifying prospect, but he was determined. Titus had made a sweeping gesture and gladly suggested he look himself. The butler would not have done so if Fallon was hiding in her bedchamber.

Which could only mean that she had already gone out.

Warrick could not imagine where. She probably had a dozen invitations. She could be anywhere in the city. She could be with anyone. Dozens of men wanted her, desired her. Just the thought of her smiling at one of those men, flirting with him, dancing with him, made Warrick want to smash his fist into the nearest wall.

Since that wall was his father's, he refrained, but he was aware he was scowling deeply, and his parents' guests were giving him a wide berth. He'd been a fool, but he would not lose her. He would go to her tomorrow, plead forgiveness.

He was not going to make a mistake he'd regret the rest of his life.

"Warrick?"

He turned and looked down into the smiling face of his mother. Only she would dare approach him when he was so obviously annoyed. And only she would bring someone with her—Lady Edith.

Lady Edith curtseyed prettily, and Warrick was forced to bow and say, "Good evening, Mother. Lady Edith." This was why he avoided balls. The inanities of societal expectations irritated and bored him.

"Your father and I are so pleased you have come," his mother said.

Warrick refrained from rolling his eyes. Of course they were pleased. He had not brought Fallon with him. They thought they had won. He glanced at Lady Edith—his prize—and bristled.

"We shall speak after the next dance." His mother patted his arm. "I will leave you two alone. I'm certain you have much to discuss." And with that, she turned and swept away.

Lady Edith gave him a small smile. "It's a lovely ball," she remarked.

He sighed. Now he was going to be forced to make idle chitchat. "Yes." He glanced about, pretending to take it all in. The ballroom looked much as it always had, in his mind. He could remember sneaking down here with his sisters and brothers as a child to watch a ball in progress. Even then he could not see the appeal of crowding into a rectangular room to dance or yell over the strains of an orchestra. He *had* envied the ball goers' supper. His parents rarely allowed the children to partake of sweet apple tarts, candied violets, or any of the other sugary confections on display in the supper room.

But now, as he looked at Lady Edith, he remembered how his sisters had sighed over the gowns and the chandeliers and the forms of the minuet. Doubtless, Lady Edith had done the same. "It is lovely," he replied, glancing about and studying the guests for the first time since arriving. He really should have been looking for the man who wanted him dead instead of brooding about Fallon. He couldn't very well win her back if he had his throat slit.

There was the Duke of Devonshire. He had the funds, but why would he turn traitor? And there was the Marquess of Bynum, but Warrick knew he was searching for an heiress to marry, which meant he would have sold the rubies, rather than offered them to a hired killer. Unless he had another motive—

"Mr. Fitzhugh?"

Warrick dragged his attention back to Lady Edith, realizing belatedly he was being rude. "I beg your pardon. Is it time for our dance?"

She smiled. "No." She was a pretty thing, but she did not fire his blood. "There is something I wish to say, and I hope you will forgive me if I am blunt."

He raised his brows. "I appreciate bluntness, my lady."

"I know about your friend." She notched her small, pointed chin up.

He frowned.

"Your lady friend."

"I see." Now this was interesting.

"I do read the papers," she remarked, "and I have seen several items about you and a certain woman, of late."

"Go on," he said because the color was high in her cheeks now, and he could not help but wonder where she was headed with all of this.

"I wanted you to know that should your parents' dearest wish be fulfilled—"

So much for bluntness. He had to untangle that veiled reference to matrimony.

"—I would not care if you continued your friend-ship with the lady. After the birth of a son, of course."

Now this was bluntness, and he spoke without

thinking, "So you are saying you do not mind if I am unfaithful?"

She blushed. "I cannot say I would not mind at all, but I understand how the world works." She made a sweeping gesture toward the ballroom. "And I admit I have a desire to taste some of it myself."

Ah. So she intended to take lovers herself. He stared at her, tried to imagine himself wed to her. Tried to imagine her as the mother of his children. Would he mind if she spent her evenings locked in the arms of another man?

No, he decided. He would not. Which meant she was giving him the perfect solution. He could marry Lady Edith, have his parents' approval, and have Fallon too.

Except Fallon would never consent to actually becoming the courtesan she played. He would lose her.

Warrick was vaguely aware the music for the waltz had begun, and he offered his arm, as if by rote, to Lady Edith and led her to the center of the ballroom. It had been some time since he'd danced a waltz, but it came back to him quickly, and Lady Edith was light on her feet and perfectly graceful.

"I can see you are thinking about my proposal," she remarked.

"I…" He did not know how to answer. *Was* he considering it? "My lady, do you mind if I am equally forthright?"

She took a breath, then shook her head. God forbid he truly be blunt, or she would probably faint. "Why do you wish to marry me, knowing I love another woman and I will be unfaithful?"

She shook her head and looked over his shoulder. "I would be honored to—"

"No. We are being honest."

"Because I am tired of husband hunting," she answered, and he was impressed with her frankness. "And I like your family. They are warm and genuine, and my own sorely lacks those qualities."

"Thank…" His mouth went dry as the doors to the ballroom opened. The light of the chandeliers sparkled off the bold blue and red gowns of the women entering the ballroom. But his gaze was fast drawn to the woman in the red. It was Fallon, and she was breathtaking. He missed a step and had to force his feet to keep moving. He wanted nothing more than to stop and stare at her.

No, that was not true. He wanted to walk to Fallon, take her in his arms, and kiss that lush red mouth. He wanted to pull the glossy brown hair from that elaborate twist and bury his hands in its considerable weight. He wanted to see her eyes cloud with passion and her skin glow with a fine sheen of perspiration from their lovemaking.

"She is pretty," Lady Edith remarked, her voice sounding as though she were calling to him from a tunnel underneath the ballroom somewhere.

Warrick stared at his dance partner. *Pretty* did not begin to describe Fallon. *Seductive, exquisite, necessary*— these were words that came to mind.

Behind Fallon, Lord and Lady Sinclair entered, and he knew, quite suddenly, where Fallon had been this evening and how she had gained entrance to this ball. Dalton would not dare refuse entrance to the Iron

Countess, even if she did bring two courtesans with her as guests. Lily, who Warrick saw was standing beside Fallon, leaned over and said something. Fallon's gaze swept across the room and collided with his. His heart hammered in his chest and a longing like none he had ever known took hold of him.

"Mr. Fitzhugh," someone said. "You are squeezing my hand too tightly."

He glanced at his partner, but not before he saw the flash of pain in Fallon's eyes. Her gaze slid away from him.

"No." He wanted to shout the word. He wanted to tell her this was not as it appeared. But then he saw his mother, the smug look upon her face, when she should have been horrified at the presence of not one, but two courtesans in her ballroom. Standing beside his mother, shaking her head as though she'd expected this, was his sister Louisa.

And he knew that this was exactly as it looked, and his mother finally had her way.

Twenty-two

"I'M LEAVING," FALLON SAID TO NO ONE IN PARTICULAR, though she knew the countess and Lily could not help but hear.

"Oh no, you are not," the countess said.

"Lily, my dear." Lord Sinclair held out a hand. "Would you care for a refreshment?"

"I would, thank you." She took his arm, and the two of them walked away.

"Some friend you are!" Fallon called. How could Lily leave her in this moment? Fallon couldn't stop her traitorous gaze from straying to the dance floor once again. Seeing him there, dancing with the blond beauty, was worse than she ever could have imagined. And she had a vivid imagination.

He was waltzing with her—this woman who could be none other than Lady Edith. He was holding her close and whispering in her ear and no doubt falling in love with the woman. How could he not? She was everything Fallon was not. She was tall and willowy with pale porcelain skin and golden blond hair. Her cheeks were a pretty pink, and everything about her screamed nobility and breeding. Warrick belonged with this woman, a woman of his own class. Fallon had only to see him with her to know it was true.

"I do not have to do this. I'm leaving."

"No," Lady Sinclair said. "You will stand here with your head up and be the strong woman I know you are. Remember appearances can be deceiving. We, of all people, know this to be true."

Is that what the countess thought? That Warrick waltzing with Lady Edith was for appearances' sake only? Fallon was far from certain. But there was one thing she was sure of. She would never hold her head up in another London ballroom, drawing room, or dining room if she did not do so now. So she gritted her teeth, forced her lips into a smile, and tore her gaze away from the picture of the man she loved holding another woman.

She focused elsewhere. Unfortunately, the person who came into her vision was none other than Lady Winthorpe, Warrick's mother.

"Lady Sinclair," Lady Winthorpe said, neatly cutting Fallon. "How good of you to come. You must sit beside me at dinner. It has been so long since we have had a real chat."

"I am afraid, Lavinia, our chat may have to wait," the countess said. "I imagine Fallon"—she put her warm, gloved hand on Fallon's arm—"and Lily will be at my sides."

"Of course," Warrick's mother said without so much as a glance at Fallon. "If you will permit me, I will call on you soon."

"Do. I am certain we will have much to discuss."

The refreshment table where Lily stood laughing at something the Earl of Sin said was looking most inviting. "Excuse me," Fallon began. "Would you like me to fetch you—?" She inhaled sharply.

Beside her the two countesses ceased their chatter and turned to watch Warrick's long legs eat up the distance between them. He was coming to speak to her. She knew not what it meant, and she dared not hope.

She dared not trust him. Hadn't she done that once before? And look how he had betrayed her.

"Fallon," Warrick said as he neared. Lord, but he made it difficult for her to breathe—or think or stand. She was glad of her full skirts because her knees were wobbling. He was so tall, so broad shouldered, his features so terribly intense. Those eyes, when they fixed on her, caused heat to swirl through her. She prayed she did not swoon at his feet and make a complete and utter fool of herself.

The ballroom was eerily silent when he stopped before her. The orchestra had not begun the next song, and most of the guests were watching the scene between the earl's son and the courtesan.

"Fallon." Warrick reached out to her, but somehow she managed to force her legs to step back. She did not want him to touch her. All would surely be lost then. He frowned, obviously mistaking her gesture to mean she no longer wanted him. She wished, with all that she had, that was the truth.

"I am so pleased you're here," Warrick said.

Fallon gave a bitter laugh and gestured toward Lady Edith, standing a little ways away. "You have an interesting way of showing your pleasure."

He had the audacity to appear confused. "I came for you. Titus said you were not at home."

Now Fallon was confused, but before she could ask what he meant, Lady Winthorpe spoke, "Warrick, how could you be so rude? You have completely abandoned Lady Edith."

"She's fine, Mother." He reached for Fallon again, and this time she allowed him to grasp her hand. "I should have gone to see you sooner. I should have sent word."

To her horror, Fallon felt tears well in her eyes. She blinked them back. "When you did not come…"

"I know." He squeezed her hand. "Never again doubt I love you."

"Warrick!" Lady Winthorpe shouted. "Stop this at once. Do not say something you will regret."

Warrick's gaze never left Fallon's. "I don't regret my words to Fallon in the least. I love her, Mama. You will either have to accept her or deny me." He knelt, still holding her gloved hand. Whispers and gasps punctuated the ballroom. "Fallon, will you do me the honor of becoming my wife?"

"Play something, you bloody imbeciles!" someone was shouting. Fallon thought it might have been her future father-in-law.

She grasped Warrick's hand. He did love her. He really did. She could see it in his face—the way his brow creased because he worried she would refuse, the way his hand trembled lightly in hers. Warrick loved her. Why had she ever doubted him? Never again. "I will," she said. "I will."

"No!" Lady Winthorpe hissed. "No, I will never accept her."

"Lavinia!" Lady Sinclair said sharply. "Do not say something *you* will regret. If you would just give the girl a chance—"

"Open more champagne," the Earl of Winthorpe was shouting. "Where are the footmen?"

Warrick stood and pulled Fallon into an embrace. His arms were so warm, so comforting, and she knew she was home. He loved her. He really loved her.

The cork from a champagne bottle popped off with a loud boom, and Warrick stiffened. Fallon started for a moment as well, but the little surprise she'd felt passed quickly. Warrick's body, on the other hand, stayed rigid. She knew, without being told, what had just happened. "Warrick?" She stepped back. His eyes were glassy, his face pale. "Warrick. Not now. You're all right. It was a champagne bottle."

"What is going on?" Lady Winthorpe was asking. "What did you do to him?"

"Remain calm," Fallon said, laying a reassuring hand on her arm. "Is there somewhere quiet we can take him?"

"Why? What is the matter?" his mother asked.

"I can't find him," Warrick said, his voice flat and strangely emotionless. "He's not here."

"Warrick. You are in London. You're safe," Fallon said, keeping her voice level.

"He's not here. Dear God, the bodies. The blood. I can't—I can't find him!"

Fallon jumped out of the way as Warrick reached for a nearby chair. He flung it aside, then knocked over a table. A footman stepped in his way, and Warrick hit the man, causing him to drop his tray of champagne flutes.

The orchestra screeched into silence, and a woman screamed.

∽

It was him. Finally, Warrick saw the boy. His once fair hair was now matted and caked with dried blood, and the youth's body was buried under a mound of corpses. Warrick bent, pushing the dead aside, uncovering the boy.

He wasn't dead. No, he couldn't be dead. He was wounded. That was all. Warrick would get him out of this hellhole and get him the best medical care available. He was not dead.

He pushed the last corpse off and lifted the boy into his arms. His form was so light, so thin. It was hardly the body of a man, much less that of a soldier. "Open your eyes, goddamn it!" he said, brushing dirt off Edward's cheek. "Open your eyes."

Edward's eyes fluttered once then twice. "Warrick," he choked out. "Told you we'd get them frog…" His head fell back and blood trickled out of his mouth.

"Edward?" Warrick said. Edward didn't stir. "Edward?" Warrick cradled the limp body to his chest. "Please," he begged, uncertain whether he was begging God or Edward. "Please."

Another explosion rocked the battlefield, and the ground beneath him shook. Shouts of "Retreat!" sounded, but Warrick did not flinch. The enemy was closing in, and he didn't care. He wanted them to kill him. He deserved to join the ranks of the other corpses surrounding him.

His brother was dead. He'd failed to protect

him. Failed in the only thing that meant anything to him.

"Warrick." Someone was speaking to him. He ignored the voice, laid the body down, and prepared to lie down beside it. They would die here together.

"Warrick, come back to me. You're in London. You're safe."

But he wasn't safe. He could never be safe again. His world was irrevocably changed into a nightmare, and he could not make it go away by waking up. He laid his head down on the filthy ground and closed his eyes to sleep—*to die, to sleep, to sleep...*

"Warrick, please."

He blinked. "Fallon?" She could not be here. She was not part of this.

"He's coming around. Some brandy, perhaps?"

"Fallon?"

"Warrick, I'm here."

He blinked again, and brandy burned a path down his throat. Fallon was kneeling in front of him. She was so beautiful. She was so perfect.

"I left him," he rasped. "I had no other choice."

"It's all right," she said. "You're home. You're safe."

"No, you don't understand. I left Edward on the battlefield. I left him to be picked over by the vultures and the thieves. I left him with the other corpses."

He heard a gasp but could not turn away from Fallon to see who it was. "You did what you had to, Warrick," she said. "It's over now."

Looking into her dark eyes, he could almost believe it. "I tried to get him out," he said, taking her hands. They were shaking, or was that his own hands? "I carried him as far as I could, but the French were coming. I would have preferred to die there by his side, but one of our generals rode up behind me. He ordered me onto his horse. And I went, Fallon." His voice broke. "I left him there. Alone."

"No!" It wasn't Fallon who spoke. He turned to see his mother coming toward him. He glanced around, realizing belatedly he was in his father's dark-paneled library. Fallon tried to move away, but he would not release her hand. His mother took the place on the couch beside him. Tears sparkled in her eyes. "Warrick, no." Her voice filled with anguish. "Thank God you left Edward. If you had not, we would have lost two sons. Edward's death was unbearable. To lose you as well would have killed me." She pulled him into an embrace. "Warrick, I do not want to lose you."

"Forgive me," Warrick whispered, closing his eyes. His mother smelled like lavender. It was a scent that reminded him of softly crooned lullabies and kisses goodnight.

"There is nothing to forgive. We never blamed you."

Warrick thought of his parents' reaction when he'd returned from the war and informed them of Edward's death. His mother had sobbed uncontrollably, while his father had ordered him out of his sight.

"We were shocked and devastated, Warrick," his mother said. "We all said words we did not mean."

Warrick felt a hand on his shoulder and looked up to see his father, standing behind the couch.

"You were with him at the end, son. That means everything."

"I'm sorry," Warrick said.

"So am I," his father answered. "For a great many things."

Twenty-three

FALLON WANTED TO MOVE BACK, TO GIVE THE FAMILY a moment's privacy, but Warrick would not release her hand. And then, when she looked up, Lady Winthorpe was smiling weakly.

The smile made Fallon nervous. She sincerely hoped Lady Winthorpe hadn't just concocted some scheme to rid herself of her unwanted future daughter-in-law. Permanently.

"I'm sorry," Lady Winthorpe said. "What is your name again?"

Fallon glanced over her shoulder. No one was behind her. "Mine?"

Warrick's mother nodded.

"Fallon."

His mother frowned slightly. "Is that your Christian name or your surname?"

"Both."

"Oh. How… interesting."

"Mother," Warrick said, rising and pulling Fallon up with him. "I was quite sincere in my proposal to Fallon before"—he waved a hand—"before all this. If she is not welcome here, I will take her and go."

"Warrick," Lord Winthorpe began.

"I'm sorry, my lord. But my mind is made up."

His mother stood and went to stand beside his father. Fallon wished there was something she could say or do to keep the inevitable from occurring. She did not want to be the reason Lord and Lady Winthorpe disowned their son.

"Warrick, I think we should discuss—"

He squeezed her hand. "No. I've made my choice, Fallon." He looked into her eyes. "And it's you."

The love she saw in his eyes was so evident, she could not have said more even if she'd wanted to. She could only pray he would not come to resent her in time.

"Our minds are made up as well," the earl said. Warrick looked a great deal like his father—same intense eyes, same broad chest.

Lady Winthorpe nodded. "We are quite resolved on the matter, in fact."

"I have no intention of losing another son." The earl stepped forward, and Fallon stepped back. Those were ominous words. But then the earl held out his hand. "Welcome to the family, my dear Fallon."

Fallon stared at the earl's outstretched hand and then glanced at Warrick. He was smiling.

"You can take it, my dear," the earl said. "I won't bite."

Fallon hesitantly offered her own hand and shook the earl's. "I... I don't understand."

"After Warrick left yesterday, we both agreed we did not want to lose him again. We resolved to do whatever it took to keep him," the countess said. "I thought I could scare you away, but now…" She looked at Warrick. "Now I see you are exactly what he needs. The way you calmed him." Lady Winthorpe dabbed at her eyes. Fallon stared. Was Warrick's mother crying? "You were so strong and steady. I am certain Warrick is fortunate to have you," she finished.

The earl was nodding, and Fallon felt tears well in her own eyes. "Thank you." She had never been part of a family before. She did not know if this one would ever truly accept her. But this was a beginning. She looked at Warrick, and her heart was so full of love, her chest ached. It was a new beginning for both of them.

∽◦◦

Warrick couldn't have been more pleased with the way his mother and father had embraced Fallon. When the small group returned to the ball, his mother made a point of taking Fallon by the elbow and introducing her to all of her friends. The looks on those ladies' faces were priceless, and yet Fallon bore it all with dignity and aplomb. She was the true lady.

He lifted a flute of champagne from the tray of a passing footman and smiled at her from across the room. He wasn't going to acquire a special license, he decided, as he sipped the cool liquid. He wanted to marry her properly with banns, a full church, and a wedding breakfast. He imagined a wedding like that would take some time to plan, but his mother had planned four weddings already. She could practically do it in her sleep.

"I see your mother has suddenly grown fond of our Fallon," a lady said.

Warrick turned to see the Iron Countess beside him. "I'm not surprised. Fallon is special."

"Yes," the countess agreed. "Yes, she is. I've always liked her in ruby red. It suits her, don't you agree?"

Warrick nodded. "I do."

"You should buy her real rubies, Fitzhugh. Large ones." She laughed. "Do not look so concerned. I don't mean anything as large as those three monstrosities the Duke of Ravenscroft is so fond of, but something substantial, perhaps set—"

Warrick grabbed the Countess of Sinclair's bony wrist. "What did you say?"

"Take your hands off me, boy. If you have that much of an aversion to jewelry then—"

Warrick released her. "No. That's not it. You said something about large rubies. The Duke of Ravenscroft possesses three large rubies?"

"You won't convince him to sell them, if that's your plan," the countess warned him. "He informed me he has plans for the rubies, though we all thought he lost his fortune on war speculation. The rumors were he'd lost a great deal of money. He'll probably have them made into a wedding gift for his new duchess. Poor Darlington."

Poor Darlington was correct. Andrew, the Earl of Darlington and Warrick's friend, was the eldest son and heir of the Duke of Ravenscroft.

And his father was a traitor.

"Excuse me," Warrick said, scanning the ballroom for Ravenscroft.

"He's not here," the countess said. "He departed while you were indisposed."

"I see." Warrick's gaze fell on Lily. His mother had left Fallon's side for a moment, and Lily had taken her place. The two ladies were laughing—and, he wagered, drawing the eyes of most of the men in the room. "Excuse me," he said again and crossed the room to join them.

Fallon smiled at him as he approached, and he had the urge to simply sweep her into his arms and then away from all of this. They could go to Italy or Greece, where they'd be safe. But that wouldn't save the other Diamonds in the Rough, and he had an obligation to his men.

"Countess," he said to Lily. "Might we have a word before you depart this evening?"

"Of course." Her gaze was searching.

"I have an assignment for you."

She sobered. "I see. Why don't we meet in the library at midnight?"

"I will see you then."

Lily moved back and was quickly claimed by a young gentleman for the waltz that had just begun.

"What was that all about?" Fallon asked. "Assignment? Rendezvous in the library? Should I be jealous?"

"No." He took her hand and swept her into the waltz, relishing the feel of her warm body pressed to his. "I know who the traitor is, and I need Lily's help catching him."

"Who is it? And how is Lily supposed to help you catch him? I don't understand your relationship with her."

He spun her around. "We have worked together in the past."

"But in the past you were… but Lily is not… Warrick, I don't understand."

"Understand this, my beautiful, noble, enchanting fiancée. I love you." He pulled her close—far closer than was proper. "I love you." Taking her face in his hands, he leaned down and kissed her gently. "I love you."

Acknowledgments

Friends of mine who are not writers often tell me they are amazed at what I do. They find it astonishing I sit down and write three books a year. I hate to tell them I'm really not amazing at all. I only accomplish writing any book because I have a lot of help.

Who helps me? My family. My mom, my dad, and my sister are constantly supporting and encouraging me. My parents often babysit as does my wonderful mother-in-law. My husband gives up precious time with me so I can work and helps out in so many ways.

My friends buy my books, attend my signings, and understand when I can't chat or go out because I have too much work. And then when I have a break, they are always happy to welcome me back into the fold. I want to acknowledge just a few of these awesome friends by name—Laura, Tina, Tera, and Sharie. I also want to thank my RWA chapter, especially Vicky and Nicole, and my "writing" friends, Robyn, Margo, Emily, and Ashley.

I'm part of a fabulous community of professionals. I blog with some of the best women around. Thank ou to the Jaunty Quills, the Peanut Butter on the eyboard moms, and the Casababes for always being the other side of the email.

There wouldn't be a book without the fabulous oanna Mackenzie and Danielle Egan-Miller. And the book wouldn't be very good without Deb Werksman and the rest of the Sourcebooks team, especially Danielle Jackson, Cat Clyne, Susie Benton, and Rachel Edwards.

And then there's maddee, Jen, and the whole crew at xuni.com who always make me look put together. Gayle Cochrane, my wonderful assistant, is so creative and talented. She makes me look inventive and tech savvy.

This book is dedicated to my readers. Thank you to all of you who faithfully comment on my Facebook pages, reply to my tweets, loyally follow my blog tours, and, oh yeah, buy my books. I especially want to thank Melanie Bernard, whose response to a Facebook plea for suggestions led to the title of this book. I really do have the best readers!

About the Author

Shana Galen is the bestselling author of fast-paced adventurous Regency historicals, including the *RT* Reviewers' Choice *The Making of a Gentleman*. Her books have been sold worldwide, including in Japan, Brazil, Russia, Spain, Turkey, and the Netherlands, and have been featured in the Rhapsody and Doubleday Book Clubs. A former English teacher in Houston's inner city, Shana now writes full time. She's a wife, a mother, and an expert multitasker. She loves to hear from readers; visit her website at www.shanagalen.com, or see what she's up to daily on Facebook and Twitter.